Hob Hurst's Daughter

I0667851

Ophelia Finsen

Also by Ophelia Finsen:

Lovers of Old Films
This is Living
Society of Lost Causes
The Women of Jimanac
Skye
The Romanian
At the Upper Villa Tyde
Perception
You Stole My Thunder
Bella Donna
George

The Yorkshire Saga
Hob Hurst's House

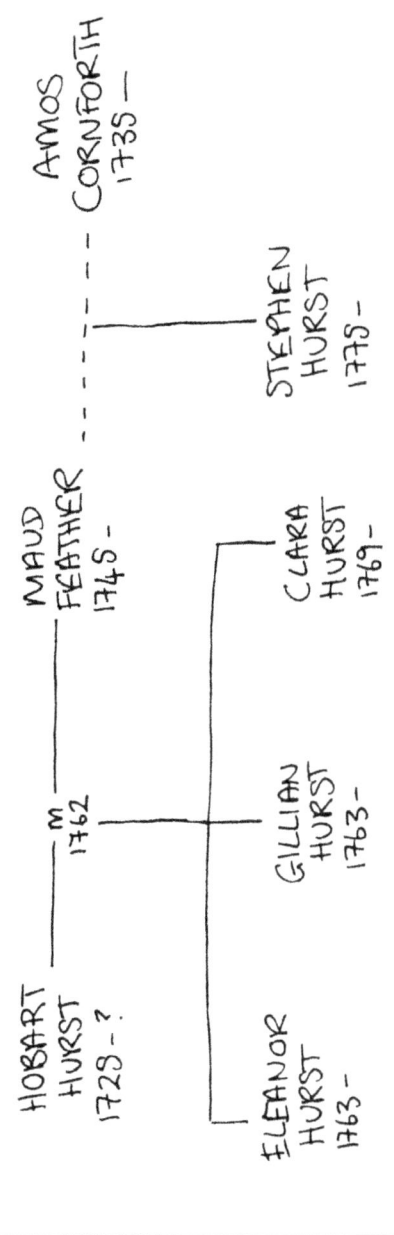

AMOS CORNFORTH 1735 –

MAUD FEATHER 1745 –

STEPHEN HURST 1775 –

HOBART HURST 1728 – ?

m 1762

CLARA HURST 1769 –

GILLIAN HURST 1763 –

ELEANOR HURST 1763 –

The heavy knock vibrated through the farmhouse. The aged timber door shook with an intensity of violence. This was a door that had withstood harsh winters and relentless gales. It had stood against winds that battered the North Yorkshire moorland.

The farmhouse was on the hill above the village of Commondale. Set apart and lonely, yet adamant it would not be moved. It was cold yet still that night. The two women in the kitchen looked at one another with a sense of foreboding. Perhaps if they ignored the knock, life could continue on its tentative but hopeful path. Someone started to hammer on the door. The ironwork of the lock rattled against the timber.

Ellen Withers, housekeeper, scullery maid, cook and manager of all other domesticities, slowly placed her knitting on the kitchen table and looked at Maud Hurst, lady of the house. They had feared such a day, but as the months went by, the fear lessened and normality had pushed them into a false sense of security.

"We must answer it," Maud spoke feebly. She looked pale. She could feel her fear in the old healed crack in her skull, between nose and teeth. It was an old wound sustained during an overeager dental attempt by a blacksmith years ago. She had been in her teens, working as a housemaid in Haworth. What had started as a little toothache had ended as permanent damage. Her life had changed considerably since then but the scars clung to her, sending out warning signals in times of stress. She was not yet quite forty and yet had lived more than a lifetime, or at least it felt that way. She was a woman for routine and the quiet family life, not for the drama and upheaval she had been pushed into. She brushed her dark hair back, tangles of white strands from the temples showing strongly. There had been little conviction in her voice, and her housekeeper, near enough closest confident for the last two decades, had not left her chair yet.

Ellen nodded, realising that was as much as an order as she was going to get from Maud. She stood up and limped towards the door. She was only one or two years behind Maud – Ellen never being completely sure or interested in exactly how old she was – and carrying her own wounds. A broken ankle she had sustained from a beating years ago had never healed properly. The old damage remained chunky and clumsy against her other dainty ankle.

Catching her breath and summoning courage, Ellen put her hand to the door.

"Stephen was not coming back tonight?"

"No. He was to stay down at Gillian's," Maud spoke of Stephen, her youngest child at the age of eight. "He was seeing something of the smithy with William."

"Good."

The door thundered again in its frame as if a bull were charging it. Ellen wrenched open the door and let the autumn night air in. Two strangers leered on the threshold, for a moment silenced by the sudden opening of the door. Perhaps they had been expecting more of a fight. Rough looking men, unwashed and with wind tangled hair, layers of clothing and mud-splashed boots from the trek on foot up the valley to the village.

"Master of the house in?"

"Mr Hurst is not at home."

"Expect him soon?"

"He has not been back for months and we have not have word..."

"Like hell you haven't," one of the men interrupted. His accent wasn't from around these parts. They were from London and a long way from home. Something important must have brought them up here. "Out of the way, you old trollop." He pushed Ellen to the wall and barged into the farm house. Furniture seemed to shrink back against the stone work as his sweating form entered the fire crackling kitchen.

Maud jolted up abruptly from the kitchen table.

"You his misses?"

"I..." She ought to have more of a presence about her, but Maud had never really made the transition from kitchen maid to merchant's wife.

The man grinned at her. "Mrs Hurst, I presume. Where's the old bastard?"

"My husband is not at home."

"You say that but I don't believe you." He snapped his fingers. "You," he spoke to his walking companion. "Search the house. I bet he's hiding somewhere."

Ellen darted forward indignantly as the second man went for the door into the rest of the property. "Here, you can't..." her protest was interrupted as the man in charge grabbed at the back of her collar and swung her round like a bat, flinging her towards the stool by the range like rags to the ground.

"You mind yourself, Missy. Mr Hurst owes us money and we're not to be trifled with, do you understand?"

"If Mr Hurst owes you money, your grievance is with him. He does not conduct his business from here and we have little ready money."

Ellen couldn't help but raise her eyebrows at the coherent sentence from Maud. Something in the situation and the way the men behaved had brought out her defence. Ellen could see how Maud's lowered hands were shaking. This was the last stand. Maud was terrified, rooted to the ground, and the slightest movement from the man would break her attempt at authority.

"I have not seen him for a good many months and I am not sure where he is. His business takes him all over the country. He has offices at Whitby. I could send word..."

"We've already been there," he snarled. On the face of things it was confident aggression, but he unconsciously went for his shoulder. Ellen had to wonder what had happened at Whitby. There would be plenty of money in the office at Whitby to pay any debts off, so why were they here? They hadn't gotten what they wanted, Eleanor must have seen to that somehow. However bold Eleanor might be, Ellen didn't think she'd have the physicality to stand up to these two and get them off the premises. Whatever had happened, she was sure Eleanor wouldn't have sent them up here. They must have gotten the address, such as it was, from some other source.

"Nothing doing," the man continued, his hand dropping from a tender shoulder. "But I will have recompense. I have lost a lot of money."

"That is not my problem."

"Oh, but it is." He abruptly marched up to her, noting the quivering back step she made in response. Another stupid woman. He could see the family resemblance with the girl they had found in Whitby. "Way I see it," he continued, grabbing her shoulder and shaking her till she cried out. "A woman is a man's property when she marries him. And if the ready coin isn't here, we'll be taking other property."

"You get off her." Ellen went at him with a rolling pin only to be batted to the floor again. Maud started to sob and tried to pull away but was pushed up against a wooden pole near the range. Her cheek pressed against the age-old markings of older traditions, long since a part of the building before she was even born.

He pressed himself up against the woman, enjoying the terror and sweat he could feel emanating from her. She was a scrawny thing, only just the right side of being all bones. Elegant, tall but utterly lacking in conviction. "I'll take a part payment now, call it a retainer of sorts," he growled into her ear.

A door banged open and the second man returned. "She wasn't lying, there's not much coin in the house, just this." He bounced a purse, the household money, in his hand. Ellen looked up and was distracted by the strange thought that Mr Hodgkins' wage was in there, and wouldn't he be angry to know it was gone. In any case, where was Mr Hodgkins? He lodged in a separate building on the farm, but surely he ought to have heard the noise and come out to check. He always had been an unreliable and untrustworthy rogue. If it wasn't of personal benefit, he wouldn't entertain the idea of lifting a finger to do anything.

"Found these though." The man held up a couple of pieces of jewellery pilfered from Maud's dressing box. He held a ruby ring and a medieval Spanish necklace with dark blue stones and beautiful goldwork. "Ought to fetch a few bob back in town."

"Those are for my girls," Maud whimpered.

"They're for us now, and they're a start. Now come along lady, fill in the rest of my instalment and we'll be on our way." He gripped the back of her neck like a vice with one hand whilst working up her skirts with the other. Maud let out a shriek and tried to get away, scratching with her hands, sometimes hitting him but mostly the air until he swung her around and flung her face down on the kitchen table, knocking the wind out of her. She felt her skirts being thrown up over her back, covering her head as if to offer a small kindness and shield her vision. She would not have to watch.

Ellen started to shout and was back onto her feet, grabbing at whatever kitchen implement she could to protect her mistress. The younger man pocketed the stolen jewellery and pinned Ellen's arms to her side, dragging her to the other end of the table as they both watched the man violate Mrs Hurst by the range. Ellen writhed and sobbed and cursed the men, remembering every vile word and curse she had learned as a girl up in County Durham from listening the working men grow drunk in the taverns. Her language only proved amusement to their attackers.

The man looked up from Maud's quivering wreck and grinned like a cat. "Take a fee yourself. Call it interest, for I'll wager it'll be some time before we're paid in full."

Maud's face was drenched in tears, slick against the wood. They'll be back again. We'll never be rid of this nightmare and this will be our punishment. And all for a man whom she had never loved. She had felt obliged to at first for rescuing her, but ultimately he had made her life a misery. She felt her flesh resist and burn. She had four children, given birth three times, and certainly been taken many times by her husband when she had not wanted it, but this was by far the worst.

Ellen was spun around in the man's arms, her giddy desperate face held so close she could see the nuances of changing colours in his iris. There were red veins showing faintly in the whites of his eyes. Then she was tossed on her back on the table like a lump of dough with her legs pinned against the edge of the table, kicking futilely against the shins of long leather boots. The man ripped open her bodice, then took a knife and hewed apart her stays and blouse, wrenching it open and laughing at her humiliation. He made crude comments about saggy trollop's tits, grabbing at her breasts and pulling at them, before he got down to the business of rape. Ellen was a spinster, but no innocent. Relations before marriage were officially frowned upon, but in the business of real life, plenty of adult men and women had taken part in the fields in summer, in haystacks and barns. But it was mostly consenting and not like this.

Mercifully it was over quickly, and with final threats, the men knew they needed to get moving before anyone had chance to sound the alarm, or worse still, they had the bad luck of meeting with those they had fought with earlier. They had taken their pleasure, a little coin and some jewellery to be pawned off for the time being. There was a property in Derbyshire they had been advised of where Hobart Hurst might be in hiding, then after that it was either back to London or away to France to catch up with their money. Or to write it off as a lost cause.

Outside a full ivory moon was revealed as the clouds pulled apart. The leader started down the hill towards the village before the younger man pulled on his sleeve. "We don't want to show our faces down there," he said. "There are only two of us. Who knows how well these country folk stick together. We go over the moors. Get ourselves to Saltburn."

"We need to get to Derbyshire."

"We need to get away from here first. I'm not meeting up with that pack of Scotch thugs again, and I'll wager you don't want to either. I know a man or two who's worked out of Saltburn with a bit of smuggling. We'll get a boat, get ourselves back to London."

The older man considered for a moment, then nodded. For now the cause was to make themselves scarce. They needed to put miles and deniability between themselves and this farmstead. Out of sight and out of mind. "Away to the moors then. As you say."

They headed north east of the lonely farm property, striking up onto the hills and onto the open moorland. The wind had died down to little more than a sighing gasp and the moon peered its gibbous face down from the sky. They were quite content with their booty; in fact it was better than expected, especially after what had happened in Whitby. Hobart Hurst Esq. was a cunning man, and no one supposed there would be a fortune stashed away anywhere so obvious as his home. Or at least one of his homes. No one person could account for the full spread of Hurst's property and business acquisitions. The only person who knew the full extent was Hurst himself, all that knowledge and plotting compacted into his overgrown head. He would be present for a month or two, then vanish elsewhere, sometimes for only a few weeks, sometimes it could be six months or more. He was always careful not to annoy any creditors, any staff or contractors too much. He needed to know he could trust on their good will and eagerness to make more money on his return. The fact that there were still bills unsettled in London, which normally would have been dealt with months ago, had started to make his local contacts uneasy. These two men, Jacob and Andrew were more impatient than most and a little less scrupulous than the majority. They knew when something had gone wrong, and they knew when a man would no longer be showing his face. They could only speculate as to whether Hobart had left on his own accord, died or another hand had decided his fate for him. There would be a lot of claims to the estate, and theirs, being less than legal, would never be heard. They needed to deal with the matter themselves and promptly, and be grateful for what they could get. And if Hurst was still alive, when he heard what had happened to his wife, he might think again on the matter and return to settle his debts. It was difficult to be sure exactly what had happened, but both men knew from experience that life would give you nothing. They lived by the mantra that you had to go and take what was yours, and when nothing was for you, you took what belonged to others.

An old sheep path cutting through the knee-deep heather took their feet and led them through the moorland. The rough branches scraped at their boots as they marched across the moonlit landscape, wanting to get as much distance between them and the village. The younger of the two men, Jacob, led the way. He knew some folk from Saltburn to the north and had been up this way a couple of times. Andrew, the older, had a good sense of direction and tended to land on his feet. But he was a Londoner and used to the hustle and bustle, people crammed into rooms, narrow alleyways so subtly slipped in between buildings that one could often miss them when hurrying down the street. But this great emptiness, with neither a tree nor a building nor a person in sight frightened him. It was as if he were running through a strange nightmare, one that would never end. In every direction the stretches of moorland lumbered endlessly.

"Will it take us long to get to this smugglers' den of yours?" Andrew called to his thief compatriot.

"Three hours or so. We'll be there before day break." Jacob looked back over his shoulder for a moment without breaking pace. "You getting nervous?"

"I don't like this landscape."

"Men have gotten lost here at night, never to be seen again," Jacob laughed. "I know where I'm going and the moon will light our way."

But for how long? Andrew looked across to the east as they began to take a more direct northerly direction. There was mist building eerily over the moorland, a strange band not quite touching the ground, and finishing perhaps two heads above a man. The night had been clear a moment ago. He looked behind him. The mist was even thicker and all sight of the valley was gone.

It must be sea fret, Jacob reasoned as he watched the mist loom up ahead. This was not a place to go roaming at night if one was not familiar with the terrain. It had been some years since he had last been here, but he was sure he could remember the route. Of course there were dangers on the hills. It was disorientating how the heather moorland went on and on – it deleted the more obvious landmarks for one to navigate by. Then there were the bogs that opened up with enough rain. Not that they were so bad, one could usually pull oneself back out if one had the misfortune to stumble into one.

His thoughts jolted as he caught sight of a figure up ahead. There could not be folk out on the moors at this time of night. He broke into a jog, nervy of who else might be here. He had no desire to bump into the Scots, and certainly didn't want any witnesses catching their direction, or a scout dashing back for the troops to hunt them down. Ignoring Andrew's protests that they did not need to run all the way to Saltburn, he hurried after the figure, catching flashes of movement through the curls of mist. It was a lithe figure, slender built and dressed in flowing clothes. Long hair. A woman. Nothing to worry about, but now that he had started the chase he couldn't help himself. He wanted her.

Andrew could sense that Jacob was agitated over something, but he could not see anything. Nothing had changed apart from the mist, and running about in this weather was liable to get them off track. "Fire in your breeches?" He joked, trying to make light of the situation, but his voice sounded strained and revealed more of a fear than he had realised. There was an unnatural air creeping up around them, the temperature had dropped and he did not feel well.

Jacob suddenly cried out and seemed to drop to his knees. Taken by surprise, Andrew did not slow down, but went stumbling after, and yelled out when the ground seemed to open up and swallow him. He could feel the heavy weight of something under him, something solid, and realised that was Jacob's leg. The thick mud sucked downwards at his body, the filthy water splashed up at him. They were already thigh deep in a blasted bog. "Some guide you are," he shouted at Jacob, trying to right himself and pull himself out of the bog, but he only seemed to wade deeper out. The mist was up around them, even the shape of Jacob starting to melt away into the air.

At first Jacob was angry with his foolishness, running straight into a bog. Then he was angry with Andrew's heavy buffoonery, falling straight in after, and on top of him as if to drown him in this filthy northern ditchwater. Then he caught sight of the figure and forgot everything else. He started out for the woman. She was crouched on a hummock of windswept grass, a higher, solid piece of earth out of the bog. The mist curled around and outwards from her as if emanating from her very essence. What little moonlight managed to filter through caught on the long tresses of silvery locks. The colour of age, but it was a youthful, sparkling face of blank curiosity that watched him.

It was such an energy drain to pull a leg forward through this bog. Jacob reached out a hand towards the strange woman. "Help me, blast you," he said. "Will you watch a man drown here?"

"Will I?"

There was something not quite right about her. He stopped within arm's length of her and gazed at her. There were moss green velvet ribbons in her hair and she seemed to be dressed in a jumbled collection of rags.

"Who are you?"

"Who am I?" She seemed surprised by the question. "I am Atheleys."

Atheleys. What kind of a name was that? At least she could talk. She would be persuaded one way or another.

"And you are..."

Ah, a desire to communicate. He'd master her yet. "I am Jacob," he told her. "And you're helping me out of here."

"Oh no." Atheleys reached out, her busy little hands going for the top of his head. "You'll be going to sleep, you and your friend," she said as she started to push down. "A long, long sleep. For you are already dead."

The last thing Allan MacCaskill wanted to be doing just now was scuttling about on the moors in the dark. He wanted to be away in his bed. He ought not to have veered off from the main route through North Yorkshire. He should have continued up the central belt of the country and got himself back home to a wee village near Falkirk. But his second cousin, Angus MacCaskill, had been persuasive that they head across to Whitby, and if nothing else, this diversion had certainly been eventful. Stories to tell on future winter evenings certainly, but he'd still rather be in his bed now.

It had been a relief when they got to the busy port town of Whitby to hear the sea, smell the salt, and the fish, and the strange odours of whale blubber. It was a salve to his heart to be back by the coast. These last thirty odd years he had been a mainlander, over near Falkirk, albeit as a drover he was away from his home a lot. But Allan was a Shetlander, and had lived there until he had been a young man in his late teens and had been drawn away to visit relatives in Southern Scotland. The sounds of the north still resonated with him; glimpses of languages he had not used for many a year, the old Celtic tongue of Gaelic, now frowned upon and repressed by a government keen on its crackdown after the Jacobites and Culloden; and a more northern, stranger hybrid of Norn, clinging to those sea battered rocky islands with memories of its Scandinavian past. They twisted in his memory whilst his tongue would only speak English.

Ahead of him Angus walked with that girl who seemed to be the cause of a lot of this trouble. Eleanor Hurst, admittedly a fine looking woman, had turned Angus' head. A married man ought to have known better, but he had known Eleanor since she was a lass, playing the fiddle in Chequers Inn where the drovers stopped en route to the south of England most years. In an ideal world Angus should never have married Anna, but the rules were strict on getting the droving licence, and real life and acute need had pushed ahead of any silly romantic ideas he'd had of heading down in to Yorkshire in a few years and courting Eleanor. At least courting her properly and respectfully. Instead he longed for that he ought not to have, and it had been eating away at him up in Scotland, all along the drove down to London, and during the summer work in the countryside around the capital. A band of them, five in total, had headed off to Whitby, in no particular rush to get home, and with a good year's earning done, a little ambling on the way home to take in the country felt in order. They had only arrived in Whitby that day and this was not exactly what anyone had planned.

So here they all were, dragging themselves through moorland in the night, the quickest passage from Whitby on the coast to the little village of Commondale inland up the Esk valley. Heather scrub tugged at clothes and scratched at leather boots as they walked. The occasional grouse burst out of the heather when a foot thundered down too close to their hiding place, making the walkers jump with the sudden explosion of panic. The other men laughed at he who had unsettled the bird, what a big Jessie for letting a little bird make him shite his breeches.

It was all very jovial along the line, but Eleanor could not settle, and her feet would not move quickly enough for her mind. She needed to be back at her childhood home to be certain nothing had happened to her mother or her young brother, Stephen. The boy was only eight years old, and despite growing up on a farm and being raised with a cruel and indifferent father, Hobart Hurst, or the Hob as she liked to think of him, Stephen was an innocent to the world, and could only see the good in people. Even so much as an unkind word seemed to break his heart. She did not want to imagine what might happen if those men, those criminals the Hob had had dealings with back in London, would do if they got to the family out on the moors. They were after their money, but they were also after sport and she had seen in their faces what they had done to weaker people in the past. The fact that they had not been successful in Whitby would only make them more vengeful.

"Eleanor, I'm sure they're perfectly safe. How would they have known about the house?"

"They knew about the office in Whitby."

"But that's part of the business."

"Aye, part of the business, and even I don't know what he's got down in London." She glanced back at him and wanted to say something more. She closed her mouth and focused on walking instead. Angus and his fellow drovers had arrived shortly after the men from London. She had not been expecting any of them. She was still not sure how she felt about them arriving unannounced. It had been months since she'd last seen Angus, and that had not been in happy circumstance either. Trouble seemed to dog her these days.

There was a figure standing by the path as it curved in readiness to start downwards in the direction of Commondale. The mist they had seen crusading over the moorland had dispersed, and yet the figure remained hazy, as if it wasn't quite there, despite the moonlight providing enough light to see. Angus put a hand out to Eleanor's arm as if to put her protectively behind him, but she irritably shook him off.

"It's only Atheleys," she muttered, bypassing him and hurrying up to her friend for news.

The men muttered amongst themselves, but continued walking. Eleanor told them to continue to the village and she would catch them up. The girl-woman beside her, in a dress of rags that spoke of poverty and great riches simultaneously, watched them go by with curiously sparkling eyes. They'd been all over the country and seen a great many things, but this was a strange place at night.

Allan felt a shiver ride down his body hair, and as he passed by the loitering newcomer his eyes widened. They ought not to leave Eleanor alone here. He overtook a couple of the other Scotsmen to reach Angus. "That's a trowie," he hissed. "You can't leave Eleanor with her."

Angus glanced over at his second cousin. The man was brought up in a world of superstition and folktales, old Celtic lore of fairies and magic, remnants of Nordic trolls and elves.

"Fairies, elves, the little folk, call them what you will. You ken what I'm saying."

"I think they call them hobgoblins round these parts." Angus looked back to where Eleanor was talking to the strange woman. The two were walking slowly, picking up the end of the line. "But that's just one of Eleanor's friends, one of the locals."

"Aye, one of the local what?"

A Hobgoblin? Angus had heard all the stories himself growing up. Be mindful to say thank you when you pass over the old stone bridge, or the fairies will curse you. Stories of babes swapped with fairy babies, changelings that would howl and wail. Strange lights in the forest. Old tales for children, but how much was of flesh and blood he was uncertain of the older he grew. What a man could not see was hard to believe in. The silver haired girl certainly looked a little odd, but isolation would make an oddity of anyone. If she lived like a hermit out on these moors, they could hardly expect her to look like the enlightened worldly folk of this new age. If ever he had seen a real hobgoblin, he was sure it had been Eleanor's father – a short, gnarled cunning man with a head out of proportion to the rest of his body. And even then he was just a human. "Children's stories."

"I know a trowie when I see one. Don't let Eleanor follow her to the hills, else we'll nay see her for seven years."

"Allan, you're letting the dark play tricks on your mind."

"I am not."

"It's a bit late for a walking party," Atheleys commented idly as she fell in to step with Eleanor. "It's been a while since you were last here. Not since..."

Distracted from her current goal, her thoughts went back several months. "Is he...?"

"You can't," Atheleys said, already knowing what Eleanor wanted. "You can't see him." She clutched onto Eleanor's forearm as if imparting great secrets. "He's just behind us but if you look back he'll be gone. You must never look."

In other words dead. She wiped at her eyes with the back of her hand. She'd had the running of the Hob's business concerns in Whitby to distract her mind from the matter the last few months. Whitby, the old whaling port where it was more acceptable for a woman to deal with finances, bills and traders, for the men of the households would be gone for so many months on the whaling boats. Someone had to keep the homes and businesses going in their absence. So many said a woman's place was in the home, and that females hadn't the head for numbers and business, but Eleanor found she coped quite well despite the so-called handicap of having a woman's mind. And now she was away from her ledgers, she must focus on something concrete. "We have to get to the Pines," she said, moving her gaze back into the direction of home. "I have to see that Mamma is well."

"Is she sick?"

"There were two men..." she stopped speaking for a moment and looked to Atheleys. There wasn't a thing that grew, lived, died or happened on the moors that Atheleys didn't know about. "Did they come this way? Have you seen any men on the moors?"

Atheleys gave a coy little grin. "There's always men on the moors. I've seen many."

"But this night. Men not from these parts."

"Greedy and grabbing. All they saw was theirs."

"They were here?"

"They still are."

"Out on the moors?" Eleanor felt herself looking around in a panic. Please don't say they were too late.

"They'll always be here now."

Atheleys' innocent comment had foreboding undertones. Eleanor looked questioningly at her childhood friend but received nothing but a blank, innocent expression in return.

"Look." Atheleys pulled away from the path, suddenly distracted and striding through the heather. She crouched down and parted two of the shrubs with her hands.

Eleanor raised her eyes to the night sky of stars. This was not the time for a natural history exploration. Atheleys had been like this when they were children, suddenly distracted to look at rocks on the floor, strange tiny plants clinging to the ground that would eat insects, abandoned windswept feathers and broken eggshells. What could she have found now? It was too late in the year for nests.

"We don't have time for this."

"Look!"

Groaning, she cast a glance at the line of Scotsmen who were getting further away before hurrying over to the crouched Atheleys. "What is it?" She peered into the opened undergrowth, a little surprised to see someone's hidden stash of treasures. Her brow creased in concern as she took in the finer details of the cloth purse. It looked like the one her mother kept the housekeeping money in.

"So pretty." Atheleys lifted up the gold necklace with the heavy dark blue stones. Followed by a ring.

"Those are Mamma's," she started, almost an accusation. Why do you have them here? Atheleys' keen little face told her all she needed or wanted to know.

"You should keep them safe," she told Eleanor, passing them into her hands, followed by the money. "Otherwise those jewels will be kept in the house no matter what happens."

"What could you mean by that?"

But Atheleys was distracted, back on her feet and running after the Scotsmen. "Make haste," she called over her shoulder to Eleanor. "You need to go home."

Eleanor put the treasures into her bag and started to run. By the time she caught up with Angus, Atheleys had disappeared into the moorland.

Maud had fallen to pieces. The recent attack was certainly not the first, for over the years she had taken on a lot of trauma and shame and weathered it all. Yet everyone has a breaking point, and she could no longer be philosophical and continue with ease.

Life had certainly not been easy for Maud Hurst. She'd given birth three times, to four children: the twins, then Clara, then finally Stephen. So she was accustomed to pain. To rebuke those few who scorned complaints over childbirth as if it were nothing, Maud always had in her back catalogue the infamous dentistry incident that had permanently damaged her upper jaw. Humiliation and shame had unintentionally been her life's business. She had fallen pregnant with the twins whilst an unmarried maid servant. Her children had been taken from her when Gillian had married without consent. Maud had been beaten and raped by her own husband, although there were plenty who said violation was impossible within a marriage. She knew that people in the village gossiped about her. She was an odd woman on the village outskirts living in a usurped family home and married to a stunted little man who some joked came from the other side. She'd taken it all and continued with the hard work, running the home, playing the role of dutiful wife and mother. All for a vile little man. This rape, punishment again taken on his behalf, had been the final straw and the haystack collapsed. Maud had sobbed until she was dry and withered, then become catatonic, sprawled out on her bed and barely breathing. All she had managed to say was that this was their divine retribution, a punishment to even things out.

Punishment indeed, Ellen Withers thought. Over the years she'd taken more than double the punishment to cancel out all the wicked things she had done. Besides, surely the good deeds ought to cancel out the bad. Ellen didn't believe there was such a balance in the universe; if there was certain people wouldn't be placed in such positions of privilege as if they were a breed apart, and get away with all they did. In a just world she was sure women wouldn't be considered less worthy than men. She'd seen what work and lives women got themselves through, and she'd met few men who were up to such a challenge.

Despite the intended humiliation of the violation, Ellen was quick to move on after the men had laughingly left with their booty, threatening with vagueness that they'd be back for full payment sometime if Hurst didn't sort his affairs. When she felt ready to drag her carcass bones from the kitchen table, Ellen tottered to the open front door and spat out into the night. Let them rot in hell.

With the ripped sides of her bodice flapping open, she went out into the darkness to the farm pump. She worked the pump handle to draw fresh water up from the well, surprised to see that her hands were shaking. She was not going to let a couple of worthless old villains unsettle her mind and dignity.

There was a candlelight flickering from the window across the yard. So Mr Hodgkins, the farm manager hand-picked by Hobart Hurst, had woken at some point, and kept himself in his own separate lodgings. So much for the honourable protection of men. She doubted he could get a good look at her chest in this light, but she scowled and cursed him nevertheless, before bending over the pail to scrub at her body and remove every last feeling of those vile hands on her flesh. Back in the main house she threw her dress onto the fire. Never mind that she had precious few dresses and that had been one of the better ones. She did not want to see it again, not after that filth had taken that which had not been offered. She had just dressed herself again, feeling as though at least on the outside she'd look as though she was calm and in control, when the door began to thunder. Maud's sobbing picked up in intensity. Ellen gritted her teeth. The bastards were back for more? She went to the range and picked up the fire poker before going to the front door.

"Ellen, Mamma? It's me, Eleanor."

"Eleanor?" Ellen wrenched open the door, in as much a panic as if it was her own child out in the night. At nineteen Eleanor wasn't a slip of a child, but Ellen had been with the family since before the twins, Eleanor and Gillian, were born, and still thought of them as babes. On hearing her voice she remembered that the intruders had said they'd already been to Whitby. What had they done to Eleanor before trekking across the moors to have their way with Ellen and Maud?

"Eleanor, are you all right? Those men didn't...?"

"Those men?" Eleanor started as she found herself tugged into an iron hug from Ellen Withers. "Oh no, I'd hoped they wouldn't know about the farm. I didn't tell them."

"Someone will have told. They didn't hurt you?"

"No. As luck would have it, the drovers arrived only a minute or so afterwards and..."

Ellen's face darkened as she noted the men loitering in the shadows behind for the first time. Angus MacCaskill she recognised all too well. His manner and his look suggested he was a decent sort, and some of his actions in the past had confirmed this. She wasn't one to judge too harshly, there were plenty who got in the family way outside of marriage. But he already had a wife at home. He should never have touched their precious Eleanor. The other men she didn't recognise, but they looked how she imagined Scottish drovers to be. Weathered outdoors men, more with beards than not, in long all-weather coats, good sturdy boots, and hats that would keep the rain out of their eyes. And a memory that contained every toll road and every awkward alternative route to avoid the fees scattered across the country. They would know fifty ways from Falkirk to London and back again, have seen more places and folks in a year than most would know in a lifetime.

"Miss Withers," Angus started.

"Don't you *Miss Withers* me!"

"Ellen," Eleanor scolded. "If they hadn't come when they had, I don't know what might have happened. There was only me and Lucy Ann in the house. I don't know who those men from London were, but they weren't legitimate tradesmen or merchants. I don't know what he'd involved himself in down there. I didn't get involved with the London work much."

"You should not still be seeing him."

Eleanor sighed. There were more pressing things at hand just now. "This is the first time I've seen Angus." She hadn't been able to take a moment to think how she felt about his arrival, for she and Lucy Ann had been in a corner in the kitchen when the Scots had arrived and they'd simply been thankful for the rescue. Eleanor had been ready with the poker, Lucy Ann with a pie dish, and they would have fought for themselves and each other, but Lucy Ann had the emaciated look of a child despite the fact she was close to Eleanor's age, and Eleanor wasn't a match for two brutes such as those. "The men, they didn't..."

Ellen averted her gaze and pulled back from Eleanor. Now she felt the shame. Knowing that other people knew what had been done to her. Especially in front of these men. "What's done is done," she muttered, pushing the door fully open. "They are gone now, with what little money we had. It is the middle of the night; you people ought to come into the kitchen where it is warm. There is a broth on the range."

This fact garnered a murmur of approval from Angus' comrades, and the rabble piled into the house. Drovers were generally known for their reliability and honour, despite Angus' past behaviour. There were good reasons why there were such requirements on a man's life before he could get the drover's licence; on age, property and marital status. These men took letters, money, farmer's stock and goods up and down the country. People trusted them, and they needed that good name and trust above else or their trade in droving would not last long. They'd all be safe in the farmhouse now.

The Scots clustered around the range, sorting out the broth and bread. They'd not eaten upon arrival in Whitby as planned, and were ravenous. Allan assured Ellen with a gentle touch to the arm that she need not serve or mind them. For a moment Ellen had been blushingly flattered by the kind attention before she remembered he was a drover and there'd be an old Scottish woman at home for this man who was clearly far too old for her any old way.

"Where is Stephen?" Eleanor looked about for her younger brother. He was only eight years old and very much the protected baby of the family. Stephen had a mild, angelic nature and could see nothing but the good in people. Harsh words hurt him. He would not have survived those men and what they might have done.

"He's down at Gillian's this night. He's seen nothing. They don't know about him."

"Thank God. And where is Mamma?" Eleanor caught Ellen's eye. They were at the side of the room, away from the hungry men. "Ellen, what happened?"

The humiliation swept back upon her. She couldn't speak of it, to admit that she had been so vulnerable. Ellen shrugged her shoulders, as if to say these things couldn't be helped. "Two men came here. They were loud and threatening. They made off with your mother's money, her jewellery."

"Did they..." Eleanor didn't know how to phrase it, and almost didn't want to know. She had noticed the dress burning on the fire. "...do anything?"

"Your mother is inconsolable; you should go to her."

In the master bed chamber, Maud was bodily flung across the bedspread in a most distraught way, face down and catatonic. She had sobbed violently until her body was wrenched of all moisture, and now she merely breathed and lay, staring at nothing with glassy eyes. She did not show any signs of recognition when Eleanor slipped into the room and crouched down by the bed, clutching at her mother's hand.

"Mamma, Mamma, are you well?" she whispered loudly, feeling distress when her mother did not even glance in her direction. She tugged at her mother's hand and Maud's pupils shifted a little to look blankly at her daughter. Eleanor was an adult, and looking after herself and her father's business in Whitby these days, but seeing her mother like this put a fear in her that dragged her back to her childhood years. "Oh, Mamma, what did they do to you?"

Maud merely sighed and looked to the bedclothes in front of her face.

"I have some good news," Eleanor scrabbled in her bag, looking for some cheer. "Look, the household money," she proclaimed, holding the purse up to Maud's face. "And here's your ruby ring." The little light that filtered into the room barely glanced off the red rock. Maud gave no sign of having heard her. "At least we got these back," Eleanor waived, feeling her eyes welling up with tears. She took her mother's hand and struggled to move the fingers apart to get the ring on. It was like working with sticks. "And your necklace."

Something seemed to snap in Maud's mind when she saw the blue stones of the Spanish necklace. A memory of when she had first been given it, perhaps. Remembering Hobart setting it around her neck. A pre payment for what he would do to her. Her eyes met Eleanor's gaze. "You must take it."

"What? No, this is yours," Eleanor protested as Maud pushed the necklace back to her.

"You must. It's your inheritance."

"Mamma, there's nothing wrong with you," Eleanor's voice sounded thin.

"Take it now before people take it from you." Maud pulled her hands in under her body like a cat, to be such Eleanor couldn't force the necklace on her. She closed her eyes and muttered something about how she needed to sleep, and that was the subject matter closed.

Eleanor sat back on her haunches and regarded the necklace. It was very beautiful, and there was such craftsmanship in it. She didn't think it had ever really been established where the Hob had acquired such a piece. But she had vague, unnerving feelings of some of the trouble the necklace had caused the three adults of the house, Maud, the Hob and Ellen Withers, at one point. Reluctantly, she slipped the necklace back into her bag, then returned to the kitchen to join the others and see if there was any broth left.

It was surreal catching sight of Gillian in the village. As if seeing what an alternative set of circumstances in life could have offered Eleanor. Although they were identical twins, there were fathoms of difference between them, not just in what life had dealt but in their spirit and aspirations. The young woman he saw with the basket caught in the crook of her arm was serious and pious. She looked unhappy, as if life was bitterly playing against her, no matter how hard she tried. And so she would punish herself, to make herself more worthy. Her face was thin and sternly set, her hair carefully flattened and pinned out of the way, her bonnet covering her face as if she did not wish the world to look upon her. He had moved to speak to her, then thought better of it and remembered his chores in the village. He knew all about Gillian from long conversations in the past with her twin sister, Eleanor, but he had never met the girl. Judging from her body language she would not want to talk. In fact it looked as though she did not want to talk to anyone, keeping her eyes low and scuttling along the edges of paths, as if she were afraid her existence might be confirmed.

Later, when he'd walked back up the hill to Pines Lodge, with the extra eggs Ellen Withers had requested, he'd found Eleanor outside perched on a barrel and gazing out to the moorland. "Eleanor?"

She looked over to him, still held back in her thoughts. Forgetting that she was supposed to be furious with him, she relaxed into a smile. It soon dropped when she saw the look on his face, as though all was forgiven, and they could continue with whatever their relationship could be called.

Angus hung back for a moment, not sure if he ought to let her be. Anna had been a marriage of convenience to get the licence, but it was Eleanor he had thought of all down the drove, all those months in the south working. "I thought I saw you in the village," he started, trying to disarm her with pleasant conversation.

Eleanor creased her brow. "I've been here."

"I'm guessing it was your sister. You, but not you. She looks severe."

"Oh," Eleanor nodded and returned her gaze to the moors. "Gillian was always the dutiful, dependable one. She's been married years and still not managed to have children, she..." her thoughts dropped off, remembering the last time Gillian had spoken to her. Such bitterness and hatred, for her own twin sister had committed the double sin of falling pregnant outside of marriage, and falling pregnant unintentionally first time whilst her sister had been trying and failing for years. Gillian was a very Christian girl, but with every failure in life she would become more devout, thinking that if only she followed the Bible a little more closely, all would be well.

Her attention was gone, as if to say he was dismissed now. He needed to make his peace, and gain a little hope if nothing else. He stood beside her, leaning against the stone building wall and looked out to the moors. "Who was the lassie we met on the moors last night?"

"Just a friend."

She didn't want to talk to him. It made breaking the ice awkward. "Allan thinks she is a trowie."

Eleanor glanced at him.

"You know, the wee folk."

No response to that, not even a laugh of derision, as if the talk of goblins and fairies was utter nonsense in this age of enlightenment. Angus wasn't sure whether it meant she would not talk to him or didn't want to admit that the lass wasn't of this world. Would she really believe it? Most people didn't believe in these things, up to a point, but out in the country, they wouldn't push a superstition too far, leaving out food with an embarrassed downcast glance. Just in case.

"How long does it take to get to London?"

He was surprised by her sudden question. "From here? Depends how you go. If you're walking, droving, riding, on the post carriage..."

"I can afford transportation."

"Why would you be wanting to be away down to London? It's a big place; many aren't to be trusted down there..."

"I can look after myself. I need to go down and look for the Hob."

"The Hob?" More wee folk. Trowies and goblins. "Oh, you mean your father," he realised. He'd heard Eleanor refer to her father as the Hob before. Perhaps it was an abbreviation of Hobart, but probably more to do with the man's appearance. "But why, we already know what's happened with him."

She looked at him as if he were an idiot. "No one knows that we know."

"But London..."

"Two thugs from London turned up wanting money and retribution. No one I know has seen him for months. No sight, no letters. If I truly didn't know, I would be heading for London now. I have the address of his office and I need to find out."

"Aye, I suppose. But Eleanor, you're just a young woman. You can't go travelling down there on your own."

"I've coped with much more than folk assume I'm fit for," she snapped.

"I don't mean it like that. But a young unmarried woman."

"I'll just tell them I'm married. It's not like you can tell from looking at a person."

He took the stab. He deserved it, probably more, but he didn't want to get into a cycle of apologies now; not when he was hearing the start of some harebrained scheme of going to London to play detective. Country folk had no idea of what the world was like down there. "A married woman would be with her husband."

"Not necessarily."

"I'll go with you."

"You're not my husband."

"We can lie about it."

"You certainly can."

They held one another's gazes, not quite sure in which direction they wanted to take this. It felt as though this was a decisive moment. Either they would part and never see one another again; or they would accept a life of sin. They couldn't return to how things had been before. Still, given their history, they were rattling through the seven deadly sins at a steady speed. He wasn't sure what to say to make it right, only that he didn't just want to walk away. He started to open his mouth, no words, let alone sentences ready, and was saved from saying something impulsive and stupid by the slow arrival of an old hag thumping her way up the hill.

"Who's the witch?"

"Angus!" Eleanor hissed at him. She slipped off the barrel and hurried over to the elderly woman. "Old Marsden," she greeted the woman. She had seemed old when Eleanor had been a little girl; old even when she had helped with the delivery of the twins. Now she gravitated with ancient wisdom, creaking bones and an increasingly gummy and wrinkled smile. "What brings you up here to us? You should have sent word."

"Someone needs to see to your mother. She is not well."

"I..."

The woman patted her hand. Reassuring. Not the kind of help you have the knowledge to give. "I have something for the pain here."

"But how did you know?" Eleanor wondered as the woman continued past her and up to the house. She continued to turn on her heel, watching Marsden walk by, before her gaze settled on Angus. "Did you say something in the village?"

"Do you think I'm a complete fool?"

She shook her head. "It's Old Marsden. She always knows what's going on without being told."

"Witches as well now?" Angus scoffed. "Nothing travels as well as bad news. Someone will have seen those crooks in the village. Probably asking for directions."

And the news had spread. Not just around the village, but surrounding villages and hamlets, outlying farms and manor houses. Late that afternoon the local magistrate rode up on his horse to offer his condolences at the crime and to offer his help. The gossip had set minds working and tongues wagging. Everyone was trying to remember the last time they actually had seen Hobart Hurst in the area, scuttling across the moors at night, taking payment, dropping off orders, or striding out along the river towards Whitby. No one was sure but the general consensus was that it had been a long time.

Whatever Marsden had brought, it had taken some effect upon Maud. She was not back to her usual self, but she was able to sit up, speak and even take a little sustenance. She and Eleanor received the Magistrate in the parlour. Ellen Withers scuttled to and fro in the kitchen, trying to get the tea and cakes together whilst clearing up after the Scots and cursing at Angus whilst he tried to make himself useful. The other Scots had taken their leave. Now that the trouble was over, they were keen to head on home. A drover always had itchy feet for the road, and if a place was not home it did not feel natural to linger too long. Angus remained. Regardless of what Eleanor might say, she would not be going to London without him.

"It is an outrage that this has happened at all," the Magistrate declared, as if his disapproval would make all well. "This is a tranquil land of decent people. That such thieves should come and treat our locals with such disrespect. May I assure you that word is out and when these blaggards are apprehended..."

"Thank you," Maud, tired and perhaps a little doped up, managed a weak smile. "It is most reassuring to know that you are here to keep an eye on law and order."

"Well, yes, indeed," the Magistrate gruffled. He had seen Hurst on many occasions, and shared laughter and a glass or two of port on most of those, but he had had little dealings with the wife. An oddly meek yet confident lady. Surprisingly together despite the rumours he had heard. No doubt exaggerated. "I do not wish to vex you further..."

Eleanor's eyes narrowed slightly. Anyone who started a subject like that was bound to bring woe to the table.

"...but the fact is that this dreadful incident has brought certain facts to my attention. As far as I can gather no one in the valley has seen your husband for many months. May I ask if you have heard from him?"

"Not for months and months," Maud sighed.

"And is such a time lapse normal?"

"Not this long."

The magistrate's brow creased. He was wondering why the family had done nothing. Eleanor could see the thought flitting through his eyes. "I haven't had correspondence from him for many months," she interrupted. She could see on his face that he was a little put out that one so young and unmarried would step in to the conversation. A woman at that. "As you probably are aware, I manage the family concerns in Whitby," she continued. "I've had no word for a long time. My father had talked of perhaps doing some business in France, and I suppose I had assumed he had crossed the channel. I have to admit the day to day work had distracted me of how much time had passed. And when those villains..."

"Yes, indeed. One is busy, then suddenly another season has passed. But the truth of the matter is that I am now concerned. Concerned for your father, your mother..." he looked between the two women. "For if something has happened to Mr Hurst..." he quickly held up his hand. "Please do not upset yourself yet, Mrs Hurst," he added, although there was no need. Maud was not worried about her husband. "We must think to your..." She really did not seem to be all there in mind. He looked back at Eleanor. "We must consider your mother's safety and how things will be in the future. Villains aside, there could be genuine debtors and contracts unfulfilled. And of course the legalities of ownership..."

He was hinting at the possibility the Hob might be dead, Eleanor realised. And the Hob owned everything. Then what? "You don't think...?"

"I don't know what to think," he admitted. "But I have taken the liberty of hiring a man I know. A man from Leeds. He has a canny and enquiring mind. He will be going to London, but will also wish to speak to you."

"Speak to us?"

"Trust me, this man is very adept at piecing together a puzzle. If there are any clues to be had, he will find out what happened to your father."

"What if he can't?"

"Then the seven year rule will have to be applied. Before your mother can be declared a widow." He misread the distress on Eleanor's face. "Don't worry about your father, I am sure he is well, but he must be found. And if it is to be the worst, then we must look to the last will and testament, so that everyone knows where they stand."

"He had written..."

"Oh yes," the Magistrate nodded gravely.

Eleanor felt sick. They could be left with nothing, not even the roofs over their heads. "But in that case we would have to wait seven years?"

"Well, only if he cannot be found in one state or another. The law requires seven years to be sure."

Seven years, she thought. We have seven years to make our necessary arrangements.

London overwhelmed her.

On her first evening in London, Eleanor plunged the depth of her youth and ignorance. She had considered herself worldly. She worked in Whitby and dealt with Baltic traders. She negotiated trade deals with strange men who spoke bizarre sounding languages. If they came from another country, London felt like another world. The Londoners could see she was naive and only had a basic general knowledge of the ways of the world. They could see that Eleanor was essentially the definitive of gullible. People could tell her anything and she would believe them. Eleanor felt like a gasping new born fish, wide-eyed and with a memory of only a few seconds. If a man approached and claimed to be the Hob, she'd probably believe him. Which was quite ridiculous, for Eleanor knew for a fact that the Hob was dead, and had been in such a state for many a month. It had been an accident, a moment of blind fury but given the particular circumstances no outsider would believe it. They would talk of murder and shake their heads and Angus would swing from the end of a rope. And for what? To bring retribution for a man who had made all their lives a misery? He was best off dead. The only issue seemed to be that even from beyond the grave, his presence, or lack thereof was making life very awkward.

From Commondale they had walked over the moors and down into the Vale of Mowbray to meet with the post carriage at Thirsk. From that point they had travelled in cramped carriages all the way south to London. Angus had navigated their route with a thoughtless amble. The time and the miles, the changing scenery left Eleanor quite in awe. And this was only heading down south. Think of the north, think of all the places he had seen on the drove. Their little lives of Commondale and the Esk Valley were but a speck in the world. Even Angus's travels were all contained within one island. There were tales of even further: the whalers who went to the ice seas to hunt those great blubbery beasts. There were great ships bringing in timber manned by sailors speaking strange languages, of Estonian, of Russian and Dutch. Seafarers who carried a stillness emanating from endless miles of strange, ancient deep forests. And further beyond this was the entire globe. The pride of Whitby was one of its trained sons who had set sail and never stopped. Captain James Cook, apprentice trained in Whitby. Only to be butchered in '79 on some island an unimaginable length away from where he began. The notion was up there with fanciful ideas like going to the moon. The immense potential of it all gave Eleanor itchy feet. If she'd been born a man she would have wanted the drover's life. She couldn't have that, but she desperately wanted something akin to it.

Dreams of travel and the massive world bubbled inside. In contradiction what surrounded her was the immense and yet claustrophobic and puzzling London. There was so much to see and think on. She was swept up by whatever she was told. Going along with any old lie. She turned from the window and watched as Angus shut the door. "You could have just told them I was your sister."

"You look nothing like my sister, and I am very glad of it."

"So I'm Mrs MacCaskill now?"

"There are worse things to be."

"And what will happen with this man the magistrate has hired?"

"You weren't wanting to wed him as well?"

"Angus!" Eleanor hissed. "You know what I mean. If he comes to London and finds out a Mrs MacCaskill has been visiting the Hob's offices, looking into the business arrangements; he's going to be wondering who she is. No one at home thinks I'm married because I'm not. It will bring scandal on my head and attention to a situation we were hoping would lie quietly beneath the stones."

"It will be well. And it is not your neck at risk."

"Don't." She turned back to the window. Tears pricked at her eyes. She had been so strong, keeping busy with the work, keeping focused. She did not think of the night the Hob died, the night when her own boy passed, or the loss of her first love, when she learned he was already married. She should have thrown him out in Whitby. She could have given a terse thank you to his friends for helping with those rogues, then set Angus on the road north to Falkirk. She shouldn't have anything more to do with him. And the very thought broke her heart all over again.

She wiped at her eyes with the back of her hand. "And I don't know what you think we're going to do with this room in the inn."

"This is our base. We have to stay somewhere."

"As man and wife?" She looked to the solitary bed in the room.

"I am not going to take advantage of you; I hope you know me better than that..." he caught her look and let the thought stop there, quickly moving on. "I will be sleeping in the chair here. You don't know what business your father was involved in. Those two that turned up on your doorstep could only be the beginning. I'm not leaving an innocent girl..."

"I'm hardly innocent."

"Eleanor, please. You cannot continue to attack me like this. I will leave as soon as I have you out of London and you will never see me again, but I would much prefer to remain in your life. I made a terrible mistake."

"A terrible mistake?"

"When I married Anna."

The woman had a name. She did not wish to hear it. Eleanor smoothed down her skirts for want of something else to do with her hands. "I am tired," she finally said, not able to meet Angus' eye. "The journey has been long and there is much to do tomorrow. I will need my wits about me."

"Aye, get some rest." He supposed that was the best he could expect for now, and at least it wasn't an outright no. Angus slumped into the chair by the fireplace, and watched as Eleanor climbed fully dressed into bed. A sensible man, a realistic man, would see the light and sneak out in the night, he told himself. These ties ought to be severed. He was quite sure he'd still be there in the morning.

It was not just one morning they had at the inn, as it transpired, but several mornings. So started the serious game of investigating Hobart Hurst's secret little business empire, pretending to care and acting as though they did not know where he was or what had happened to him. The first place to call on had been his office, which was the only address in London Eleanor had prior knowledge of. She had corresponded with the chief clerk, a certain Walter Tilling, on matters of business, and goods being sent north or south depending on requirements. In reality Walter Tilling matched his handwriting as a slight, spindly creature with a tendency to lean to a life he could not afford. His spending habits were immediately apparent from the frilled shirt sleeves that peered out from his jacket sleeves. It was not the best attire for someone who spent a lot of time writing in ink. He was visibly shocked when he realised that Eleanor was his employer's daughter. This was not how he had imagined the offspring of Mr Hurst. For a moment he flattered himself of great alliances, leaning in towards her with a twinkle in his eye before he caught a look from the man accompanying her, and leaned back again as if at the whim of a gentle breeze.

"Miss Hurst, this is..."

"Mrs MacCaskill," the man gruffly corrected him.

Eleanor's lips formed a thin line.

"Oh, my apologies, I did not realise congratulations were to be had for your recent nuptials," Walter fawned at her. His mind was always ticking over. Hobart Hurst hadn't been here for months. Things had continued well enough without, Walter minding London, and Eleanor Whitby, but now that it was possible that Hobart Hurst would be out of the picture for an undetermined amount of time, this put Eleanor effectively in charge. "Your father had not mentioned it the last time he was here, but then it has been some months since he last set foot in this office."

"When did you last see him?"

"It would be last year now."

"I know he talked of going to France, to the continent, but I am not sure if he went ahead with those plans."

"I would not recommend France. There is trouble brewing there, this is what we hear. The last I know he was heading for home, to the marital home, close to Whitby. At least that was what I told..." Walter faltered on the nudge from Eleanor's sharp eyebrows. He realised that something up north must have happened to cause this visit. Something unpleasant. If he would take a guess, it would be the stupid and slightly desperate. Those whose business practices were a little less than legal. Jacob and Andrew were a couple of thieving thugs, but there had been an arrangement with Mr Hurst that Walter had not been privy to. His absence occurred before business was concluded, and they had turned up at the office sniffing out money. Walter feared the wrath of his employer and did not want them taking what their busy hands liked. This was Hurst's problem, and the sooner they had left Walter Tilling alone, the better. He had suggested they get themselves up to Yorkshire and seek their recompense there.

"Told who?" Good grief, Eleanor thought, was it this spineless frippery who had sent those thugs to attack and rape her mother? "London's criminals?"

"I am not privy to all your father's dealings. And it would be slander to make such wide sweeping judgements on people when one is not completely certain..." His defence was faltering and neither

Eleanor MacCaskill nor her husband looked impressed. Walter wheedled back to his place behind the writing desk. "Mr Hurst owns two warehouses at the river. The dockyards attract many types of characters, you understand. The two..." he paused, having been about to say gentlemen, but it did not seem to be the right word. "They had an understanding with your father and led me to understand that they had not yet been fully paid. I do not know the details of such an arrangement and could not pay on something I had no knowledge of, so I suggested they dealt directly with your father and sought him out."

"You sent them up to deal with defenceless women?" Angus sounded disgusted.

Walter shrunk into himself. "I was of the understanding Mr Hurst was still up north."

"We have not seen him since last year either. No word has been heard." Eleanor said curtly. "It would seem that my father has gone missing without us noticing. A man has been hired to look in to this matter. To find him."

"A man? Hired?" Walter looked questioningly at the Scot as if to ask if he was the said man. The Scot returned his gaze stonily. Perhaps not. It was good to know that the matter would be looked at properly, by a professional man. "Quite sensible in the circumstances. But if there is a man hired to investigate, then I am not certain why you yourselves are here?"

"With my father missing, and remaining so for an undetermined length of time, his business must be attended to on the assumption he is incapacitated. Therefore I think it acceptable to assume I will manage..."

"A woman in charge?"

"I assure you it is quite acceptable in Whitby as the men absent themselves for months out on the ships. And I have managed well enough these past few years. I deal with the warehouse, the whalers, the blubberhouses, even traders from far off places such as Russia. And you and I have managed admirably via correspondence to keep things moving. I will assess what business is ongoing in London. If you could give me the addresses to the warehouses, and any other notable places, I will make a tour. I will also need to see the accounts..."

Walter visibly paled.

"Will that be an issue?"

A woman checking his work? If she had still been Miss Hurst, this could have been a golden opportunity to realign the matter to his benefit, but if the girl was now a married woman, there was nothing here to be won. The best scenario he could aim for was to make her content on matters, so that she might leave and let him run things how he liked. A little private profit was not strictly speaking what Mr Hurst's business was about, certainly not for the employees. But London living was expensive and Walter had a certain lifestyle to keep up. "I am concerned by the thought of you visiting the warehouses. For a lady of such..."

"I will be there. No need for concern." Angus interrupted.

There was a tense moment of silence. "Very well," Walter nodded. "Let me make you a list."

The warehouses did not bring up any anomalies, although Eleanor had not been minded to look for problems. She was distracted by other fury, reminded by it every time she heard Angus' voice. It made it hard to concentrate on needling out secrets and discrepancies that did not wish to be found. When Angus had joked that she looked vexed to see things were running smoothly, she had almost attacked him. When this man hired by the magistrate arrived in London asking questions, the name of Mrs MacCaskill was sure to pop up. Mrs MacCaskill, Hobart Hurst's daughter. But she wasn't married. It would raise suspicions, and would be the ruin of them all. To which Angus had replied they could just get married down here in London where no one knew any better. Between the droving road and spending months in Whitby, he'd only have to go up to Falkirk once a year at the start of the drove. It could be done, and no one would know. No one but God, she had said, although as the words came out of her mouth she knew she wasn't convinced by that argument. There were stronger women, certainly her sister, who believed in the sanctity of God and would never betray such a solemn oath, even if they had not been party to the first promise. But Eleanor was not saintly, and the longer the suggestion bedded down in her mind, the less she could argue away from it. She would not be able to hold out forever, and by the time they were departing London, some weeks later, they had been married in front of a God who did not send down thunderbolts or dispatch a last minute messenger to confirm there was an impediment. On the journey back to Yorkshire, she was to all intents and purposes, Mrs MacCaskill. If the legality of the matter was ever investigated, it would be proved otherwise, but in the meantime she had a ring on her finger, a new name to sign, and furthermore, unknown to everyone, a new life forming inside.

The news of Hobart Hurst's unexplained absence from life and business spread organically across the land. Gossip and chatter moved from village to village as it has done since the beginning of time. Most of the time it was precipitated by the non arrival of payment or goods or both. Word got around that the headquarters had been temporarily moved to Whitby and a daughter was keeping an eye on things until the master reappeared. Many laughed at the idea, but headed across to the coastal port or sent correspondence, some hoping to get more than they deserved from a foolish girl who couldn't possibly understand the ways of the world. Instead they were met with a shrewd businesswoman, a married woman, and one who was expecting what most of the world and society would consider her first child.

Some arrangements were of a more odd nature, classed as a gentlemen's agreement. It felt inappropriate to go cap in hand to the daughter. Especially when the matter regarded another daughter who had been given such obvious advantages over the young woman who was now in charge of the purse strings. Better to bring the contract to an end, now that Hobart Hurst was no longer available to instruct on proceedings. And so it was, in the following spring, that Clara Hurst found herself on a cart with her packed luggage, leaving

Thirsk and rattling her way back to her early childhood home in Commondale.

Clara Hurst, the only true daughter of Hobart, was now a young lady of fourteen years and on the surface a perfect picture of good manners, breeding and exceeding beauty. Most who had met her father simply could not believe that they were related. She had sweet blue eyes and golden blonde hair that fell to her waist in natural waves. Long dark lashes that would flutter and smile in pretended innocence, and a sweet voice that was pitch perfect. She was a beauty and had been aware of the fact since birth. She was a little coquette for attention, who had disregarded her lessons by a private tutor from London whilst still living at home on the farm property in Commondale. In a move both to improve his daughter and punish his wife for misdeeds relating to the other children, Hobart had made arrangements with a businessman living in Thirsk. For a fee, Clara would live with the family and have the benefit of the tutor hired for the family's daughter, so that the two girls could be schooled in the art of being proper ladies together. Clara would see more of the world and civilisation, and eventually grow into a valuable tool for forming an alliance to expand the Hurst business empire through marriage when the time was ripe.

At the age of eight Clara Hurst had been sent to live with the Mowbray family in the market town of Thirsk in the lower plains further inland. She had not taken to the governess, a Miss Boye, who had her eyes set on marriage with the widowed father until an unexplained condition removed her hair. The father lost interest after that, although the woman remained to continue schooling Clara Hurst and Annabel Mowbray for some time before the reminders of a fate not to be became too much. Clara had enjoyed her position in the house, and although she never learned as much as when she had spent her days back in Commondale with Old Marsden, she was finding her feet and settling her place in decent and polite society. Andrew Mowbray, Annabel's elder brother, was taken with Clara from their first meeting and it was a situation Clara was only too keen to encourage. Andrew was away at boarding school a lot of the time, but she was always waiting whenever he returned for the holidays. And how she grew and blossomed between each parting.

Her horror was acute when Mr Mowbray informed her that the funds her father had provided for her keep had run out, and despite numerous attempts, her father could not be contacted. Regrettably she would have to return to her family home until the matter was resolved. Clara felt a panic in her stomach. It was only a few weeks before Andrew, now seventeen and becoming a man was due home for a visit, and she felt it was imperative to be here so that lesser beauties such as Bethany Middlewell, could not distract his attention. She had tried to persuade Mr Mowbray with what little warning she had been given, that her father would soon rectify the situation, but she could tell from the man's stare that nothing but ready money in his hand would be enough now. On the morning when she was to leave she had tried to get the little housemaid, Mary Harker, to run an errand on her behalf to at least keep the problem of Bethany Middlewell in its place, but the maid had been stubborn and unusually inflexible towards Clara that day and refused to do anything. On any other day Clara would have reported such insolence to be sure Mary, a girl the same age as herself, but less fortunate in life, was reminded of her place and her duties, but there was barely chance to catch a breath before Clara found herself clutching her fine hat to her curls in the wind and starting out on the journey back to Commondale.

With the glint of silver buckles on her shoes as she was helped down from the cart, Clara looked miserably across the farm of Pines Lodge, a place she hadn't seen in years and had felt no desperation to return to. Most girls would have been overjoyed to see their mothers again, but Clara was a particularly resourceful and self sufficient creature, and as long as she had someone, anyone to flatter her vanity, she did not need her family.

Mr Hodgkins, the farm manager, had been on site as the cart rattled in. He strode across and looked Clara up and down as she was helped down by the driver. "Well, you've grown."

Clara wrinkled her nose in distaste. She had a vague memory of Mr Hodgkins, hired on the day she was sent away from home, and did not like the man. Not only that, but he offered little potential in the case of advancement and wasn't much use to her other than getting her luggage down from the cart, which she instructed him to do so. Closing her parasol, she hooked the handle in the crook of her arm and carefully stepped her way in-between sheep droppings to the main door of the house.

She reached up with one lace-gloved hand to knock on the door just as it was opened by her elder sister, Eleanor. The two young women were taken aback by the unexpected appearance of the other. They had not seen one another since they were both sent away from home on the same day. Some six years had passed, and they were both very much changed. Clara eyed Eleanor's abdomen, which was swelling with life. That was going to annoy Gillian greatly.

"Why, sister," Clara started insincerely. "I see congratulations are in order, both for your recent nuptials, and your more recent condition."

Eleanor regarded her younger sister silently. She had never completely trusted the angelic little face, even when she had just been a babe. Whether that had been completely due to jealously, when she and Gillian had been demoted to old news with the arrival of a new sweet child on the premises, or the feeling of trouble pending, she was not sure. She had never wasted any time worrying or analysing the reason for her feelings. "I did not expect to find you paying a visit," Eleanor said. "I thought you were very well settled in Thirsk and had quite forgotten where you had come from."

"I have a letter for Papa," Clara said, as if this was explanation enough. She raised the aforementioned paperwork so that Eleanor could see it but not take it from her. "Or if he is not here, Mamma may read it."

Eleanor looked quizzically at her. "Of course he's not here."

"Mr Mowbray has tried to contact Papa on several occasions and has been unsuccessful. The money has run out and..."

"Oh, of course." Eleanor already looked bored. "Let me have that letter. I will have to access our funds and then write to him."

"But it is for Papa."

"He's disappeared. Did Mr Mowbray not explain this to you? We're all trying to locate him and no one has had any success. In the meantime, as I'm based in Whitby, I am looking after the financial matters. Mamma will look after the farm here at Commondale."

Clara felt a little ball of horror in the pit of her stomach. Eleanor in charge of the family purse? This did not bode well. She wasn't miserly with money, one could surmise so much from the elegant cut of her clothes. But she had never been one to fritter, and she could not be relied upon to attend to each and every one of Clara's whims. "But what will happen to me whilst you are corresponding? My education is not complete..."

"You can stay here and learn housekeeping with Ellen." Eleanor had to quickly turn around to hide her smile as she saw Clara's unabashed utter horror at the thought of slumming it in the family home. Her pretty little hands take part in manual labour? Clara was too fine and too well brought up to be anything other than a wife, a wife of a rich man with a staff of servants to attend to all the day-to-day drudgery of living.

"Did I hear Clara?" Maud came through from the kitchen. It had been several years since she had seen Clara. Although she kept in touch with short, vain little notes, Clara had never come back to visit after she'd escaped to sophisticated Thirsk. "Oh, Clara?" Maud stumbled upon herself as she gazed upon the stunning young lady at the threshold. "You are an utter picture."

Clara collected herself and put her best smile on as she approached her mother. The woman had aged since she had last seen her. There were white hairs at her temples and creases around her eyes. A weight of worry pulled at her shoulders. A simple woman who would never fit the proper role of a woman married to an entrepreneur such as their father. She looked provincial and simple. Clara had outgrown her mother in many ways.

"Mamma, what has happened? Mr Mowbray has been unable to contact Papa..."

Maud's eyes dropped. "No one has. He has disappeared. We are not even sure how long he has been missing for he does travel so with his work. Everyone assumed he was at one of his other lodgings.

The magistrate has hired a man to look in to it, to try and find your father."

"And has he picked up his trail?"

"Not yet."

Eleanor shuddered and kept herself to the background of the kitchen so that no one might see her face. That man had been to Whitby a month back. Having worked his way through the Hob's other places of business, he had finally reached the northern port of Whitby. The moment she looked up from the ledger and saw the stranger in the office, she knew it was the investigator hired by the magistrate, and furthermore that he was no fool. The interview had started off easily enough, on a professional manner, asking all the usual questions. He was working out a timeline of the Hob's movements. Then he had stopped writing and looked up at her with a new expression. She couldn't quite decide if it was disgust or pity.

"I've already spoken to your mother, you understand."

"That's only to be expected."

"I know what you've done."

Something dropped out of Eleanor's usual confidence. She did not move, for she knew if she did, her weakening knees would betray her. She thought of that early morning, piling the rocks back up at the place where they had hidden the Hob's dead body. Ellen Withers' was strong-minded, she would not have broken, but after everything that had happened, Maud was crumbling. Had she just confessed the entire incident without thought? Maud had moments when she struggled to live with what they had done. A confession might ease her mind, but there were many other lives that could be ruined because of that vile little man.

"Mrs MacCaskill."

"Yes?"

"I noted during my time in London that you rather married in haste." He pointedly looked to her stomach.

Eleanor relaxed. Was this just to be a moralistic snub? He knew she had become pregnant around the time of the marriage and suspected the baby came first, the ring second. If that was all he had, there was no need to worry. There were countless marriages that started this way, and as long as the wedding preceded the arrival of the baby, no one needed to worry.

"What I'm not certain of is whether you knew before hand."

Was he to accuse her of lying to Angus to get him wed? As if she hadn't been sure of her pregnancy.

"But he knew."

"Sorry?"

He had left the comment hanging in the office like a threat. He looked quite comfortable with the silence and the seething unbalance he was causing this woman. Watching her as if at a game of cards, trying to read the undiluted facial actions to translate her inner thoughts. "He's a drover, this Mr MacCaskill. They have to be married already to get the licence..." he held up his hand as she went to say something. "Ah, Mrs MacCaskill, I've already looked in to it. Been to Falkirk. I have seen the register with my own eyes. He was married long before he got to you. That church wedding of yours led to no legal union and technically that's a bastard you're carrying."

A wave of nausea swelled upon her. She had to think. She looked around for somewhere to sit, searching although she knew the exact layout of the room. Carefully lowering herself into the chair, she closed her eyes for a moment. This man was thorough, frighteningly thorough. Nothing was missed. He'd found out about Angus, and that wasn't even part of his remit. Had he discovered the truth about the Hob, or was he merely harbouring suspicions and scratching around for potential motives.

"Bigamy," the man said simply. "That's what they call it. When a man has one too many wives. It's illegal you understand. Seven years hard labour if you're caught. I hear they've opened a female gaol in York as well this year."

Not as bad as the penalty for murder, Eleanor thought. The threat of prison, however many years, was not to be trifled with. She rubbed the space between her eyes. How ought she to play this one? "What are you intending to do about this?"

"Nothing."

She looked up sharply.

"I'm not condoning what's been done, but it's not what I have been employed to do."

"But then why did you go all the way to Falkirk?"

"Following up leads. I'm still not settled as to whether you knew beforehand or not, but given that you're in the family way, I suppose you had to make arrangements as best you could. And as no one seems to have any idea what's happened to Mr Hurst, or where he might be, I have to follow up on whatever I can. I shan't lie for you; if it ever needs to be said, then I shall say it. But I believe your family will be in for some rough years."

"Rough years? What have you found out?"

"Precious little. Many anecdotes and trails that lead me to dead ends. I have not yet found your father and I am not certain that I will now. This is a great vexation..."

"So he's just vanished into the air?"

"Hardly. But I am of the opinion that he is no longer with us."

Eleanor's eyes widened. "You think he is dead?"

"Oh yes. Perhaps he travelled somewhere and expired and the people neither knew who he was or what to do, so they simply buried him. I understand your father travelled a lot. Although it is just as likely that he came to a more sinister end."

Eleanor put her hand to her mouth, feeling as though she were about to be sick. Not from the thought of the Hob being murdered, although she could see what the investigator was assuming; but rather from the sensations of pregnancy. The man wasn't stupid.

"I do not wish to upset a lady in your condition, but I believe the truth must be faced. Of course without any certain proof, the statutory seven years must be born out before the assumption can be made and your father declared dead."

Seven years, just as the magistrate had informed them in the parlour at Pines Lodge. It would hang over their heads like an axe for seven years before it could come to conclusion. And until then debtors would appear, agreements would be broken and letters would keep appearing begging for money. Eleanor considered the letter she had just taken from Clara. She really wasn't inclined to bow down to her sister's every whim, for Clara was very spoiled and always had been. But it would probably be best to write to Mr Mowbray and agree on something going forward, for Clara would be best out of everyone's hair.

"Oh Clara, my sweet." Maud, who had never seen anything but perfection in Clara, had taken her girl by the hands and was leading her through the kitchen. "Do come and say hello to your brother Stephen."

Stephen, a sweet and mild mannered boy of nine, looked up from the book he was reading and smiled at Clara. He had been so young when she had been sent away that he barely remembered her. He had a heart of gold and saw only the best in people, which was a good and a bad thing, for his little heart would not be able to stand it in the future when he learned the duplicity of people.

Clara regarded the boy, and for the briefest of moments her eyes narrowed in jealousy. This was her usurper, he who had taken the place of the baby of the family. A sweet angel, and a sweet but dumb and trusting heart to go with it. "Why, doesn't he look like that man who used to work here," she declared, to the horrified silence of the room.

The barbed comment completely passed by Stephen. Eleanor glared at the back of Clara's head, wondering what poison the Hob had been pouring into her ear whilst she had been away in Thirsk. Perhaps he had said nothing, for Clara always had an uncanny ability of knowing what was going on. Sometimes she just knew. And it was true enough, there were resemblances to their previous farm manager, Amos Cornforth. He had been laid off the same day the children had been sent away and Mr Hodgkins had arrived. From what she remembered, he had left Commondale a few months later for a position on a farm at Haworth, where Maud's people originally came from.

Eleanor glanced to her mother and watched her try to keep the shake in her hands hidden. If that investigator was hounding down every lead, every motive for why anyone might have wanted to do away with the Hob, wouldn't that be a reason also? There were a lot of people and many more reasons why the Hob had death wishes upon his head. The truth of his end was duller than all the possible melodramas. It had been an accident born out of fury. Angus had never intended to kill the man. Hobart had tripped backwards, knocked his skull on a spike and that was that. Combined with the fact that the Hob had beaten an unborn child out of Eleanor the previous night, no one would believe them if they had told the truth. Besides which an accident and a dead man were still manslaughter at the very least. The Hob wasn't worth any more deaths, misery or compromises.

"Clara." Ellen Wither's voice was particularly sharp in the soundless kitchen. She made everyone jump. When Clara had been born, she had been just as besotted with the child as Maud had, but time and a sharper mind had opened Ellen's eyes a little. "Why don't you go down to the village and visit your sister? It's many a year since you last saw her."

Clara's fixed gaze moved from Stephen to Ellen, then across to Eleanor. "Mrs Longbottom? Does she not come to the house?"

Eleanor ignored her.

"Not that often, she is a busy wife," Ellen spoke. "But she will not know you are here. You were not expected."

"Surely not that busy. She does not have children." Her gaze dropped to Eleanor's stomach.

"I don't have children either and I never stop till I reach my bed," Ellen snapped. "Running a house keeps a woman busy and Gillian has to help William out with his work. Now away with you. Stephen, you run along and show your sister the way, then you can go play with the other boys in the village."

Stephen closed his book and jumped up, eagerly taking Clara's hand and dragging her to the door. He couldn't wait to show off his elusive sister to the village, as pretty as a china doll. He would bring about a reunion between her and Gillian. Perhaps that would bring some smiles back to his sad sister.

Eleanor watched them leave, her arms folded. Trouble. That was the only word for Clara. Trouble.

Gillian was not thrilled to see her younger sister. Her distracted glance in the direction of her siblings was so underwhelming that Stephen felt he had done something wrong and was near to tears. The chill from Gillian wasn't as bad as when the twins came into close contact, but this was hardly a warm, happy meeting.

Clara remained calm and stood tall and straight, her blonde waves gently flowing in the breeze. Her layers of petticoats ruffled, the beautiful fabrics of her skirts gleamed in the sunlight. If she hadn't seen Eleanor's positive glowing and fashionable self respect, she would have been convinced now that marriage was nothing but a drudgery designed to crush a woman's soul utterly. Gillian looked like a morose ghost, dressed in plain and dull clothing, as if she were a nun of some strange order that allowed for union with a man.

"Why don't you run along, Stephen," Clara suggested. "Go play with the other little boys. Let us girls catch up."

He didn't need to be asked twice, and ran back along the track to the village. When William, Gillian's husband was at home, he didn't mind coming here, for William was happy to show him different aspects of blacksmithing. But Gillian carried a misery that held her aloof from everyone.

"It seems you have taken very well to the fineries of city life," Gillian finally spoke, setting the pail of water at her feet.

Clara sniffed in amusement. City life! As if Thirsk was a beating metropolis of the country. Still, there was a mix of jealousy and disapproval in Gillian's tone, as if a fine dress was an obvious sign of an ungodly life. That was nonsense, because if drab was godly, Gillian ought to have all that her heart desired, and it was clear from her face that the years had not been kind. Gillian and Eleanor were the same age and yet Gillian looked as though she had a decade on her sister. "And how is married life suiting you? Of course, it has been some years now since you were wed to your sweetheart. I just saw Eleanor and it seems it suits her very well."

"Eleanor," Gillian muttered, her face souring. "I doubt she managed to get down the aisle before she already had that baby in her womb this time."

Clara's eyebrows shot up. This time? Were there family stories she had missed out on?

Gillian was not inclined to explain; her fury was not for Clara's benefit. "She is ungodly and does not deserve all she gets. She ought to be cursed!" She burst out in anger, surprising even herself by the venom. It was an inopportune moment, for one of the village women was coming up by the river from the bleach mill. The villager suppressed a gasp, for no one locally heard or saw much of Gillian Longbottom at all. It was a shock to hear her shouting curses.

Clara smiled to herself, watching Gillian stumble over her embarrassment to have been caught out by one of the locals, and furthermore with such unchristian behaviour. She wrung her hands on her apron, as if to wipe the stain from her flesh, before distractedly turning and heading for the shadows of her home. She seemed to forget that Clara was even there, so caught up in her own trials of woe as she was. What a ridiculous woman, Clara thought as she followed without invitation. She had so much, all that she had dreamed of as a child and yet she was too busy longing after what she did not have to be able to appreciate all that she did possess. "I had expected to find you happy, sister dear," she said, following Gillian into the small kitchen. "I remember from when I last lived here in Commondale that your greatest wish for so many years was to marry William. You got that wish, although it seems the rest of us were punished for you doing so without father's consent..."

"It's not a proper marriage," Gillian moaned. "Not what William wants. He wishes for children, lots of them. He is a good man, with a lot of guidance to offer, and I have not been able to provide."

Clara said nothing and watched her sister fuss about the kitchen. She had either not heard Clara's barbed observations or was unconcerned by the fact that her sisters had been sent away from home as soon as her own bad behaviour had come to light. Their father had been furious when he heard of Gillian's devious behaviour in getting married without permission. The punishment reaped on those innocent parties had worked in Clara's favour, for her prospects had widened greatly since going to Thirsk, but it had never seemed right that everyone but Gillian had been punished. It was even worse that Gillian chose to ignore the fact.

"I would have thought this would be the ideal situation."

Gillian stopped fussing over the few pots in the kitchen and looked at Clara as if she was mad. "This is a hell for me. What can you mean?"

"You wanted to marry William. He was your heart's desire. You live with him without the distractions of small children. You two can be in a permanent wedded bliss. I see these women tugged down by countless children, and all it involves is never ending work and no thanks. The husbands become blind to their wives. Surely it is better to remain at the point you are at."

"You're just a child, Clara, you know nothing of the meaning of marriage," Gillian scolded. "There needs to be children. That was always what William wanted. That was why..." she dropped off. Time and thoughtless comments may have rid her of her childish fantasies but there was a large gap between knowing the miserable truth and being able to utter and acknowledge it to another.

Oh yes, Clara remembered. There had been Megan before Gillian. William was quite a bit older than Gillian, in fact there was a good ten years between them. Originally he had been sweethearts with a girl called Megan from Osmotherley, a village away at the edge of the moors. They had been all set to be married, then there had been an accident and Megan had taken a fall. Oh, she was recovered, but the doctor had advised that she would never be able to bear children and she had rejected William. The next thing anyone knew, Gillian and William had been sneaking off to a distant church every Sunday in readiness for a secret wedding. And they were married when Gillian was still just a girl. The years had passed, and no children had appeared. Perhaps William was regretting his choice in life. Who could say?

"Well, I can't say I understand you," Clara said, ignoring Gillian's put down. Clara understood the world and the minds of men a lot better than Gillian gave her credit for. "If I were married I would much prefer to be in your situation, than like some milk cow pumping out babies. Think of all the work, and how it would be a drain on your looks. I know Eleanor looks very well on it, but then she has money from working with father in business. I suppose she'll have a nursery maid and wet nurse to help her, so it won't be too much of a chore, and of course she'll already have a house keeper so she doesn't have to worry about all the domestic tasks." She gave Gillian's home a glance. It did not need to be said that if Gillian had children, she would have to do everything on her own, house and babe.

Gillian sat down by the window, quite a picture of misery. "Without children there is no point in my being."

Clara pursed her lips together. Very well, stupid sister, she thought. Old Marsden had taught her many a technique with the plants from back in the day. It had been years since she had spent most days with the old wise woman, but she hadn't forgotten a thing. And Clara had a natural talent for manipulation. "Let me make you a brew, of herbs and goodness. To help bring some cheer to your mood."

"That is not what I need."

"That is what you shall get."

Clara went out to forage and brewed up the tea which they both shared before she went back to Pines Lodges. Gillian hunched over her cup, nursing the brew with a desperation she didn't want Clara to see. On her way out Clara slipped a little bundle of knots, twigs and leaves up on a ledge on the inside above the front door. Gillian may well moan, but she had ended up exactly where she wanted to be. Things had not worked out so neatly for the other Hurst children. Clara had grown to be a refined young lady, only to be stuck back at this moorland farm with no opportunity or chance for further education. Waiting on her sister, Eleanor, who had control of the purse, in the hope that a new agreement with Mowbray could be reached.

Luck followed Clara in those days. The magistrate, friend to Hobart Hurst felt obliged to keep a friendly eye on the family. He particularly felt bound to them whilst there was uncertainty over Mr Hurst. It needed conclusion, either the investigator found Hurst dead or alive, or the seven years were up and legally an end could be enacted. When he heard that Clara had been sent up due to funds from Hurst faltering, he offered the young lady the opportunity to spend the summer at his manor house whilst the family made arrangements with the Mowbrays. Eleanor wrote to Thirsk to explain the situation and enquire what might be done for Clara's future. Thinking he might take advantage if a young woman had been left in charge, Mowbray attempted to overcharge Eleanor for Clara's tutor and board, making plans on what he could do with the extra money. Eleanor was no fool, and pretended to be surprised that someone would take advantage of a family's particular trouble. In the end she negotiated a lower sum than her Hob father had originally been paying.

Over the long summer months Clara lived in an unfamiliar but fine building, with servants to attend to her needs, and every comfort seen to. There was no tutor to nag her about improving her studies and accomplishments, and as the magistrate's own children were much older than she, they had all been married off and left home for many a year. One daughter was visiting the mother for some weeks, along with a new baby, which was a pink faced howling brat that only continued to convince Clara that children would ruin a woman's life beauty. She was ever more certain that Gillian was mad.

Without guidance, tutorage or company, Clara was left to her own devices, and would often wander into the library, working through the Magistrate's extensive book collection. Whenever he happened upon her, she was either reading a trifling novel or looking at a dry legal tome, and would tell him how she struggled to make sense of it all. When she was sure that she would be undisturbed, she went to the older books, shelves where the special collections gathered. There was a print of a much older book, written hundreds of years ago that had caught her attention. *Malleus Maleficarum,* a book originally written in the 1400s on the continent, and in Latin, engrossed Clara in solitude for weeks. She had studied some Latin whilst in Thirsk, and now her understanding of the language accelerated as she soaked up the book. Most of it was laughable, and the hatred of women that seeped through the pages made her sneer through narrowed eyes. The Witches Hammer, as it was referred to in English, was a guidebook supposedly to everything one needed to know on witchcraft. What witches did, how to spot them, how to interrogate them, and how to kill them. Such nonsense, but people had truly believed it all. Now that they were nearing the end of the 1700s they lived in enlightened times and the belief in witches and other folklore and superstition was dying out as people were shown the truth through the scientific revolution. No one had been executed for witchcraft since 1722. Burnings, hangings and major witch hunts were just frightening tales of the past. Still, Clara reflected as she worked her way through the *Malleus*, and other curious works in the Magistrate's collection, it was an interesting thought experiment to wonder how one might work the general populous up into a frenzy to believe such things. So much so that they might act on such beliefs. Under the surface, communities wouldn't completely deny the old ways for fear of bringing ill fortune upon their heads. People were like sheep, so willing to be lead without thought.

As autumn approached, Clara was reinstated at Thirsk and the twins made progress with their offspring. Gillian discovered that after her many years of empty harvest, she was now pregnant. She missed her regular bleed but put it down to an illness that took her. She felt nauseous most days and often threw up. Nothing made her feel better and she was sure she was about to be taken in death. She was worthless as a wife to William. It was her punishment for her failure. When she eventually dared to speak of what was happening to someone, Ann Longbottom, William's mother, assured her that rather than death, this was much more about life. Ann would be looking forward to becoming a grandmother yet again.

Gillian's outlook on life and state of mind improved immensely, and in expectation of their first child, the couple began to grow close, full of hope of how their lives would finally be. They no longer felt that there was something wrong with their union. Despite her joy, she was still unable to try and make peace with her sister. Eleanor had no ill will towards her, but Gillian had shunned her for so many years. Naturally there was the matter of the first out-of-wedlock pregnancy, which had mercifully ended in miscarriage as far as Gillian was aware. But underlying that had been an intense jealously of her sister's fruitfulness, and Gillian could not reignite contact for fear of anyone realising the root of her anger. So the twins remained estranged, even when Eleanor's first child was born. She had a son, named Stewart and a healthy, hearty and solid boy was his father's pride and joy. He was a particularly long baby, eliciting exclamations and comment from all the women locally to Eleanor's property, and promised to grow into a tall man.

Clara's considered opinion on the matter proved to be true, for Eleanor had the funds and the lifestyle for an easier motherhood than Gillian. She ran the Hob's business, but had Mary-Ann Argument to keep house, the washing sent out to Mary-Ann's mother, and a cook to prepare much of the food. Gillian had to do everything on her own. And whilst for many years it appeared as though Eleanor was the fertile of the two, it would be another three years before Eleanor had another child. Gillian, much to Clara's satisfaction, fell pregnant when William so much as glanced at her, and was having a child virtually every year.

Her first was a son, born the year after Stewart. He was christened William after his father, and named little Will at home to avoid confusion. Gillian did not immediately take to motherhood, and struggled for some time with what she ought to be doing with the baby. It cried and spun its little limbs around like windmills, its eyes screwed up and its mouth widened further than seemed natural. Gillian had assumed everything would come naturally, for she was a wife and her purpose was to provide William with children, and yet, after a long labour, when the little boy was passed to her, she felt a wave of gushing horror. She did not know what to do with the creature. William, her husband, was more involved than many men, and happy to jiggle the lad on his knee now and then after work, but for the long days she was alone with the babe and expected to continue to keep house at the same time. Her mother came down into the valley to stay with her the first couple of weeks, and her little brother Stephen was very good at running errands. Each day he would scamper up and down the hill, between Pines Lodge and the Longbottom cottage, to deliver parcels of food prepared by Ellen Withers. Ellen came down occasionally, but struggled with her limp to manage the walk frequently.

It had been a lot of years since Maud had tiny babes to care for, but the routines and lullabys returned to her without hesitation. Maud's quiet nature suited the patience newborns needed. Little Will was a scraggly and complaining child who would not eat a lot yet was never satisfied, and suffered from a great deal of colic. Yet he survived, unlike Gilly Longbottom's first child, who was born shortly after Little Will. The child did not get enough food, whether due to her own unwillingness or her mother's inability to provide enough, it was impossible to say, but the child withered and died within the first ten days of its life.

Maud helped Gillian to learn how to deal with the baby, and manage the household chores at the same time. After a couple of weeks when Gillian felt ready to face her old life alone again, Maud moved back up to Pine Lodges. It bemused her to consider that at 39 years of age, she was now a grandmother twice over, to a little boy in Whitby and a little boy in Commondale. It was a lucky turn of events that Gillian picked up the ways of her new life so quickly, for by the time little Will was two months old, she was feeling the old sickness upon her again. Her mother-in-law, Ann Longbottom was a little surprised, as she had always believed the suckling of a little one delayed the coming of another pregnancy. If Gillian was being sick now she must have fallen pregnant almost as soon as Will had tumbled from her womb. But with child she was indeed, and the following year she gave birth to a second son, Jeremiah, who was calm and happy where Little Will had screamed, and had a very hearty appetite. But just as with Little Will, no sooner was the baby out than another had started to grow. Villagers commented on Gillian's sudden burst of fertility and wondered what she'd taken to eating. Others noted that she had married extremely young and perhaps her body had simply not been that of a woman until now.

William Longbottom Senior celebrated the birth of his first daughter, Mariah, in the same year that Eleanor MacCaskill gave birth to her own daughter. Eleanor's daughter Elizabeth was a laughing and chattering little baby, long before she was able to make any words with her mouth. She had an easy manner and was comfortable in the company of strangers and family alike. During a visit to Commondale, Eleanor made a first tentative visit to her sister for three years, so that the cousins might meet for the first time. She went down to the little house, Elizabeth in her arms and little Stewart toddling along holding on to his grandmother's hand. Gillian was polite but distracted and showed little interest in her niece, nephew and sister. Mariah, a screaming furious baby was distraction enough. Then there was little Jeremiah who had just learned to walk and was too eager to see what was happening in his Papa's work shed, the smithy. Little Will ran about constantly getting under her feet. The washing was never ending, the house was never quite clean and the money didn't always stretch to the heartiest of meals. Not that it mattered to Gillian, for she had already gone off her food. She looked drawn and tired, far older than her sister, and with a secret misery that number four was already setting its territory in her womb. In contrast Eleanor positively glowed with motherhood, enjoying her two laughing children. She was unhindered by the thought of housework and laundry, for she could afford to pay people to deal with the chores. It was the early summer and her husband was away on the drove, so she had no need to worry about falling pregnant again so quickly.

The wider Hurst family was blossoming and as the years went by people thought less and less of Hobart Hurst and where he might be. Those who knew forced the knowledge from their minds. The only one who really cared to any degree was Clara Hurst. Yet she was too busy focusing on her lessons with the tutor in Thirsk, making eyes at Andrew Mowbray, the elder son, when he was back from his school, and making mischief with the maid, Mary Harker, when she had opportunity. That continued until Clara was eighteen and Mary Harker left her post at the household for a new life in York with her family. She did not particularly miss the maid. Clara's first and main concern was herself, for she was quite a conceited young lady, and her relations with others tended to revolve around what they might do for her. Now and then in quiet moments in the night, she wondered where in the country her Papa might be and why he had never come back for her. She had never been in any doubt that she was the jewel in his eye. It must have been something very serious for him not to have come for her. She feared he was dead and yet she felt his spirit still existed.

Little Stephen Hurst, who had never really known his father-by-name did not miss Hobart. He enjoyed an idyllic childhood growing up in the dale. He helped William in the smithy, learning some of the blacksmith trade, and in the summer he would help at the local farms when they had their sheep shearing days. Farm workers from all around would descend on one farm to soldier their way through all the sheep. Around the yard piles of fleeces mushroomed ready for market.

With Hobart gone so long, Mr Hodgkins felt his position of power on the farm destabilise. The wife, Maud, seemed less and less in servitude and fear of him, and after two years of Hurst's absence, he had finally realised that old ugly gargoyle wasn't coming back. The money was good, but Hurst's licence to bully the women of the farm had expired, and he was bored of the dale. Mr Hodgkins left the estate, giving Maud Hurst little notice, and went across the moors to Farndale to take up a new position with a better salary. He had been there two years when one afternoon walking the high moors, he came across one of his charges, an injured sheep that was beyond repair. Not wishing to waste a resource, he slit the creature's throat and gutted it, before tying the legs together with a cord and slinging the carcass across his shoulders for the walk home. There was a fine piece of mutton here and it would see him nicely through the coming winter. North of Lowna Bridge he sat down at a large boulder to rest, slinging his cargo onto the top of the rock in readiness for an easy move back onto his shoulders. In his eagerness to rest, he had not checked the sheep's position on the rock, and as he lent back in the autumn sun and rested his eyes, the carcass lost balance and came tumbling over the edge, hitting Mr Hodgkins with a heavy, startling thump. In the battle between slumbering man and dead beast, the two became entangled quickly. The cord between the legs pulled down against Mr Hodgkin's scraggy neck. The more he struggled, the heavier the heap pulled against his windpipe, and he swiftly lost consciousness. The strangled remains of Mr Hodgkins, contorted under an eviscerated sheep, were discovered by the stone a day later by a passing tinker.

When Mr Hodgkins had first abandoned the farm, Maud had been all for contacting Amos Cornforth. He had been the previous manager, now settled in Haworth many a year. Maud wanted him to return to his ancestral home, but Ellen persuaded her otherwise. Returning an old lover and Stephen's biological father to the farmstead at this stage was not a clever move. They did not want to set tongues wagging and until those seven years were up, Hobart was still technically alive and Maud was still technically married. Better to keep temptation out of the way and leave potential, yet false motives out of the sight of people who may grow suspicious. They took on strangers at the hirings on yearly contracts, and kept the property running at a steady and modest pace. Perhaps when he was fully grown, Stephen would be able to take over the running of the estate. Perhaps, they hoped, as all the scattered Hursts relaxed into a routine of security and serenity, believing that all their troubles and trials were long behind them.

The first notes of brewing troubles sounded the year Gillian's twins, Harriet and Agnes were born. Gillian was now a worn-out but experienced mother at the age of twenty five, with four other children running about the house. Little Will was four, Jeremiah three, Mariah two, and Joseph one. Maud was often down at the cottage helping out. At the farm there was only Ellen and Stephen, now fourteen and there was not so much pressing that Maud couldn't be spared. Besides which, as the lady of the house, it was quite acceptable to leave a lot of the household running to her employed housekeeper, Ellen Withers.

Clara was now nineteen. She was a young women and in the market for a husband. She was a stunning beauty of angelic proportions and countenance, and much spoken of in all decent society in the county. Although her fortune was under some question, what with her poor father missing all these years, there was no question that the family were still thriving, for the business was still running, now controlled exclusively from offices in Whitby. No one, not even Clara, knew what allowance would come with her hand, but all the local young men hoped that it would be plenty, and coupled with her good looks, there were many who hoped to win her.

Eleanor MacCaskill of Whitby had proved to be not quite as fertile as her sister, and had two children, Stewart at five years of age and Elizabeth at three. Elizabeth was a vivacious and chattery little beauty with dark hair, who had made great friends with Jayne Argument, a little girl of similar age. Jayne was Lucy Ann, the housekeeper's little niece. She would often come with her aunt to work. She and Elizabeth would play together in the kitchen, and later have great fun running through the narrow alleys and yards of the steep sided, cobbled and leaning whaling town of Whitby. Stewart had a healthy appetite, and was growing rapidly, tall and strapping already at five. There were many who mistook him to be an older child. Their father, Angus MacCaskill, a Scottish drover, was at home from the late summer through winter before heading back up to Scotland in the early spring to prepare for the year's drove. All the women of the household missed him, although in Whitby it was not so uncommon for families to miss their men for months on end, what with the fishing and whaling ships that set sail from the harbour. Those left behind got on with all aspects of running the household and it was acceptable for a woman to deal with money and business.

The twins had each settled into that wedded, domestic routine that had seemed so far away and foreign to a memory of young girls helping their Mamma with chores in the house. Maud was content to think that both her twin girls were settled in life. Both had a set of fine children, if only Gillian were able to cease in the childbearing a few years to give herself a break. Both were married to older men, and had their own homes, although one might say Eleanor's life was more of her own to enjoy given the finances to pay for domestic help, and the very fact that she only had two children to Gillian's six. In regards to the marriages, Eleanor certainly enjoyed a much better relationship with her husband. William Longbottom had once daydreamed of a happy household full of children but the reality of six children under five was very different from the sunshine filled image he had once carried in his head. His wife had no time for him, the children were forever shouting, and there was barely enough money to go around all the hungry little mouths. He did not have a moment's peace to think and none of the children were particularly inclined to listen when he sat down to impart the wisdom that he had built up over the years. He found himself taking on more contracts that required him to work away from his home-based smithy, just for some peace and quiet, and to avoid his wife, who he could barely look at without making her with child again.

When a joiner from Kildale he knew asked if he'd be able to work over the north-western edge of the Moors for a couple of weeks, William did not even pause to consider whether Gillian would be happy with the arrangement. Of course he could help. The joiner, John Mansfield had a number of orders for carts and wagons to make for various villages in his area. To make a good cart a joiner needed the help of a competent smithy, especially to get the wheels rimmed. It was often outdoors work, with a pit for the hot coals dug into a field, and the wooden wheel pinned out ready for the iron to be fitted around. Then there were the hanging bolts and angle parts to fit the moveable parts together. William and John would go from village to village for a few weeks, getting the contracts completed as they went.

The final cart required was a little one-pony cart ordered for a spinster who had come into some money when both parents had passed away. The woman was keen to increase her mobility and independence. William had assumed an old woman when John had briefly mentioned the customer. When the spinster in question approached as they were working in a field up the hill from Osmotherley village, he felt his age, and the time of his youth and his dreams rushing back at him. The spinster was a couple of years his junior, but at thirty or thirty-one, an unmarried woman was considered most definitely an old maid. The years had been kinder to her than they had to Gillian, and she actually looked younger than his wife. Skipping multiple childbearing could do wonders for a woman. But Megan always had a calm and angelic countenance. She and William had been betrothed, but she had broken the engagement after an accident that had left her unable to have children. And so he had swiftly married his little sister's childhood friend whilst she was still a child herself, on the promise of a great hoard of children and a new focus on ongoing life. All that had come to pass and yet it had not become what he might have hoped.

He forgot what he was doing when he saw Megan making her way up through the field, wading through thick grass that would soon be chewed down to the sod by the rotating cattle herds. He felt the anticipation of his youth swelling up on him, remembering when they had been shortly to be wed, and it all felt as though it was only yesterday.

"Why John Mansfield," Megan spoke as she reached the joiner. "I wasn't expecting you for two more days."

"Miss Hammond. Getting through the work quicker than I thought," he said, doffing his cap. "The work goes easier when you have a good smithy on your team."

This comment gave her pause as if she had not noticed the second man in the field. She looked up to William and was visibly shaken when she recognised him. Although they had lived within a day's walking distance of one another this past decade, they had very consciously never chanced upon one another. He had been so eager to take this commission that he had never stopped to think that it might bring him too close to Osmotherley.

It was just a moment of shock, then Megan broke into a wide smile. "Why, William Longbottom..."

"Megan Hammond."

John Mansfield looked from one to another, wondering how they sounded so well acquainted, then mentally slapped himself for forgetting that piece of gossip he'd heard years ago about an engagement that hadn't worked out. William was a married man now of course, but with a crowd of children and a household to keep, women could lose their attraction and men's eyes could start wandering. Not that John ought to turn down work because of old romances. Both Megan and William were adults and able to control themselves.

To William it felt and looked as if no time had passed. "You look very well."

She smiled graciously. The same could not be said for William. He had certainly grown more since she last knew him, broadened out. He looked weary with responsibility and burdened by day to day reality. But there was still the same young William in his eye. "It is good to see you again, William. It has been too long. I hear you have been blessed many times over. Six children, I understand?" There was an underlying pain in her voice as she spoke, but she was determined to convince that she had moved on.

William faltered, knowing what she thought. "Yes, I..." He did not know what to say. That he loved his children was in no doubt, but the low discontent felt intense now. "You never married?" The words were out before he had even consciously thought over them. If Megan Hammond had married, the gossips would have gotten word to him sooner or later. To question it was to poke an old wound open. The thought of her married to someone else was painful.

Her gaze dropped. "No, I never... you know why I couldn't. Besides there was only ever one man for me."A silence, mournful over what might have been, settled between them. She looked up again, forcefully bright. If you pretend that all is well, eventually you might believe the lie. She had missed out on a life she had dreamed of, but tried to focus on the alternative positives reality had brought her. It had been a tragedy that her parents had died, but the little money she inherited and her lack of children gave her a freedom many women her age could never experience. "It is good to see you again. I do so miss our talks and it would be very nice to catch up. I live just down the hill from here, at the little cottage..."

"I don't think that would be appropriate," William interrupted her. "People would talk."

"I miss talking to you. It never stopped us before."

I wasn't married before William thought sadly. "I must get on. These wheels won't rim themselves."

"Yes, of course." Megan backed away. One could not retrieve what had been lost. She was not quite sure what she had been attempting. She was a moral and sensible woman, who had a great respect for the vows of marriage, even if she hadn't been the one swearing eternal love.

William returned to his work in a fever, not stopping until the working day was done and the wheels were all rimmed. He and John returned to their lodges for the night, John sitting downstairs with the local farmers, swapping gossip and old tall tales of the dales. William went to bed but lay awake. He had taken an oath before God, and Gillian had been a good wife to him. Six children, a great brood, just as agreed when they had sneaked out across the moors in the early morning to arrange their nuptials. But seeing Megan had reminded him how much he missed her. He sometimes wondered if he had made the wrong choice.

When night was fully settled and the darkness complete, he gave up and left the inn to walk out in the fresh air. It was just to clear his head, he told himself, but he automatically started up the hill and soon found himself at the cottage door. Megan was perched on a little bench at the front of the property, shawls wrapped around her body and a candle burning low beside her for company. They looked at one another but didn't utter a word. Megan picked up the candlestick and walked into the cottage. William loitered for a moment, still held back by the moral goodness he had always prided himself on. It was no use, and he closed the door on his way inside.

"What on earth is she doing?" Eleanor peered out of the back kitchen window incredulously. Ellen Withers was hunched forward in the little walled kitchen garden they had created a few years ago, ranting to no one and shaking her head with glee.

Since they had officially and publicly admitted the Hob's missing status, the family had been able to relax. Gradually, and subtly, Maud and Ellen had introduced new things to their home to make their lives a little easier. Although they couldn't take things as far as they wanted by reinstating Amos Cornforth as farm manager just yet, there had been other things they could do. Eleanor had persuaded them to invest in a pony and trap, so that they might be able to get about. Ellen Withers walked worse with every winter, and although it was no hardship to putter about the house and yard, her ankle could not take a long walk to any of the neighbouring villages. They had also added a small walled area to give protection from the moorland winds and created a kitchen garden. Fruit trees were being trained up the walls, and there was a variety of fruit bushes, all of which led to a richer and more colourful diet in late summer and autumn. Both the women tended the garden, but it had been Ellen Withers, more out of fascination rather than any sense of duty who had taken on an almost obsessive habit with the fruit bushes after a long talk with a widowed carpenter from Egton. The two had fallen in to conversation when they'd met at a hirings a couple of years ago. Ellen had accompanied Maud in search of a new farm manager. Maud would have said that a new romance was sparking, for Ellen had been like a woman possessed after the conversation, except that her amour was directed at the garden. She spoke of the carpenter and his opinions, and always kept an ear to the local gossip to know when he would next be Commondale way so that she might accost him. Rather than a mutual infatuation, rivalry of a friendly nature with an undertone of personal honour was a better description.

"It's all Caleb Lyth's fault," Maud explained, joining her daughter at the window.

Caleb Lyth, Eleanor thought, the name was vaguely familiar. "He's a carpenter, isn't he?"

"From Egton."

"Egton? Catholic?"

"I'm not sure." Maud only gave lip service to attending church and showing an interest in religion, despite her daughter, Gillian's horror at her mother's disinterest in the word of the Lord. And as for denominations, she was very apathetic. It was all the same God, why did people need to squabble and judge?

Egton was a village much further down into the Esk Valley where houses clutched to the sides of a steep valley rolling down to woodland and the river. There were still Catholics in Egton, which was something considering the historical persecution of Catholics in previous centuries. Their endurance was probably connected to the fact that Father Postgate had been born in the village. He was long dead now, but had lived an eventful life, trained on the continent as a Catholic priest before returning home to administer to the needs of fellow Catholics in his native tracts. He'd eventually been arrested and executed in York a good hundred years before Eleanor was born, but his name was still known in the area.

"I've got it well packed." Whilst Maud and Eleanor had been pondering on Catholics, Ellen had completed her task in the garden and returned to the kitchen, carrying a small box, clasped like the holy grail between two hands. It appeared to be full of wood shavings. She set the box on the kitchen table, popped a top on and then tied it all securely together with string. "I have to get to Egton."

Eleanor smiled. "Are you missing Caleb Lyth?"

Ellen rolled her eyes. "Don't make sounds of such trivial things. This is very serious."

"Shall we go tomorrow?"

"No, it must be today. Stephen can get the trap set up now for me. He's over at the Applecross farm tomorrow helping, and you know I can't walk so far as Egton on my ankle. Stephen?" She almost roared the young lad's name, and after a moment or two the lad came bounding across the yard and into the farmhouse.

"Get the trap set up."

"Yes, Ellen." Stephen, still with his almost cherubic curls, breathlessly bounded back out of the farmhouse to do as he was bid.

"Ellen, what on earth is going on?"

"I'm going to show Caleb Lyth, that's what," she said.

"I don't understand what the desperation is in aid of. What's in the box?"

"Never you mind, Mrs MacCaskill. You come along with me and we'll get ourselves to Egton."

"Ellen, maybe Mamma needs work doing," Eleanor laughed. Not that Maud ruled Ellen like a member of staff. They were like family really, as much a part of Pine Lodge as the moorland that surrounded the buildings. "Besides, I have Stewart and Elizabeth to mind." She waved a hand at the window, through which they could see the two children chasing the chickens.

"I can watch them," Maud offered quickly. She knew for a fact Ellen was terrified of driving the trap, and she had no desire whatsoever to be dragged over to Egton. She knew exactly what was in that box for she had listened to nothing but from Ellen for the last month. "You go with Ellen. It will be nice for you to take a break from work, the children and being inside. Get some fresh air."

"Right, that's settled. We're off." Ellen bustled outside.

Eleanor eyed her mother warily. "I feel there's something you're not telling me."

It took them well over two hours to travel across to Egton. Eleanor was relieved when Ellen told her that Caleb Lyth lived in the upper part of the village. She had been worried he'd be in Egton Bridge at the bottom of the valley and not been looking forward to getting the trap down that steep incline to the river and the rest of the village. They kept to higher roads across the moors, Eleanor driving the pony whilst Ellen clutched her box to her as though the survival of mankind depended upon it. Ellen directed her to a terrace of cottages, the carpenter's property highlighted with the scent of freshly plained wood radiating from the open door. Eleanor brought the pony to a halt and hopped down to tie the reins to a tree by the side of the road. Ellen waited in the trap, and Eleanor helped her down, first having to accept the box, setting it to the side to be certain it would not be dropped whilst Ellen descended from the trap. As soon as she was on terra firma and with the box back in her hands, she was shouting for Caleb Lyth and marching up to the house. Eleanor followed in amused bewilderment.

A man who had once carried a head of thick dark hair now strung through with more grey than he liked to consider appeared in the doorway, wiping his hands on his work apron. He had a square face with a broad, unassuming mouth that seemed to be set in a smile even when he was not especially happy. He looked a little perturbed as to who was shouting until he saw the limping figure of Ellen Withers marching up to his house.

"Why, Miss Withers, this is a surprise. You're a long way from home."

"You said it couldn't be done," Ellen started, skipping the pleasantries. "That a woman didn't have the eye or the patience for it. And I tell you Mr Lyth, you are wrong. For this is the best that has ever been." She held the box aloft.

"What are we talking about?" Eleanor asked.

Caleb nodded to her. "I don't believe we've been introduced."

"Mrs MacCaskill."

"Caleb Lyth at your service."

"Never mind all that. Come inside and look at my gooseberry."

Eleanor's eyes widened. "You've dragged me all the way over the moors to Egton to look at a gooseberry?"

Caleb started to laugh. "You've not come to see my goosegogs."

"And we had it with us all this time?"

"I'm here to prove a point."

Caleb and Eleanor followed Ellen into the workshop. She roughly cleared the workbench of wood shavings with her forearm and then set the box down. "I tell you, it is the image of perfection. Even and round and not a blemish upon it. It is the best gooseberry you have ever seen."

"Ellen, have you gone quite mad?"

The lid was lifted in hushed reverence, the wood shavings carefully picked away to reveal the green shiny orb, complete with short prickles, nestled in its holy bed. The skin was a light glowing lime green, with fine lines to show veins. Ellen carefully held the severed stem by thumb and forefinger and lifted the fruit up into the air. It was very large for a gooseberry, and certainly the largest Eleanor had ever seen, but she still didn't think the size warranted such a desperate ride across the moors at the drop of the hat.

Caleb was not in agreement. His eyes widened. "Bloody hell," he burst out, forgetting there were women present. "That must be the biggest goosegog that ever there was."

"Didn't I tell you so?"

"I will have to fetch Mr Rathmell; he must see this," Caleb declared. "Mr Rathmell takes his goosegogs very seriously," he added for Eleanor's benefit.

"I can assure you all I do not," Eleanor muttered to his retreating figure. "Ellen, is this the honest truth that I have been dragged here over a gooseberry?"

"You know as well as I do how seriously people take their fruit growing."

"But to travel..."

"These lot compare their harvest, seeing who has managed to grow the largest, the most perfectly formed. When I purchased my gooseberry bushes from Mr Lyth he mocked me and said my fruit would never come to nothing. Being a woman I wouldn't have the patience, and besides which, everything would be straight in the jam pan."

"But I don't understand. Is there a prize?"

"A prize? Why no, this is more important. We're talking about honour."

"I'm not sure what we're talking about."

A small, rotund man like a mole in dark trousers, white shirt and moleskin waistcoat, entered the building with Caleb. He adjusted the spectacles perched on his nose before approaching the rumoured fruit, then spent a good five minutes examining the gooseberry from all angles in revered awe. "It is a beauty," he finally concluded.

Ellen nodded as though justice was being done. "Is it not the biggest gooseberry you ever did see?"

Caleb nodded eagerly, Eleanor looked bored, but Mr Rathmell was contemplative. "It is difficult to say. Certainly one of the largest. I remember a particular specimen perhaps twenty years ago, by..." his words drifted off as he smiled at the memory of the fruit. "But we took no measurements and the mind can be a tricking beast. Things can be remembered as bigger and better than they were."

"Ought we not to measure this and make note of its particulars?" Ellen asked.

"Perhaps a commemorative plaque?" Eleanor said flippantly.

"Or an award?" Caleb suggested. "We could have a record of the best from each season."

"But what would be classed as the best?" Mr Rathmell considered. "One would have to draw up a list of guidelines, rules as it were, by which the goosegogs could be judged."

"Who would draw up such rules?"

"A society could be formed perhaps?"

Heaven help us, Eleanor thought. A gooseberry society. "The proof will be in the eating."

"We won't be eating this!" Ellen shrieked. "It's far too precious."

"You'll be wanting to keep the seeds." Caleb advised.

"Indeed," Ellen said, looking back to her prized gooseberry. "But only when it's no longer fit to be looked at."

It was growing dark by the time they returned to Commondale. Stephen quickly helped them get the pony freed from the trap and away in the stable before he was away to bed himself for it would be an early start the next morning for him. Eleanor stayed up a little longer to talk with her mother by the fireside whilst Ellen sat and admired how the glowing light from the fire warmed up the green hues of her most prized of fruits.

The gooseberry obsession continued, and the following summer with a couple of promising fruits swelling on each bush, Ellen Withers was almost beside herself with the prospect of being able to show Caleb Lyth what for a second time in a row. It was a year of spectacular fruiting, for along with Ellen's little green pride and joys, Gillian gave birth to her seventh child, Prudence, and Eleanor had her third, a little girl named Muriel who immediately showed her Scottish heritage with shocking red hair. It would come to pass that she was born on a noteworthy day, for across the seas of the English Channel trouble and rebellion were brewing in France, culminating in a prison break that kick started a revolution. It was a revolution that sent fearful shockwaves throughout the English gentry, and had the armed forces mustering in readiness for trouble on the homeland as well as abroad. Although people talked of the news and shook their heads at the thought of those passionate but over-top-Frenchmen, in the Moors and in Commondale in particular, life continued at its regular pace, following the rural calendar of crops sown and harvested, lambing, sheep shearing and the gathering of fodder for winter.

Little Stephen Hurst, now fifteen, was not the tallest of boys and did not yet meet his sisters in height. At such an age he ought to have been properly apprenticed for several years now, but instead he darted merrily about, helping out wherever he could, and too cherished by his mother to be released to adulthood. All the girls were away from home, the twins with families of their own and Clara manoeuvring herself towards an advantageous marriage. Stephen was a homebody with no greater ambition than to see his mother smile. He helped William Longbottom with smithy work from time to time, although the frequency lessened as William worked away from home more and more, quoting a need to earn more money for all the hungry mouths he was responsible for. Gillian was too busy to give his absence a second thought. With blacksmithing possibilities waning, Stephen learned more about the running of the Pines estate. It was a possibility that he might take the farm on properly when he came of age. Such hopes were also tied up with the dark question over the end of Hobart Hurst. When he was declared dead, body absent but by the law of seven years of silence, they would know what the intention had been regarding inheritance and distribution of property. There was only one more year to wait and then the family could be satisfied the nightmare was well and truly over.

When not helping at home, Stephen would run across to the Applecross farm over the other side of the valley, where he had become great friends with the middle son, Albert Applecross. The lad was a year older than Stephen, and was broadening out into a man, although still with the tender-cheeked look of a boy. Stephen was in utter adoration of his friend, and sometimes struggled to focus on the task in hand, so keen was he to watch every move and nuance of the lad. A couple of the labourers working to contract on the farm joked that Stephen made Albert a very adoring wife, which set Albert swearing furiously, although he did not avoid Stephen for he enjoyed his company very much. And things could have continued very happily thus had certain events not happened that year at the farm shearings.

The entire flock was to be sheared in one day, and a great number of men descended on the farm for wages and to get the task in hand completed in good time. Stephen was on site at the crack of dawn ready to help. He and Albert worked as a team, getting the sheep in the queue through and sheared, between the two of them swinging the beasts around and under control to get the fleece removed quickly and skilfully. The sun was strong and as the day wore on the men grew sweaty, slick rivers sticking shirt fabric to skin and outlining contours of muscles and body form. Stephen found his eyes regularly creeping across to look at the shape of Albert's chest as he worked, and had to force himself to get his mind back on the job on many occasion.

By the early evening the job was done, and the two lads, glowing in exhaustion, were up on the hillside, slouched back in the heather, and gazing out on the view back down into the village.

"It were a good day's work." Albert was enlivened by all that had been done. He took the final swig from his beer bottle before discarding it in the heather and leaning back on his elbows in a self-satisfied manner. "Those fleeces will bring father a good profit."

"We've worked hard. To look at us you'd think we were drenched in water." Stephen could feel the youthful energy radiating off Albert's flesh. The presence, as they slouched side by side on the moorland, woke him up, setting new ideas racing and impulses dancing. He wanted to reach out and touch that shimmering face, perhaps run a finger along the contour of his cheekbone and then taste the salty residue.

Albert just laughed. "It's the sign of a proper working man. We're no layabouts."

"We're laying about quite well just now."

"Stephen Hurst, you know fine well we worked hard today. I bet we cleared through the most fleeces of any man there today. We earned that bottle of beer and rest."

Albert turned his head to look at Stephen and was surprised by how close they were. Stephen leant up on his side and peered in at Albert's face as if he was a newly discovered gem stone. The focus of his silence was a little unnerving, like the moment before thunder. Stephen could not help himself, and his impulse took over any common sense. He bridged the final gap, curiosity desperate to know what it would be like and he kissed Albert full on the mouth, feeling the droplets of sweat that had gathered in the dip above the bow of his upper lip. There was a time, which felt like an age but was in reality only a second, when Stephen pulled back, his heart still full of the goodness of man, smiling at the idol of his eye. Albert was as stone, with no expression, and perhaps Stephen had assumed that his trusted friend could never turn under any circumstance.

The second ticked past and Albert's expression formed, a sneering ugly face. Whatever he had thought when the lad's lips had touched his, and however nice the sensation had been on an earthy level, he had heard too much talk from the other men in the family. There was joking at the inn about such dirty ungodly things . He felt disgust at Stephen and disgust at himself that he had momentarily allowed himself to enjoy that quiet and unexpected moment of intimacy. "You dirty little sodomite," he sneered, wrinkling his nose and glaring as he watched Stephen's face turn from joy to fear. "I always knew there was something wrong with you. You get away from me now."

Stephen scrambled away as Albert lashed out with a heavy tired arm.

"Get away with you, you dirty bastard!" Albert shrieked, his discomfort increasing. "I ever see you again, I'll tell them about you. All of them. Do you know they do to sodomites? Do you know? There's laws for a reason."

Stephen staggered to his feet and started to stumble away, feeling his eyes fuzz up with tears.

"Your mother would die of shame and disgust if she knew what you are!" Albert shouted after him. "You get away from here, Stephen Hurst, else I make sure you never bother another soul again."

When Stephen did not return home that night, Maud assumed he was staying at the Applecross farm. He was probably so shattered from the day's work that he did not have the energy to walk home. Either that or there was too much celebrating for a man to think of walking home. By the second night she guessed that he had joined the group of men travelling around the local farms powering through the seasonal shearing. When four nights had passed, she had to go out to find him. He was a grown lad, but he was still her baby and such an innocent trusting soul. Stephen was such a thoughtful boy, he would have told her where he would be if he were able to do. She fretted over illness and accidents, but if that were the case, surely the Applecross family would have sent word.

Maud walked down to the village and back up the far side of the valley to the Applecross farm. She passed by the younger lad, Albert Applecross, whom she knew was good friends with Stephen. She went to ask him, but Albert just sneered in her general direction and slumped away. Boys, Maud thought to herself. So many of them went through a phase at that age, lost their respect and thought they knew it all.

Mrs Applecross was surprised to find Maud Hurst at her door, and even more so when asked where Stephen was. Why, he had only been at the farm for the day to help with the work. No, he hadn't stayed with them, and there had been no accident or illness. What did Maud Hurst think of her, that she wouldn't have sent a message if such a thing had happened? Of course she would let Maud know if they heard anything, but she didn't think Stephen had gone on to work at any of the other farms. In fact, she thought her husband had been expecting to see Stephen the following day, but he never showed his face. Maud bit her tongue, wondering why they had not come to her earlier to ask where Stephen was, and thanked the rounded and red-faced farmer's wife for her time, before heading back down towards Commondale. Mrs Applecross looked over at her eldest daughter, folded her brawny, bread-making arms across her chest and shook her head in a disapproving sort of way.

"There's something wrong with that family," she said. "I do believe they're cursed. This'll be the second disappearance. That husband of hers disappeared years ago, and now the son's just wandered into thin air. There's mischief afoot."

"None of the daughters disappeared," the daughter pointed out. "In fact, it's only the men."

Mrs Applecross raised one eyebrow as if this was a very important point. "I can't speak for Clara or Eleanor, for they are seldom in the dale anymore, but that Gillian's an odd one. Doesn't have much time for folk. It's a strange going on with that family, I tell you. I never thought they were quite right."

In truth, the supposedly long-set opinion had only just occurred to her, but as gossip loves drama, the opinion soon became gospel truth and spread its way through the village before the sun was up in its noon position. The talk was on all tongues, too busy wagging to notice the ever darkening expression on Albert Applecross's face. None of it did any good, for no one knew where Stephen had gone. It was as if he had just walked out onto the moorland and been swallowed up into the landscape. Had he been an outsider it could well be believed, for at night or in bad weather the moors could be treacherous to strangers, but Stephen had been born here. His behaviour made no sense.

Maud sent letters to Clara and Eleanor, the writing laboured as her penmanship had never been perfected, to ask if Stephen had perchance gone to them for an unexplained visit. Clara laughed at the notion and sent a distracted no back to Maud. Eleanor had no better news, but let the word out to her acquaintances to see if someone might be able to shed a little light on the mystery.

In the end, over a month into Maud's fraught suffering, word finally came of Stephen's location. The letter arrived unexpectedly one morning. Maud immediately recognised Stephen's fine and fluid handwriting. She burst out into tears with giddy joy to see confirmation that her boy was still alive, and was shaking so much that she could not manage to open up the letter. Ellen had to wrap a shawl around her and get her into the rocking chair, before unfolding the letter herself and laying it out on the kitchen table. She squinted at the writing, book-learning had never been her forte either, and slowly dragging her finger across the lines, she painfully read out Stephen's message.

He was indeed alive and well, and claimed to have had a moment of clarity working at the shearings at the Applecross farm. He was fifteen, but had no particular goal or plan for his life, merely drifting aimlessly. It was time to become a man, so he had left all that he knew behind and taken the king's shilling and joined the army. Maud had cried out at the news, unable to imagine her blessed baby as a fighting man. He was still quite a small boy for his age, and couldn't stand violence. He couldn't be in the army, not with all this trouble going on in France. It was revolution, anarchy with executions, and the gentry were terrified that such ideas would come over the channel and rile up their workers, either that or the British would have to go over to France and fight to sort the lunatics out. Either way the armed forces were preparing themselves. Anyone who showed the slightest interest would be snapped up.

"He can't go to war," Maud pleaded with Ellen, as if Ellen Withers was in charge of his Majesty's armed forces.

"We're not at war just now," Ellen tried to soothe her. "He'll be garrisoned. He'll be in no danger for now."

It was a sensible assumption to make. Stephen had told them that he had signed up with a brigade stationed at Richmond, over in the north-western edge of the Yorkshire Dales. It was a distance from Commondale and an odd choice. To have suddenly disappeared from home only to travel all that way across Yorkshire to turn up in Richmond, signed up with the army. It made no sense. The vague talk of having no direction and wanting to be a man felt like nonsense.

Stephen had been quite aware of the fact that the family estate was there for him to take over when he came of age.

Maud and Ellen were not wise to the ways of the world. They wrote to Eleanor in the hope of a solution, for Eleanor knew a great many people and understood how things like the government worked and the country was run. Bureaucracy was a great mystery to the housewives and maids of Commondale. Eleanor, with her little baby Muriel, received the letter and felt a weight of hopelessness upon her. What did they think she could do? If all that Stephen had written was true, he had signed up, and leaving the army on a whim wasn't an option. He wouldn't have bought a commission, so he would be in the rank and file and would have to serve his time unless discharged for illness or madness. But would the army really have taken such a boy? Perhaps a trip to Richmond was in order to locate her brother and find out what had actually happened. Everything about his disappearance and re-emergence smacked of polite lies to cover the truth.

Although Eleanor would eventually make her way to Richmond, it was not to be quite as she initially suggested to her mother by letter. An unexpected parcel stopped any plans. A brief and formal note explained what had happened by telling nothing. It was penned by Stephen's commanding officer, who explained that Stephen had recently joined them as a drummer boy, and had shown diligence and great potential. Sadly Stephen had been killed in action and they were forthwith returning his possessions to his family. Maud immediately took to her bed and could not be consoled. Ellen sat down at the table and quietly read through the note again.

"This is utter nonsense," she finally declared to no one. Whilst her grasp of politics and current events was slight, even she knew that no war raged on English soil just now. The commanding officer wrote from Richmond in the north of England. Where there was no fighting. Stephen couldn't have been killed in action, for there was no action. Had Stephen even joined the army, she wondered, as she went through to the study. Perhaps something quite different had happened, and this was all a trick to keep them from finding Stephen.

It couldn't be of Stephen's hand, for he was such a devoted son, who would never do such a thing to his dear Mamma.

Sitting at the desk, she picked up the pen from the writing desk, dipping the nib into the inkwell. Ellen could not write well and her spelling was quite dreadful, but she would enclose the note they had received and get Eleanor to investigate the matter. They needed to know what had really happened, and if at all possible they needed Stephen home safe and sound.

Although Eleanor had a business to manage and three young children, including baby Muriel, she took up Ellen's request immediately to find Stephen. Like Ellen she could not understand why they would write and suggest Stephen had been killed in action. It was a blatant lie, and she wondered if the letter had been written on Stephen's request as he did not want his family to find him. It was a theory that could be very plausible with many people, but Stephen was such a sweet boy, she could not think why he would want to cut all ties with his mother. Yet there was still his disappearance and this odd letter to be explained. Something was wrong. Even if the very worst had happened, and Stephen had been killed, they wanted the body back in Commondale. Whoever had written the letter was hoping it would be the end of the matter, but the first thing Eleanor needed to do was travel up to Richmond to find out how much truth there was in all this running-away-and-joining-the-army nonsense.

She left the children to the care of the nanny and her housekeeper, Lucy-Ann Argument, and hired a horse so that she might ride across the moors, up the Vale of Mowbray and into the gateway to the Dales where Richmond sat. Long gone were the days when Eleanor had travelled about the moorlands with her donkey, delivering parcels and letters. She had eventually learned to ride horses, with some help from her droving husband, and although travelling by the network of post carriages would have been easier in many respects, horseback was the quickest way to get across the country to Richmond. She was worried and did not wish to delay.

Richmond was a market town built on slopes, with streets of stone houses rolling down the hills to a cobbled marketplace. A grey stone castle on high overlooking the proceedings of the busy market town.

Upon arrival Eleanor secured lodgings and somewhere for the horse to be cared for, before getting directions to the offices of the North York Militia. They were garrisoned in the town and presumably ready for action, should the trouble over in France blow up to any degree to endanger England. She had told the man stationed at the door her name and she was here to see the commanding officer regarding correspondence that had been sent to her mother. The man had sniffed as though a woman had no chance seeing an officer, before sending word into the garrison. Eventually a man, all dressed in red jacket and brightly polished brass buttons, appeared to deal with her enquiry. At this stage they were unaware of why she was in town.

"Mrs MacCaskill, I believe?"

Eleanor, who had been left in a sparsely furnished room, turned from the window as the man entered. He looked like an officer, neatly dressed and groomed, and not someone she could imagine partaking in rough drinking songs, as the man on sentry duty probably did when his time was his own.

"Lieutenant Wainwright at your service. I was told that you wished to see the commanding officer. I don't think that will be possible, but if there is anything I could do to aid you?"

"I'm here on behalf of my mother. We're concerned that we've been sent a fraudulent letter, pretending to be written by your commanding officer. It's regarding my young brother, and as we have no other clue as to his whereabouts I must start here. Would you be able to confirm if it's a fake?"

"I am very familiar with the Colonel's hand and the brigades' correspondence. Do you have the letter with you?"

"Yes, it's just here." She passed him the folded letter.

"I have to say, this looks genuine," he said quite quickly, before he had chanced to read the contents. "What made you think it might be a fake?"

"My brother disappeared from home some weeks ago. We then received a note from him to say that he had taken the king's shilling..."

"And that would be impossible?"

"Out of character and unexplained perhaps. But shortly after we received the note you now hold in your hands to tell us that Stephen had been killed in action..."

The lieutenant paled a little at the name. "Stephen?"

"Stephen Hurst. Now, I don't claim to be following military progress that closely, but I am quite certain that no war rages here in Richmond..."

"It is terminology. Only to say that a man has died in duty. It does not necessarily mean that he expired on the battlefield, only that whilst he was serving his country. We wish to save the family from any distressing details..."

"Something is not right with this. Stephen wrote that he had become a drummer boy. I fail to see how a drummer boy in Richmond could have been killed. I'm here to find my brother."

"But if your brother has died..."

"I don't believe he is dead, but if he is, we will take the body home."

The man nodded distractedly, then took to reading the letter. He paled a little more, then walked to the window to read the short letter a second time as if to try and comprehend the meaning a little better. Eleanor watched him, noted his nervous body language and realised that he had not needed to read the letter, for he already knew what this was regarding. His issue was that he did not know what to say to her. He needed to get rid of her whilst telling her nothing.

Finally he folded the letter again and gave her an apologetic smile. "Madam, regretfully I know nothing about this."

"It is a fake?"

"No, only that I am not acquainted with the incidence."

"Something has happened?"

"No, I..." He tapped the letter in one hand, trying to buy time whilst waiting for inspiration. It was not forthcoming. "Let me go speak to my superior. I'll see if I can find someone to talk to you."

"I can't believe that you would not know what has happened to..."

"We will return shortly."

Eleanor caught him by the doorway. "Might I have the letter back?"

He did not look as though he wished to return it, loosing hold of some evidence that would be better destroyed, but reluctantly returned it to her hands.

Eleanor had to wait over half an hour before anyone returned to the room. Lieutenant Wainwright came back, rather sheepish and subdued, led by a red-faced, highly-whiskered man who looked as though he personally had a war to run and did not have the time to deal with silly women who were too stupid to understand the simple truth explained in a letter.

"Mrs MacCaskill?" The man barked as he strode through the doorway, eyeing her as if he expected her to snap her heels and straighten to attention. "Major Brodsworth. I've been told some nonsense of questions over the Colonel's authenticity. I can confirm this letter is from our Colonel and what you need to know is explained inside."

"But Stephen would never have joined the army."

"He did indeed, and regretfully he has been killed in action."

"But there's no fighting and if he was just a drummer."

"Falling rocks," the Major barked.

Eleanor was stunned. It couldn't possibly be true that little Stephen Hurst was already dead. He'd been so young, so much in life ahead of him. Just to vanish like that and then to be told he was deceased. She couldn't believe it. "We will need the body," she almost whispered. "His mother will want to bury him."

"That will not be possible," the Major said brusquely as he took her arm. "The boy was crushed and the body in no fit state to be sent to anyone's mother. We have dealt with his remains. You may be assured that this is the end of the matter." As far as the Major was concerned, that was that, and without another word, Eleanor was ejected back out onto the street.

Eleanor was convinced that they were lying and somewhere Stephen was alive, until a young drummer boy appeared at the back of the inn early that evening and assured her that Stephen was indeed dead. He'd been there at the time, so he knew for a fact. The officers didn't want to tell her anymore as they were embarrassed about the circumstances and wanted the entire thing hushing up and forgetting about.

"But this is ridiculous," Eleanor exclaimed. "I cannot believe it without the body. Tell me, where is he buried?"

"Under the ground."

"Under the ground!" Eleanor repeated in exasperation. "For goodness sake, why all this ridiculous secrecy? I am sure you are all lying." She regarded the drummer. He looked older than Stephen, as tall as a man whereas Stephen was still short and boyish. Regardless of his height, he had the same immaturity. Easily cowed by anyone with confidence. "Do they know you're here?"

His eyes widened, as if only considering for the first time how much trouble he might cause. "No, and please don't tell them I've come to you. Only I heard Stephen's sister was here and I thought you deserved to know. They daren't tell anyone the truth for fear people will think them fools."

"Can you take me to his grave?"

He shook his head.

"Please, will you not do me this favour? His mother is distraught."

"There is no grave, madam," he explained. "All I know is that his body must be somewhere underground but I couldn't even say where exactly. We couldn't find it. Some reckon that there was a cave in and he is crushed by rocks, but when I went in I couldn't see a cave in. Although I didn't dare go too far because I heard things, scared me right up and down, they did, and I was back out that tunnel. If he was still alive, believe me, he'd have been straight back out as well. I reckon it was a mad monk that got him."

"A mad monk? There's no monks here."

"The ghost of a mad monk."

"Please tell me you are not being serious."

"It's the truth." He looked around the yard, considering how much more to say. "Look, I can take you to the last place we heard him..."

"Heard?"

"It's the closest we can get to a grave. It's the best I can do for you."

Eleanor followed the lad out of the inn's yard and down side streets so that they might skirt the market place and avoid being seen by any of the soldiers. They headed down towards the river, before skirting off from the road and along a dirt track in woodland until they reached an inoffensive and featureless part of the track, marked only by a stone gatepost long out of use and being swallowed up by forest undergrowth. Dusk was falling and the birds in the trees were twittering before sleep.

The lad pointed further down the track. "Easby Abbey's not all that far in that direction. Ruined it is these days, but it was a going concern a few hundred years ago. He would have lived there, the mad monk."

"This is a local story to scare little children?" Eleanor was not impressed. "And you mean to suggest that a ghost of a long dead monk came running down this track and stole away my brother? This is not a game, you understand? My mother is destroyed..."

"Not up here," the lad was shaking his head. "Down there." He pointed at their feet. "Stephen disappeared somewhere down there."

The fact of the matter was that on investigating the castle keep, some of the soldiers had discovered a crevice that appeared to give access to a vaulted chamber below. Men that had grown up in the locality had heard stories of an escape route rumoured to exist, that ran underground between the castle in Richmond and the Abbey along by the river. It was a tale that had always been taken with a pinch of salt, for how could such a chambered tunnel have been constructed. But there was certainly a room down there which must have had a purpose, with seemingly no way in. Although the crevice through hewn rock was large enough for them to peer inside, the men were too big to slip through. In trying to find a solution, one of them had come upon the idea of bothering the drummer boys, who were young lads, and surely one of them would have been small enough to slip through.

A few of the boys had been duly woken, her informant included, and marched through to the keep. Stephen, the smallest, had been sent in first, and had managed to squeeze through and scramble into the vaulted room. They had passed him a candle and asked him to say what he saw. Very little had been the answer, other than the opening to a passage. Like giddy children, the men had exchanged glances. Perhaps the story of a secret tunnel was true. What use would it be should the country find itself at war, and they were able to get out of the castle undetected, should they find themselves under siege.

They needed to track the route and see if it really did go to the old Abbey ruins, but with only a young lad in there, it would be difficult. One man had suggested that Stephen walk down the passage drumming, so that they might hear him on the surface, and that way they could mark the route of the tunnel. The drum had been passed down to the boy, and he was advised to not be shy about giving the drum a good beating.

The lad had told Eleanor with wide eyes that it had actually worked. They had heard the drumming, and had left the castle as a furtive little group, and gone out to the Market Place. The drumming had led them along towards Frenchgate and then headed down the hill to the River Swale and out into the woodlands where they were now stood. They reached the gatepost, and then all of a sudden the drumming sound, which had been quite clear, stopped. They had waited for an age, barely daring to breathe, listening for any sound. One of the drummers had run along down the dirt track to check that

Stephen hadn't gotten further ahead without them realising, but there was no sound.

The group had returned to the castle in something of a panic, for Stephen would have to be accounted for. They had hoped to find him back in the keep, but it was very silent and empty. The lad and another drummer were persuaded to squeeze through into the room and then head down the tunnel together to retrieve Stephen. He had been terrified, although he had tried not to show it as he had wanted to be thought brave. The other drummer had tears in his eyes and could barely see. Not that they had found anything. It had been cold and dank and the tunnel went on forever. The candles didn't illuminate much, and they had called for Stephen without getting any answer. They had walked for miles, honest they had, and found nothing. Then one of the candles went out and whilst the other flame was sputtering and threatening to extinguish itself, they had heard a hiss of air coming out of man's lungs, just by their ears.

Eleanor and the lad stared at one another. Eleanor shivered. Dusk was sucking the light and colour out of their surroundings and a chill was creeping around them. She did not feel safe here.

"What happened?" she asked.

The lad did not meet her gaze, looking out into the middle distance. "I pissed myself," he admitted. "I was so bloody frightened. There was something down there, I tell you, but it wasn't Stephen. We never found Stephen and I don't know where he is now. Only I can tell you that you won't ever see him again. He is lost. They'll never admit any of this to you, for they don't like to look like fools and they think I am making up what I heard. But I know what my ears heard and the sickness in that air."

"So Stephen is somewhere down there."

"He is lost. You'd be best to make up some story for his mother if she is so saddened. But that is the truth as God is my witness and I am telling you this so that you might move on. You must be brave to have come out this way on your own, so you deserve to know the truth, but there is nothing any of us can do to get your brother back."

In many ways it was irrelevant to Maud how Stephen had died, only that he was dead. The letter had not been a fraud. That terrible thing had come to pass. Ellen Withers managed to keep her head enough to write an ill-spelt letter to Amos Cornforth at Haworth to let him know what had happened, and to quiz Eleanor as to where the body was. Eleanor told a lie and said it had been buried at Richmond. And yes, she had seen the grave. In some respects she had, for she had managed to get into the castle and be shown the crack into the vaulted room, where Stephen was last seen. It was dank and fetid down in the bowels of the castle, and Eleanor could not wait to be set free out into the sunlight again. There was an unpleasant atmosphere, an air, something inhuman emanating from that concealed room. Why on earth had they even bothered – no one was ever going to need to escape from the castle. Her brother had been lost in vain, and she grieved over his soul. Would he even find peace wherever he now was? Stephen had been such a kind hearted, trusting boy. He had not deserved this.

Maud was inconsolable. It was a torture too great to bear that a parent should outlive her child. Oh, there were so many children that died, but if they got into their teens, one could relax in reasonable certainty they were healthy and vigorous and would survive. Sadly Maud's tears and nightmarish screams in the small hours would not be the last heard in Commondale that year.

It started with Gilly Beecroft's second son, Harold, a little lad of six. Gilly Beecroft, born a Longbottom, but married these past seven years and now with three children, was distraught when her son fell ill with Scarlet Fever and was dead within three days. She did not have time to grieve, for as Harold was taking his last breaths, her daughter was fighting for her life. A fight she did not win. Gilly's siblings had visited before Harold's affliction had been diagnosed saw the fever jump across the households of the wider Longbottom family, and quite suddenly the little valley village was caught in an epidemic. In every household with at least one child under fifteen, at least one child died that early winter. At least every household but one.

William Longbottom's little tribe thrived. At the height of the epidemic he was away at Osmotherley working on a large order. Gillian was managing her hoard of six children, plus newborn Prudence, and was terrified they would be struck next with the Scarlet Fever. Yet it never happened. The children contracted not so much as a sniffle, and by December Gillian was run ragged. She dragged herself through the village and up the hill to her mother's house. The baby was strapped to her chest with an old shawl, and the other children whooped and ran, throwing snowballs at one another and laughing to see their breath steam in the air. She felt the accusatory glare of the village, watching her pass by with her healthy children, whilst other households faced a sombre yuletide.

Maud heard her grandchildren coming before she saw them, and opened the door as the band tumbled across the farm yard. She was up again from her bed, going through the motions of the day's routines, although her heart was broken. "Gillian. The children are all well?" Everyone felt as though they were waiting for the fever to hit Gillian's household. It could only be a matter of time.

Gillian grimaced. "As you can see."

Maud wrung her hands together. "That is a blessing."

"Is it?" Gillian felt wretched. "I do not feel I can do this anymore. I never knew children would be such hard work. And that the fever has not taken one of them..."

"Gillian!" Maud looked horrified. "Never say such a thing. Children, come in to the warm and see if Miss Withers doesn't have a treat for you all." She stepped out through a sudden flood of children rushing the door. She felt the chill snap at her skin. Winter's bite. She gazed out over her little empire, watching the farm manager step out from the barn and start in their direction. "Our children are gifts from God, you know this yourself."

Gillian's face twisted in sourness. "Oh, a curse on all children. I wish they were all dead!"

"Gillian, get a hold on your senses!" Maud could see out of the corner of her eye how the farm manager halted in his approach, his eyes widening as he heard Gillian Longbottom's words. It would not help the general feeling in the village when this was reported back at the inn, as no doubt it would. "You must mind what you say, show some sensitivity. There's many a grieving family here in Commondale this winter. I'm sure they'd give much to get their little ones back." She put an arm around Gillian's shoulders and was shocked at how much the bones poked out. There was barely any flesh on her daughter. "Come inside," she said, her voice a little softer. "Ellen's got a stew on and we can mind the children whilst you get some rest."

"I have chores at home."

"Chores that will wait. Everything will be easier with some rest. Let me spend this yuletide with one of my children. Stephen is lost, and we wrote to Eleanor weeks back not to come. We do not want to spread this to her children."

"If they have the same constitution as mine, there will be nothing to worry about," Gillian muttered as she allowed her mother to take her in to the kitchen. "And what about Clara? When will you see her?"

"Clara is to stay in Thirsk for the winter. I think she is quite sweet on Mr Mowbray's son. I think she will come through next year, when the magistrate comes to finalise things."

Gillian's brow creased in question.

"It will be seven years next year," Maud reminded her. "He will have been missing seven years and we will be able to legally bring closure to the matter.

"Seven years," Gillian breathed. "How quickly time does pass. And to think we never did hear anything of father all this time. I wonder where he is, what happened."

Maud looked away from her and pretended to go fuss with the stew. Indeed. Seven long years. But the sentence was almost fully served, then the magistrate would perform the necessary legalities, read out the will, and they would all move on. Permanently leave that dreadful night in the past and try to make something of the future, although with her boy gone, Maud didn't see anything in the future beyond household chores and routine.

Seven years had felt like an age, a life sentence that would never end, but the seven years did pass. The investigator had never picked up on Hobart Hurst's true trail. His final location remained a secret and many believed he had died somewhere in the country, off on one of his secretive business journeys. Perhaps it had been a deal that went wrong. Seven years of silence. Now it was time to officially declare him dead and move on.

Once the legalities were complete, a date was arranged for the reading of the last will and testament of Hobart Hurst. Clara arrived three days before the communicated date. Her early appearance was not out of a confusion of dates, or adding extra time in case of delay on the journey from Thirsk. Clara came with a companion who was keen to speak with Maud before he had to be back at Cambridge.

Clara was now twenty one years old, unmarried but a very eligible young lady. Perhaps her prospects would have been better, or certainly more nationwide had her father still been alive. He had been cultivating her with something in mind. All that Hobart had planned was lost, and Clara had been left to arrange her own fortune. She had found herself well placed in the Mowbray house, a wealthy family with an ancient Yorkshire lineage and importantly one son who would inherit all. He was three years older than she, and was studying law in the south. Andrew Mowbray would live a comfortable and wealthy life, either from his own hard work, family inheritance or both. He was a fine catch for any young lady, however, Clara had made sure many years ago that there would only ever be one hand he wished to take in front of the alter.

He had proposed, and she had accepted. As far as Clara was concerned, the matter was settled, but Andrew clung to tradition and duty, and keenly felt the absence of a man he'd never met, Hobart Hurst. He had so wanted to gain permission from the man of the household for Clara Hurst's hand. With the tragedy of Stephen Hurst's death the previous year, there was literally no man of the house, so Andrew set his mind to speaking to Clara's mother. Besides which, it was only good and proper that he meet his fiancé's nearest relatives before the happy day. Clara had been less concerned. Her family was not a branch to cultivate. Her mother was a glorified maid, one sister a businesswoman who looked at Clara with a gaze too shrewd for her own good, and the other sister a worn out hag of a baby machine. With the possible exception of Eleanor, they were not appropriate company for a sophisticated and educated young lady. Clara was embarrassed to be taking Andrew home, but he had been adamant. At least he would have to leave the day after in order to get back to Cambridge in time.

Maud had been a little taken aback by the enthusiastic and smiling young man. When he had asked for an audience, she had remained in the kitchen, Ellen Withers looking on as if she were an associate and not an employee. Clara was horrified at how familiar and casual everything had become, seemingly worse than she remembered. She had pointedly taken Andrew's arm and marched him into the parlour whilst calling for her mother to join them. If that had all overwhelmed Maud, Andrew's question felt beyond the ridiculous. No one asked Maud for her permission, certainly not beyond the children and now grandchildren asking if they might be excused to run out and play. Andrew Mowbray was a particularly pleasant young man, trusting and open, and not what she expected from someone who professed to be a lawyer in training. Still, she was just a maid from Haworth who had married her betters, and knew little of the world. What would she say other than yes? Clara clearly was happy with this arrangement and she only wanted the best for all her children. It was reassuring to see that Clara would be well looked after. Another child, along with Eleanor, she felt confident would have a happy life. Gillian, pregnant again with her ninth child, seemed to be destroying herself with the childbearing and Maud was at a loss as to how to help her.

With permission granted, Maud and Andrew fell into conversation. Clara was restless, and out of sorts in a farmhouse. It was not the type of home she was used to being in anymore. She decided to go out and take a short walk on the moors. Snapping her little parasol open as she stepped out of the door, she started up the track to the moors, enjoying the scent of heather wafting across on sun-warmed breezes brushing over the hilltops. After about twenty minutes she was out into the wilderness, alone apart from the occasional sheep head that would look up at the sound of footsteps. She watched an odd little boy dressed in rags wade out from a thick glade of heather. She paused in her walking, tilting the parasol to one side as she regarded the child. There was something oddly familiar about him although she couldn't quite place it. She knew she'd never seen him before.

"You there, boy," she called out. Perhaps he was the last in a long batch from one of the poor farm labourer families, barely dressed in the last of the hand-me-down rags that his twenty previous siblings had worn.

The boy scowled at her, then darted back into the heather and sprinted off towards the skyline.

Clara stared after him, furious that he had disobeyed her. If she had known who he was, she might have looked for a way to teach him a lesson, but aside from the fact she didn't know who he was, there was an odd aura about the child. He wasn't quite like the others here. He was from another place. She thought to ask if anyone else had seen the ragged brat when she returned to the house, but the trivial matter was soon forgotten when she found her mother and intended in quite a jovial discussion. Why did they have to go through this performance? It was quite irrelevant whether Maud was happy with the match, Clara would do as she wished. Considering how Gillian had precipitated so much misery with her own secret marriage, there could be no reason to reject such an advantageous match. Not that Maud would stand in her way; she could see immediately that Maud was very taken with Andrew Mowbray.

Clara loitered in the doorway to the parlour, unnoticed, and considered her mother. She was ageing, with strands of white hair, particularly at the temples, breaking up the dark gloss of her hair. There were lines around her eyes and her hands were rough and worn from long labour. Last week she had been legally declared a widow due to the seven year absence of her husband, and Clara wondered if Maud might not marry again. For her age bracket, Maud turning forty-five this year, she was not all that unattractive, and the combination of reasonable looks and a fine property meant all kinds of suitors would start crawling up the hill now. The reading of the will, for which Hobart Hurst had specifically requested all family members to be present for, was scheduled for two days hence. Clara wondered what her dear father would have remembered her with. It was infuriating that he had never told her, and she was unable to get a look at the will in advance. The magistrate, who had been holding the will, was following her father's wishes to the letter. All this secrecy meant that she would have to stay here for several days, with Miss Withers not minding herself or her place.

The entire situation vexed her so that Clara struggled to sleep that night. She hated being in this shabby little bedroom, which had suited her as a child, but now as a refined lady, was a joke. Why could Mamma not have added some decent curtains, a portrait or two for the walls, and good quality bedding? And the vanity table was non-existent. Clara wondered how she had managed in her younger days. Because you did not know any better, she reminded herself, as she lay in the bed listening to the patter of rain. It was a blessing Gillian had been so keen to ruin her life, for that had been the trigger to get Clara out of here and in to better society.

It was cold in bed. She was in the room on her own, and nightdress and shawl were not enough. She climbed out of bed, scampering across to her luggage (that she had been forced to deal with herself, there being no proper maid) to pull out a couple of extra shawls to wrap around her body. The paltry warmth of the bed called her back, but Clara found herself drawn to the window. Pushing aside the thin curtain, she peered out onto the rain-splashed yard. There was a full moon up in the inky sky, and wide gaps between the rain clouds, so the night world was well illuminated. Out in the yard stood a man.

Clara gave a gasp barely as loud as a whisper, and pulled back from the window, not wanting to be seen. Who would stand out there in the rain? Up to no good surely. Yet there was something odd about the determined, unmoving stance the man took, and the steady gaze at the farmhouse. He wanted her to look. She leaned forward to the window and her eyes widened as she realised who it was.

Hobart Hurst.

Her father. Missing these past seven years, and yet here he was. Mere days after their mother was declared a widow. Clara started to raise a hand to wave at him, call out, but stopped as a realisation hit her. He was there and yet he was not, for he was dead. Not just disappeared, but dead, long dead and rotted. His apparition was here, and why here? Why did he haunt? He'd died here. He was buried somewhere nearby, but in secret, in an unmarked grave. She felt her stomach tighten as another realisation hit her. They knew. They all said they did not know where he was or what might have happened, but they knew. Her family knew he was dead and they were keeping the secret for their own benefit. They must have killed her dear papa. And with the widowship legalised and the will about to be read, they would be relaxing, smiling secret smiles at one another and deciding that they had gotten away with their plans and designs. Poor Papa, who had doted on his little Clara.

Clara's eyes narrowed. Regardless of what that will said, she'd make sure things were made right. Her dear papa would have his justice.

The uncomfortable atmosphere was a depressing reality. At one time they had all lived together in this house quite happily. Some were now so miserable having being forced back to the Pines Lodge, and the rest were displeased at having to spend any time with their siblings. Is this how life affects everyone, Eleanor wondered as her gaze moved across from her prim, lady-like younger sister, Clara, to her own estranged twin, Gillian. Her own true other half, who was a drained out hag looking twice her age, and heavily pregnant yet again. If only Old Marsden was still alive, she might have been able to give Gillian something to stop her falling in the family way. Children were a blessing, but there was a limit on how much anything could be good for you.

The Hursts were gathered in the parlour as if awaiting a grand unveiling. Hobart Hurst was finally, officially dead, and as requested, all his living children and wife had collected together to hear his last will and testament. Ellen Withers had slunk back out of the parlour when the magistrate had given her a particularly stern look. Despite all the years of her life in service to the family, she would always just be that, a service. Maud and Eleanor could not have held her dearer had she shared the same blood, and Stephen had loved her like a second mother when he had been alive. Gillian was too tired and drained to have any opinion, and Clara held very high opinions on herself these days.

The magistrate gave a cough as he finished unfolding the will. "If it is acceptable to all, I will proceed directly to the reading."

Clara, fanning herself unnecessarily with a petite little folded paper fan, rolled her eyes to the ceiling.

"The last will and testament of Hobart Hurst, of Pines Lodge, Commondale and of sound mind and not under duress hereby make the following bequests on the event of my death.

To my wife Maud I leave the jewellery purchased for our joint marital life, to do with as she sees fit, although I may make a suggestion that such pieces may be passed on to my daughter, Clara..."

Clara's eyes lit up. The family jewellery. Eleanor raised an eyebrow at this. Three daughters but he was suggesting only one, and the youngest at that was treated in favour. Clara might have been his only daughter, but they were all children of Maud.

"To Gillian I leave nothing. In going against the respect of your family in marrying at such a young age to such an unsuitable man, I consider you outside of the Hurst family and therefore have no right at my table..." the magistrate's voice faltered. He knew the will was harsh, but it was unpleasant to have to read such things out loud.

No matter the girl's faults, she was certainly paying for her life choices now, and to humiliate her in front of her family was unnecessary. But then Hobart Hurst always had a cruel streak. The magistrate had spent many evenings chortling away with the old merchant, who had always treated him very well. But he was not so blinkered as to have not noticed how Hurst had dealt with problems in the wider world.

Gillian remained unmoved. "Our rewards are not material, only God can judge..."

"Oh Gillian," Clara trilled. "Are you to tell us that children are the only blessing worth having?" What a fool Gillian was, rushing into procreating servitude. It put women in no better place than the cattle in the fields. Clara had much different plans for her marriage.

The magistrate cleared his throat. "To Eleanor, whom we both know is not my natural child..."

"He's denying me?" Eleanor scoffed. She did not particularly care, may the man rot in hell, for he had always been cruel and unfeeling. It was not surprising he would want to leave this little stabbing comment for after his death.

"I bequeath nothing after my death. Despite our lack of blood, I consider to have passed you a great gift in the study of business and I am sure you will be able to look after yourself admirably when you are set out in the world."

"You get a compliment and he tries to insult me?" Gillian muttered. "And it is not I that has been immoral..."

"Gillian!" Maud scolded.

Clara grinned, watching the sport.

"To Stephen, you have already had more than you should, in taking my name. Do with it what you will."

Maud's face dropped at the mention of Stephen. Her lost, dead boy.

"And finally, to my dear girl, Clara."

Hush settled across the family, and Clara tried to remain relaxed although every nerve was straining to know what her dear papa had planned for her.

"I leave to you all the wealth. You are now the sole owner of Pines Lodge and associated land. All the buildings of my business in Whitby, London and in Derbyshire are to do with as you wish. Keep the staff or start afresh, or sell everything off and use the capital for something else. Do as you see best, and live a good life knowing your father always loved you."

Clara could not help but smile, although she managed to keep her lips from sprawling out into a satisfied grin. She could feel the surprise, the horror from everyone in the room, that the younger daughter had been left everything. The son was already dead, but when the will had been penned, Stephen had been alive and well and many had assumed that he would take over the running of the farm when he came of age. She had promised her poor papa justice, and this was an excellent start to the retribution.

Gillian abruptly stood up. "I don't know why I needed to hear all of this. I have children to tend to, I must go."

Maud shifted a little as if to follow Gillian and comfort her, but remained placid and shocked in her seat. Her chair that was technically Clara's chair now. All she had was her jewels and the clothes on her back. Was this his revenge for her infidelity that had produced Stephen? That she would be left no protection when he died. Returned to the state in which he found her. And that was his final revenge, after his miserly end dying by accident in the kitchen.

Gillian stomping out of the parlour woke people out of their stupor. The magistrate coughed awkwardly and refolded the will before setting it down on the table. His task was complete and he no longer needed to keep the document. "The terms seem very harsh, but you have all continued admirably these last seven years and I am sure you will find a way forward to mutual advantage..."

"Thank you for your time, magistrate," Eleanor interrupted. "I do not mean to appear ungrateful but I think we need some time together as a family. If we require any legal advice, we will of course be in contact."

"At your service, madam."

Eleanor glanced through the door as the magistrate left. The parlour door hadn't been completely shut. She could see Ellen

Withers sitting at the kitchen table and she knew that Ellen had heard everything.

"Well, now," Clara was the first to speak when only the family remained in the parlour. "I was not expecting that. And I was wondering what I was going to do with myself before I married Andrew. It seems I have a few new projects to keep me occupied."

Eleanor watched her sister closely. She had never trusted Clara, and she doubted that this latest revelation was going to elicit any compassion. It made her all the more grateful that she had set in practice insurances in business and in home so that she could be completely independent from the Hob's empire when the seven years were up. As soon as the clock had started ticking she had increased her salary as was only fitting for anyone taking control of the business. She had saved that money, and only last year purchased a fine town house in Whitby, into which her family, along with housekeeper Lucy Ann Argument had moved. She had also started up her own independent business trading, so that legitimately and honestly she had her own home and her own work to continue with, should the eventuality of being thrown out of the Hob's property come up. She had gotten into flax, which was shipped into Whitby from the Baltic states, and then transported up to the mill at Castleton where it was spun. The moment the flax reached Whitby's harbour, it was Eleanor's property, until it was linen ready to be sold in drapers shops. She made a tidy profit and also kept the industry going in the little villages of the North Yorkshire Moors. As well as the flax, she had gone into food transportation, buying in salted and cured meats from Houlsyke, which were sent by Wagon to Whitby and then shipped down to the markets in London.

No one responded to Clara's flippant comments. As if it were a mere trifle, and she didn't actually hold in her hands the ability to make or destroy many people's lives. "I think I need to take the air," Clara decided, standing up. "This has all been quite a surprise."

Eleanor watched her flounce out of the room. She didn't hold out any hopes for her having anything to do with the Hob's business by the end of the year, but she truly hoped there would be no trouble for her mother. Clara wouldn't need the farmhouse. She had been told about Clara's impending marriage. Naturally the couple would need a marital home, but her fiancé came with plenty of money and there was mention of wanting to go to Leeds. Clara certainly wouldn't want to settle down to the life of a country wife, and there wouldn't be much call for a solicitor here. Whatever was needed was usually dealt with by the magistrate.

Maud remained in her daze. Eleanor turned to her mother. "Mamma, if anything should happen, you must come to me in Whitby."

"Whatever do you mean?"

"If..." Eleanor paused, not wanting to utter the possibilities that were flitting through her mind. Maud was blind to Clara's cat-like personality. Oh, she could purr and make herself amicable and beautiful, but there were hidden claws. Clara took great joy in playing with others. "I have purchased my own property in Whitby. There will always be a place for you, and Ellen, should you ever need it."

"Nonsense, Eleanor," Maud responded. "This is my home, and Clara is my daughter. I have no need for concern."

Ellen Withers was not quite as confident as Maud, but when Eleanor spoke to her, she shook her head and stated that she would be wherever Maud was, and besides, they were worrying over eventualities that would not come to pass. What did any of this mean? Eleanor had eyed her cautiously and explained that the particulars of the Hob's will essentially meant that Clara was now Ellen's employer. Never the less, that evening whilst Maud retired to bed early and Clara set out writing letters in the parlour, Ellen went out back and sat with her gooseberry bushes and lamented that this might be the last year of her gooseberry reign. If she ever had to leave, she supposed she could dig up the bushes, but then where would she be going to and would there be a patch of ground where she might plant her treasures? And would they even survive the move? Probably not. And she was just hired help with no capital or home of her own at the end of the day. She had no claim to anything beyond the goodwill of other people. She was in her mid forties and still fit enough for a day's work despite her deformed ankle, but what would happen to her when she became frail and weak? Today her foundation had been given a little jolt and it had occurred to her just how alone in the world she actually was.

The following day Eleanor started her return journey back to Whitby and Clara dispatched her letters. She told her mother nothing of her plans, not even when she intended to return to Thirsk, but instead illusively loitered around the moors. Within seven days she received three letters, the contents of which buoyed her and set off a chain of decisions, the final of which was when a stranger arrived at the doorstep. A letter was dispatched to Eleanor informing her of the intention to sell all of Hobart Hurst's properties and businesses, therefore could her sister kindly quit the premises and look for other work. Eleanor crumpled the letter in the hand, a taste of bile in the back of her throat even though she had known this was coming. Thank goodness she had the foresight to make preparations for the eventuality. At least she could be with her family in her own home and continue with her own work.

Eleanor had the true measure of Clara for many years and had been ready for the decision. For others it came as a far greater shock. The morning Mary Harker arrived at the Pines Lodge permanently dislodged Ellen Wither's foundation.

Mary Harker had a shifty look about her, Ellen decided the moment she laid eyes on the girl. She must have been about the same age as Clara but certainly not of the same class. She had travelled across from Leeds on account of there being a few months work, and was here to see Miss Clara Hurst. Ellen took her into the kitchen before fetching Clara, and on returning was displeased to see Mary taking a turn around the room, picking up objects with very nimble and familiar fingers. Things tended to disappear when Mary Harker was around.

No one, perhaps not even Clara, understood the odd connection between herself and Mary Harker. The girl had just been a scullery maid at the Mowbray's property when they had first met. Mary had then moved on to a position in York, which had barely lasted a year before her nimble fingers had been caught and she'd been forced to go on the run, without even chancing to gather up her clothes. She'd been in Leeds since, struggling to get work until her old mother had helped. Clara's letter had offered a chance opportunity for a few months before she'd be away back to Leeds, for she certainly didn't want to be stuck out here on the moors all winter.

Clara had been pleased to see Mary, and had taken her through the house to show her where she would sleep. Ellen's brow had creased, wondering which room Clara could possibly mean. She did not have long to ponder on the question before Clara was back to speak to her. As the new mistress of Pines Lodge, she had some changes to make, and intended to stay at the farm until her marriage. Naturally this would mean a different way of living and new staff. She had waited until Mary had been able to get here, for it wouldn't do for a young single woman to live in a house on her own, but now that things were settled, they could step out of this limbo. She thanked Ellen for all her years of service to the family, but that Clara would not be starting a new contract of employment with her, and she would no longer be required at the farm. She could have the rest of the day to pack her belongings, then could leave the following morning.

Ellen felt as though her heart was breaking, to be so cruelly cast aside, and by a young woman she'd seen born. Suddenly she was just part of the furniture, and something to be thrown out, for it was no longer fashionable or part of the new vision. Worse was to come. Clara sought out her mother and essentially gave her the same notice to quit, although Maud did not even have the benefit of her final wages being paid, for Maud had never been an employee, just the wife of the master of the house. And just like that, Maud Hurst and Ellen Withers found themselves unemployed and homeless, cast out by their own precious daughter.

Maud cried for the rest of the day, for her heart was broken all over again by another of her children. Fury kept Ellen going, and she packed up not only her own but Maud's possessions, so that they were all ready to leave in the morning. Maud could not think straight and without any other thought of what they could do, they headed out to Whitby, passing by Gillian's on the way to say their goodbyes. They stayed a month with Eleanor, Maud gazing out of the window at the cloud ravaged skies and not knowing what to do. She wrote to

Haworth, where her own people were, and where Amos Cornforth now lived. Amos, now in his fifties, was still working the land as a tenant farmer, and replied suggesting Maud come back to her home, and do him the honour of becoming his wife. Maud gladly accepted and set off to West Yorkshire, for she felt that she could not live on Eleanor's charity forever.

A tenant farming couple would not be able to afford a housekeeper, and sadly Ellen Withers found herself at a loss in the world. Eleanor would have gladly employed her, but for the fact that she already had her own housekeeper in Lucy Ann Argument, whom she would not be without. Ellen helped out with odd jobs and took up some seamstress work in Whitby to keep herself busy, but felt herself fall into a maudlin and hopeless state. She knew she was living on the charity of Eleanor, who gladly gave it, but she had lost her home and her purpose and belonged nowhere. She had originally come from a little place in County Durham, but after all these decades and the things that had happened, could never go back. She wandered about the seafront of Whitby, watching the grey tides of the North Sea draw back and forth across the sands and thought of all that she had experienced and lost. She had worked so hard and yet in her autumn found she had nothing. The joy faded out of her, and when she went to the markets for fruit and vegetables, found herself crying over baskets of gooseberries. Thinking of her treasured little fruit bushes and how they would wither and die, for she was sure no one with such a mean squint like that Mary Harker would do anything to care for them.

Eleanor watched Ellen stumble into a pit of misery and despite her efforts, failed repeatedly at helping the woman move on from Commondale. She felt utterly inept, dear Eleanor, businesswoman and headstrong girl who got herself through any disaster no longer knew what to do. Ellen Withers was her second mother and she so wanted to do something to help her, but it seemed that some problems in the world were not to be fixed. A curse upon Clara Hurst, she thought as she tossed the wedding invitation onto the fire. She did not care if she never saw her sister again.

It was not until the following year that Ellen Wither's fortunes changed in a rather unexpected manner. Eleanor had travelled out into the moors to visit the mill at Castleton for a meeting to discuss prices and the possibility of upping productivity. She was looking at potentially getting more flax in from the Baltic States. On her way back to Whitby she stopped to rest in Egton Bridge. She went to the very inn where she had eaten a meal with the Hob all those years back when he had first dragged her away from her childhood home in Commondale. That had been the start of her education in Whitby. It was there that she bumped into a familiar man she had met once at the end of a ridiculous cart ride across the moors with Ellen some years back. Caleb Lyth, carpenter of Egton and fellow gooseberry grower, immediately recognised Eleanor and was keen for news of Ellen. Gossip being what it was, and people loving nothing better than a tragic tale, the details of Maud and Ellen's expulsion from Pines Lodge by Maud's own daughter had soon travelled up and down the Esk valley, but no one, certainly not Caleb was sure what had happened to Ellen since then. Her gooseberries had been missed, he informed Eleanor, although she had considered his earnest look and wondered if it wasn't more than Ellen's soft fruit harvest he had been pining over. Her suspicions were confirmed when three weeks later Caleb Lyth turned up on the doorstep of her house in Whitby, asking after Ellen Withers. The three of them had taken tea in the parlour before Eleanor had quickly made an excuse to leave the room. The visits had continued with surprising regularity after that day, and within a month Ellen Withers found herself in a position she had long since given up hope of ever being in. For what woman in her mid forties, past the time of bearing children, with no real money and a dodgy ankle, could hope for a proposal of marriage. But there she was, with Caleb down on one knee asking for her hand. She had told him she would need to think about it, and to return in a week. Need to think about it, she had wondered to herself that evening, as if she had any answer other than yes. She was too old to be playing hard to get, foolish woman. But Ellen Withers could not help herself and when he dutifully returned the following week, she had to make sure that it was all agreed as well as a husband she'd be getting her own patch of land at his property that he did solemnly swear not to tinker with, for Ellen was already plotting of the gooseberries she would be growing once she was settled in Egton as Mrs Lyth.

That was all in the future, but there was the time prior to Clara's marriage to be worked through. Clara's pre wedded months at Commondale proved to be busy. Things did not go as smoothly as she might have hoped with Mary Harker, and within a few weeks she was sending the girl back to Leeds. When she had been a little maid in Thirsk, Clara had easily manipulated her. Now they were evenly matched as women. Certainly Clara's more suspect, otherworldly talents garnered from Old Marsden and an inert, inborn knowledge, could never been beaten on a level playing field by Mary. Mary Harker plied her trade with trickery and sleight of hand, and when that didn't work was never above a little thieving. She listened to what Clara would suggest and teach her, but she was not in awe of her employer. She had no fear of taking the odd candlestick or silver teaspoon. Clara knew for longer than Mary realised, and even pilfered a few items back from the temporary housekeeper, but in the end she grew fed up of having to steal her own property back, and sent Mary packing. She had no other housekeeper, and it was not ideal to be a single lady living alone in a house like this, but it was Commondale, out in the countryside, and Clara didn't care. She'd be able to talk her way around any awkward situation and she was more than capable of looking after herself.

With Hobart Hurst officially dead word spread out like a firm sticky mould, creeping over the country and finding residence in ears in every tavern and back ally. The genuine tradesmen and merchants contacted Eleanor via the London or Whitby offices to have final debts settled, now that they knew Hurst was dead, and furthermore his business empire was being wound down. In truth he had nothing owing to the criminal circles, but if thieves and murderers had played by the rules they would have been nothing more than upstanding citizens. Minds started to turn back to the memory of that gnarled little man and his cunning ways. Now that he was dead, perhaps there were a few final pickings to be gathered up.

A mere week after Clara had thrown Mary Harker out of her house, a storm blew up across the moors. Rain thrashed at the buildings all day, the sky grey and sombre, the outlook across miles of moorland bleak and morose. Folk stayed inside whenever possible. Darkness fell and the wind howled relentlessly as though it were the end of the world. And it was on such a night that Clara received her visitors.

She was taken from her business in the kitchen by a heavy hammering at the front door. A bashing similar to one some eight years ago that had taken Ellen and Maud's dignity and made off with some family jewels, albeit only a temporary theft. Ellen and Maud had been frightened at such a sound, but Clara had skipped to the door in simple innocence, wondering who it might be. She did not give a second thought that she was all alone in the house.

Upon the doorstep stood a hunched and overweight old hag, drenched through, with her ragged skirts and shawls plastered to her rolled up frame. She was a mess, so dripping in rainwater she could barely see. She squinted out from the overhang of bonnets and shawls, and noted the doll-like, slender young woman in front of her. "It is a terrible night," she croaked in a high pitched, forced tone, pushing her way past Clara without invitation. "I have been waiting for my husband but he is delayed."

"Waiting up here?" Clara asked incredulously as she pushed the heavy door to. She turned and looked at the dripping trail. The old hag had already headed straight into the kitchen. "It certainly is a terrible night. Why would your husband ask you to wait out on a hill when you could be down in the valley of the village, in the shelter of an inn?"

The woman sniffed and turned her back on Clara. It was logic she couldn't easily counter without arousing suspicion. She looked in the pot on the range, bubbling with something thick like stew. "This for eating?"

Clara pursed her lips. She couldn't place the accent. It was attempting a fool's version of the locality, but covering something else. Even the locals wouldn't be so brazen as to march in to the house without an invitation and expect to be fed. "No," she answered slowly. "It's not ready yet." So that was why she'd had a niggling want to start preparing this mix this very night.

"Not to be minded," the woman, who had still not introduced herself, rustled her sodden skirts and lumped her heaving behind in the chair by the fire. "I shall wait here until my husband gets here. I expect the cart is stuck in mud."

"Perhaps."

"You the mistress of the house?" the woman eyed her. "You look awfully young."

"Do I?"

"What with your husband being so old."

"Is he?"

The old hag squinted at her. She wasn't going to get anywhere with the girl that easily. Clara offered no explanation, but turned to the bread she'd left proving on the table. She started to knead the dough, and gradually the old woman by the fire went to sleep, lulled along by Clara's humming. Clara didn't usually like to get her hands dirty. She was happy to let the cook prepare the food. But for some things, if you wanted them, you had to do them yourself.

When she was happy with the bread, she separated it and formed it into two loaves before leaving it for a second prove. Stepping around the table, she examined the old hag. She had leant right back in the chair, using the top of the back rest as a neck prop so that her head was bent back, mouth wide open and snoring to catch flies. Her legs were stuck straight out like two timber posts, shoes and the hems of her skirts dripping onto the floor. Not only that, but the trousers under her skirts were dry until the last couple of inches at the bottom where the water had seeped up. In her idleness she had let the shawls loosen and sleepily pushed up one of her sleeves, scratching at her arm to reveal a forearm full of long, thick wiry dark hair. Clara stepped up to the bloated, snoring figure and peered into the wrinkled face with disgust. An ugly old woman it could have been but this was no woman. It was a man. Here to do mischief. Just as soon as her 'husband' arrived.

Clara went back to the pot on the range, which was furiously bubbling. Boiling fat and herbs. Perhaps she had been intending on making soap. Or something else. But she knew what its purpose was. Taking down a copper saucepan, she dipped it into the boiling mix. Carefully lifting it up, she walked over to the man-hag and poured it straight down the open mouth.

The man woke up with a roar. It would have been deep and baritone, were his vocal chords not immediately burned away with the boiling fat. Inside it was a spittle and foaming blood cry that splattered down the front of his disguise. Pain scorched through him as the devil's broth burned its way through his throat, spilling out into his organs and chest cavity. His mind turned quite mad in the intense agony. His body was wrenched from the chair and flung onto all fours, vomiting up copious amounts of thick dark red blood mixed with blotches of cooling fat. His arms juddered and he collapsed face-down onto the kitchen floor, his fleshy, corpulent body gently convulsing as he died.

Clara calmly stepped out of the way whilst the stranger got on with the business of dying. She put the saucepan on the table and peered down at the corpse. She would be nobody's victim. Who did this wretch think he was, turning up at the house and expecting to take away her worldly goods and her virginity with it, as if the world owed him all that and more for doing nothing other than being thieving and vile. She would not stand for it, and wasn't sorry for what she had done. The only problem was the mess. She wrinkled her nose with disgust when she realised she would have to remove the body.

Cursing to herself, Clara rolled the dead man over and hooked her arms under his armpits so that she might drag him from the house. It was dark and stormy and there was no risk of being seen, so she boldly drew him out the front door and across the yard to the manure heap. She dropped him at the side, then took a fork to roll him in to the filth where he belonged. Job finished, she spat in his general direction before retiring to the house, careful to lock the door before going to bed.

Late at night, long past midnight the storm broke and the atmosphere calmed to stillness and the gentle pitter-patter of rain. At some point Clara woke, and lay in bed, concentrating on the silence for she was sure she had heard something. She sat up in bed just as she heard the voice again, somewhere out in the yard speaking in a stage whisper.

"Are you there, Fatty?"

Clara's eyes narrowed. Was this the husband? Was the wife to unlock the door so that they could both be in and have their way with the goods of Hobart Hurst? No such luck. They hadn't reckoned with the fact that Hobart Hurst's daughter was still alive and well. Quite bold, she got out of bed and opened the window. She couldn't see the accomplice but she knew he was there. Leaning out into the chilled damp air, she glared into the darkness. "Fatty's in the midden, you bastard!" she yelled, before slamming the window shut and returning to bed. Such was her confidence that she knew she would not be bothered again by petty crooks and thieves.

The next morning the farm manager was a little perturbed by the mess in the yard, finding the manure pile disturbed. It looked as though some heavy sack had been dragged back and forth across the yard. It must have been the storm, Clara had thoughtlessly said. She noted that there was no longer a body on the manure heap. She did not care where the man had taken the body. She was done with them.

Pines Lodge became an occasional summer home for Clara Mowbray, nee Hurst. Most of the time the furniture was kept under dust sheets, and the property minded by the farm manager's wife. The couple lived in a smaller building on the property, much to the irritation of the wife, who would have preferred a decent sized home. Mrs Mowbray barely used the house, and it would be in better condition if permanently lived in. But there was something of the dog-in-the-manger about Mrs Mowbray, and she would not share the house, even if she had no particular use for it herself. She was a fine woman who belonged in a town house, not a grounded farmhouse fitted out for working the land. Yet the villagers shook their heads, remembering how Maud Hurst, Clara's own mother, and Ellen

Withers had been kicked out of their home with only a day's warning and nothing but the clothes on their backs. And for what? So that the main farm house could stand empty for most of the year. It was not right. Not how decent folks behaved. Did not the bible say to honour thy mother and father?

Clara Mowbray settled in to married life very well. She encouraged her new husband in his work, to build up the reputation of his new firm and take on plenty of clients. He did not need to worry about working such long hours, for from the start Clara excelled in managing a household. She had a keen eye with the interiors, and kept a very presentable home in a fine area in Leeds, as was befitting someone of her husband's position. She managed the staff easily. There had been a cook who thought she'd easily get the better of such a young wife faced with running her own home for the first time. She had her own ideas about the pace of work and what ought to be expected of her role. Clara told her otherwise, which she ignored, but two days later was plagued with such nightmares she was sure she was going mad. Sleep deprived and unsettled, jumping at her own shadow, she would find Mrs Mowbray suddenly appearing with subtle suggestions, calmly pointing out the idiotic things she had just done wrong. They were errors she could not even remember she had done. Quite quickly, without thought or resistance, she slipped in to following how Clara Mowbray wanted things. When the friction between cook and mistress eased, so the nightmares began to calm down.

Clara ran a tight ship. She would never let any member of staff get the better of her. It had been particularly infuriating when she'd caught Mary Harker stealing from her own property. How dare Mary even think to do such a thing. Clara had known her since a young maid in Thirsk and had always assumed that she'd had the upper hand. She had taught Mary a few illusions and tricks, and had believed Mary was a little in awe of her. When she'd thrown Mary out of Pine Lodge she had known she would see the woman again, but not when or how. The next time she heard of her compatriot Mary was quite unexpectedly at tea in her own parlour in Leeds.

Clara was entertaining the wives of two of Andrew's colleagues. The wives were air heads, tittering and simplistic, interested in the latest fashions, marriages and recent engagements. They could discuss the merits of mauve over indigo all afternoon but one could not feel enhanced after conversing with them. They were full of gossip but no intelligence. Clara had appearances to keep up and players to control, so she went along with the mindless chatter. She had half an ear on Patricia Varsey's prattle, whilst watching the comings and goings out on the street outside, until Patricia started giggling about a silly little charm she had bought from a woman.

Clara's eyebrows had risen when Patricia had cautiously removed the little item from her purse. "Where did you get that from?"

"Why, I was just saying," Patricia continued, slipping the lucky charm back into her bag before picking up her tea cup. "But you mustn't tell my husband. He thinks such things are nonsense. He'd be so angry if he knew I'd paid for it."

"But where did you get it?" Clara persisted.

"Mrs Bateman."

"Mrs Bateman?" Clara tested the name around her teeth. It wasn't familiar. But the charm was. "And where did you find Mrs Bateman? If one wanted to see her on a matter."

"Why, Clara Mowbray," Patricia tittered. "Are you in need of a lucky charm? You did not strike me as the sort."

"Perhaps it is in hopes of little feet," Margaret Lawson whispered loudly across the room as if involved in a conspiracy. "After all, Clara has been married a year now."

Clara rolled her eyes. The last thing she needed was a child to spoil her figure and steal her youthful beauty. One did not need to spend much time with Gillian to see how much children ruined one's life. "Patricia, shall we have an outing one morning to meet Mrs Bateman?"

"Well, I could manage this Thursday," Patricia started uncertainly, glancing across at Margaret who just grinned and nodded at her. Clara Mowbray wanted a baby as far as Margaret was concerned. It wasn't coming quick enough, so she was throwing her desperation on lucky charms and fertility potions. Many a woman had clung to such superstitions as a distraction during the empty months. Mrs Bateman would be making a fortune out of the desperate.

That Thursday Mrs Varsey and Mrs Mowbray arranged for a cab to pick them up and take them to Black Dog Lane where a certain Mrs Bateman lived. It was a shabby, ramshackle cottage, with dirty curtains in the window and a step that had not been washed for months. It was not the type of place Clara would have expected Patricia Varsey to dare set foot in, for fear of catching some terrible plague or that some decent person of society might see her darkening the door.

"Well, here we are," Patricia spoke uncertainly as they stood outside. As if they had seen enough and would be heading straight back for their comfortable parlours and maid-swept floors.

Clara hammered on the door. She didn't know who Mrs Bateman was, but she wanted to know how she'd gotten her hands on one of Clara's creations. By the looks of her abode, she wasn't making anywhere near the amount of money she ought to be charging.

The door abruptly snapped open and a shrewd woman with dark hair and narrowed eyes looked out, from Patricia to Clara. She had a keen memory and recognised both women.

"Ah, Mrs Bateman," Patricia started. "You perhaps do not recall me, but you were so kind as to..."

"I remember you," Mrs Bateman interrupted. "And I don't think you've come for lucky charms. What do you want?"

Clara squeezed her lips together in fury. There were a lot of things she wanted, but not in front of Patricia Varsey. She had her husband's standing in the city to consider. "This woman is a fraud," she finally spoke, as if the voice of authority on the matter. "You would be best to throw away that charm, Mrs Varsey. For it will do you no good." And with that she turned on her heel and marched away from the cottage, a bewildered Patricia Varsey stumbling after her. Perhaps Margaret was wrong and Clara was not yet so very desperate for that baby.

Mrs Bateman folded her arms over her chest and nodded. That woman, whatever her name was these days, would be back.

It did not take long for Clara to contrive an evening when her husband was out and the servants safely away to their duties or on an evening off. Selecting a dark cloak and bonnet, she slipped out of the tradesmen's entrance and hailed a cab to get her back to Black Dog Lane. Upon arrival she could hear the muted sound of voices, signalling that Mrs Bateman had a visitor. Clara waited in the shadows for a few minutes, and quite soon a giggling young woman and her friend left the cottage, breathlessly whispering about love potions and what they hoped for the year. They'd get nothing but a case of the runs from whatever Mrs Bateman had put in that bottle.

Clara rattled on the door, and barely had time to take her hand back before Mrs Bateman had responded. Despite the trade, there was no money for a servant to answer, she noted.

"I thought you'd be back."

"Peddling my charms, I see?"

"A girl's got a right to a living."

"Isn't your husband keeping you, Mrs Bateman?"

The woman sniffed as if the very notion of a man made her ill.

"Mary Harker..." Clara started.

"It's Bateman now, on account of me being married, don't you know, Clara Hurst."

"It seems we're both married now."

"Oh yes, and what was it you were going by now? Mowbray."

Clara regarded Mary Bateman, the little maid she'd known in Thirsk, her short-lived housekeeper and now a married woman selling fake trinkets, potions and charms. Mostly fake apart from some that she must have stolen from Clara either at Thirsk or Pines Lodge. Her confidence had certainly grown as she'd moved into womanhood and marriage. Now she was over confident and arrogant. "I think I'd better come in if we're going to talk."

"Certainly, Mrs Mowbray." Mary Bateman grinned and pushed the door open so that Clara might follow her inside.

At night, illuminated by gaslight, the parlour room looked even shabbier than by day. Sickly and barely clinging on. Mary had clearly tried to decorate as if to give some sign of her otherworldly ability: horseshoes, drying herbs, grotty animal skulls displayed in glass bell jars and rocks and pebbles scattered on display as if they were fine china. Anyone genuine had no need of such decoration. The proper furniture itself was sparse and hastily thrown together. As if they had just moved in. Clara could sense the impermanence of things here. That and the dust marks and scrapings showed that the room had been better furnished until recently. Items had been taken out and sold in haste, probably to deal with a theft victim demanding recompense. Clara walked straight in and stepped up to the little fire, regarding the flames for a moment before turning on Mary.

"I was rather surprised to see my friend brandishing a little charm I'd made years ago."

Mary shrugged and settled into one of the chairs by the fire. "You weren't using them. You didn't notice they were gone. Probably didn't realise till that lady showed you."

"Thievery and lies will catch up with you sooner or later."

"Everyone's mischief catches up with them, does it Mrs Hurst?" Mary smiled.

Clara didn't like this new married Mary. The attentions of the man, wherever he was now, had given her a maturity and a confidence she hadn't carried before.

"Well now," Mary settled her shawls around her shoulders. "It's all very well for the ladies who marry wealth."

"I have my own money."

"Your husband's making plenty of his own as well. And no doubt he'll inherit a nice bit when the time comes. I remember the Mowbray house. It's all well and good for you, but my husband doesn't support me. He used to be a wheelwright. Now he's gone off and joined the militia."

"You driving him mad with your trickery?"

Mary's eyes narrowed. She did not deign to reply.

Clara decided to take a seat in the second chair by the fire and took a good few minutes to regard Mary. More confident and adult she might be, but intelligence was only middling and manipulated she still could be, only that the tactics would need to be a little subtler. In

Clara's public life she was a fine wife to Andrew, took tea with the other wives, ran a house. They were all good and decent past times, and so utterly boring. After the excitement of the chase and the romantic notions of love and adoration, marriage was proving to be very dull. A little distraction might just keeps the sparks in her mind going, and stop her doing anything rash at home.

"I don't suppose you'll have many of my charms left, if any now."

"Just the one. I'm holding it for a special customer. Not sure who it'll be yet." Mary paused and regarded Clara. "You want to make me some more. Or better still, tell me what's in them?"

Clara smiled like a cat. "Some secrets can't be shared. Besides, I've already taught you enough tricks. Do you remember the one with the eggs."

Mary snorted. "Like I have nothing better to do than shove eggs back up hen's arses. You have some funny habits for someone who's supposed to be a fine lady. I always wondered what was going on with you."

"Oh, this and that." Clara caught sight of her reflection in a tarnished copper pot hanging close to the fire. "One mustn't let life get stale. And people will believe anything. I think you and I could have some fun."

"Fun? I've a living to make."

"I think it's fair to want to enjoy one's work. Well, if you find you're in need of new charms, perhaps I can help, for a price of course. If you're wanting something a little more genuine." Clara pulled herself back up out of the chair. It was getting late and she needed to be home and in bed before anyone had chance to realise she was missing.

"Shall I pay you a call then?" Mary laughed.

"No, write to me. No, rather, not to me," she quickly changed her mind, pondering over how such an allegiance might work. "It wouldn't do to have my husband's name used in any way. I think I should use an alias. Something that sounds better."

"All right. If I need to get in touch with you, what should I call you?"

Clara considered the matter. "Call me Miss Blythe."

Whilst Clara may have only been considering mischief and amusement with her Miss Blythe charms and potions for Mary to sell on, sometimes her trickeries had more serious repercussions. Gillian's fertility had certainly been one, for the woman was now tied down with ten children, the eldest nine years of age, the youngest only a few weeks, but all healthy, vigorous and unending. Whilst it may have taught Gillian a lesson for being so bitter over her previous lack of children, Gillian was in fact too tired and overworked to have a moment to consider how her life had worked out and if she ought to have wished for something different instead. Now thirty years old, yet there were days when she felt a hundred, and her life for herself had amounted to nothing. The great infatuated love was meaningless. Yes, she was married to her sweetheart, but he was at home infrequently. Travelling to take on commissions to help pay for his increasing family, as any good husband would, but Gillian wondered where all her adoration and romance had gone. Or in fact if there had ever been any genuine adoration returned. She had certainly been besotted with William, but had it ever really been reciprocated? She wondered for a moment as she stared vaguely into the broth she was stirring before the baby started to scream again and she woke up to the present moment.

Clara's marriage was not quite the great romance either. Andrew Mowbray was intensely enamoured of his beautiful wife, and despite the fact that there were still no children from the union, continued to be grateful every day that Clara had agreed to be his wife. But he would never receive the intensity of love back from Clara, for she had always had a greater love, and he could not compete. Whilst Andrew longed for a family to complete the picture, Clara would sit at her dressing table every morning and smile at her great love, sharing that deepest secret that she had complete control over her fertility. She would not allow her figure, her looks and vivaciousness to be disfigured by children, and she certainly had no need for a brat to come and usurp the attention she received.

Perhaps in a desperate hope to drum the notion of importance of family to Clara, Andrew decided that following summer they would go and stay at the property in Commondale for a short time. He also wanted to check the accounts and the running of the farm, which rankled Clara – as if to suggest she wasn't perfectly capable of organising her family estate. Yet she smiled sweetly and fluttered her eyelashes at her otherwise astute husband, and went along with the plan. Family, she sniffed at the thought. What good was family? Her nearest and dearest had murdered her dear papa, and certainly wanted nothing to do with her now. They would not quite leave her web until she was done with them of course. But they were now spread out across Yorkshire. Her mother lived in Haworth and had lowered herself to marrying that shepherd man Clara remembered looking after the flocks in her youth. Eleanor was married to a drover and quite the businesswoman of Whitby. Gillian was a mess, and Stephen was dead. That was the extent of her family, and quite frankly they were of no use to her.

After two days in residence in Commondale, Andrew encouraged Clara to go out and reacquaint herself with the village. Didn't she have a sister who lived here still? Ought she not to go visit the woman? Besides, they had brought presents for the children, little toys for Clara to pass out. She had been sweetness and light to her husband, but had glowered at the very air as she walked down into the green valley, wicker basket full of little wooden toys held in the crook of her arm, her parasol held aloft by the other. Gillian? There was no sport or interest there, just a cautionary tale. At least if she had been forced to go and visit Eleanor, there would have been a bit of spirit to converse with. She could imagine the conversation and friction, but realistically Eleanor would probably throw her back off the doorstep if Clara went to visit. Eleanor had not communicated with Clara in any way since her mother and Ellen Withers had been tasked to quit Pines Lodge. Andrew knew that Clara had been the sole beneficiary of her father's will – the fact was hard to hide, especially from a husband conversed in the law. But she had been careful to embellish the hard truth, and had told him that with the declaration of her father's official death, and the news of the will, her mother had felt freed to move on in life and to go to her new husband's home. Ellen Withers had wanted a change, bored with village life, and in short both women had been desperate to get out of Commondale.

There was a bunch of ragged children playing outside of the smithy building as Clara approached. She didn't know who was who, in fact she couldn't have listed the names of all her nieces and nephews had she been pressed to do so. She passed out the toys and asked the children to direct her to their mother. Why, she's in the kitchen, the children had informed her with a look of astonishment that anyone would need to ask such an obvious question. Clara found her at the table kneading bread with inflamed, overworked knuckles. Tears were running down her face.

"I didn't know baking was such an upsetting task," Clara declared as a greeting as she entered through the open door.

Gillian stopped, her sparrow-thin arms like sticks pushing the dough out across the table. She looked up at Clara, loose greasy strands of hair coming from her bonnet. "What would you know about honest housework? What are you doing here, Clara?"

"I've come to visit, and to give the children toys." She gestured vaguely at the basket.

A chorus of shrieks came from outside as if to underline the point. Gillian gave a vague expression, eyebrows raised as if she didn't really care. The sound of fussing came from a worn wooden crib to the side of the room. She sighed, deflated and not particularly caring in many ways. The first child had been a joy to begin with but now that she was on number ten it was a chore. "This is a curse," she told Clara as she begrudgingly made her way over to the crib. "I am terrified I will be with child again soon, for I always am."

"And this was your greatest wish, to give William a great tribe."

"I can't do this," Gillian said, her voice growing thin. Her eyes were filling up with tears. "Did Old Marsden not teach you anything, so that..." she left the thought unspoken, but they both knew what she meant.

"There comes a time in a woman's life when she can no longer have children," Clara started.

"I will be dead before then."

Clara had a private thought which brought a cunning smile to her lips. Yes, you probably will. Whilst Gillian was calming the baby, she went to the door and stretched up on her toes. Blind fingers moved along the ledge until she located the little charm she had left there several years ago. She slipped it into a pocket and turned around just before Gillian stood up, now with baby Matthias in her arms.

"The Lord forgive me, but when the scarlet fever went through the village, I hoped it would take some of mine so that I might find some peace. But they all thrived. Every other family suffered, but we thrived. And they did give me some looks. It's not as if I want this."

"I think you have no further cause for concern," Clara told her, the seeds of an idea forming in her mind. "I will leave you in peace, sister. I see you have enough to do without entertaining me."

That evening, when her husband was fast asleep, Clara got up and went to her dressing table to regard the little charm. There was no point in wasting such a thing. She could send it on to Mary Bateman, courtesy of Miss Blythe of course, and she could sell it on to some silly, desperate woman. There would be a payment, of which Clara ought to get a cut although she didn't trust Mary enough to expect it to be as agreed. Maybe she should ask for something else as well. Why not? It was her talent they were trading off. Perhaps she could add a note in the letter that some little trifle ought to be sent to her, else the charm would not work. What sport it could be. Just what ought she to ask for?

She spent a week pondering on the issue, and finally settled on a jar of honey. She sent the request, along with the charm off to Mary, signed by Miss Blythe, and looked forward to her reward. For a couple of weeks she continued to congratulate herself on her keen wit, considering future treats for Miss Blythe, and the ever forming plots of justice for her papa. But Clara had been thoughtless, and when the month was out she realised she had hung on to that fertility charm a little too long. The nausea was debilitating, and she found herself throwing up several times a day. Distraught, Clara cursed the very thing inside of her, and tried various concoctions and vigorous movements to get rid of it. Yet it would not budge. It was not going anywhere. When the nausea had worn off, and the thing was getting to be four months old, Clara devastated that she had fallen into the very predicament she had sworn never to become a victim of, her husband finally noticed that she had not been herself and realised she was in the family way. He was delighted. Clara pinned a fake smile to her face. It would be the one and only, she promised herself. Her carelessness had cost her heavily but she would not make the same mistake twice.

Whilst Gillian grieved over the number of her lively children, and Clara sulked over the single growing foetus she could not rid herself of, across to the coast in Whitby Eleanor thrived with her ideal number of children, a happy home, and her work to keep her mind busy. There were several months every year when her husband was not at home, on account of the droving rather than the fishing and whaling that left other wives in Whitby alone for long periods. She kept herself busy and focused on her work and her children.

She had extended her dealings with the Baltic states, who brought much timber and flax in to the port of Whitby. The raw products were sold to Eleanor's business, registered under Angus' name for face value only. She followed the flax's journey to the mills in Castleton and then down to London as linen before making her final profit, and the timber was sold on to the navy and the ship builders of Whitby most of the time. The navy were busy trying to increase both the head and ship count they could consider at their disposal. Earlier that year Britain had declared war on France. From the safety of the island the ruling classes had watched the French revolution from under worried brows. The landed gentry trembled at the thought that the ignorant masses might try the same nonsense on

British soil. The execution of the French king had been the last straw and Britain entered into war against France. The navy needed its ships and men. Eleanor's Baltic timbers were much in demand.

Ships captains and merchants from Estonia would often be in the office dealing with payment and subsequent orders. Eleanor was picking up some of the language, but she had neither the mind nor the spark for languages to advance to fluency. In the meantime, a little girl who was often with her Mamma, was listening and soaking up the language like a sponge. Muriel was only four, and did not have the extrovert tendencies of her siblings. She liked the quiet, her books, and being with her mother. She already had the basics of reading, and was more than content to sit in the corner of her Mamma's office pawing through books and studying the print in great detail, even though she did not comprehend most of the words she saw. She displayed her Scottish roots in her red hair, and furthermore differed from her elder sister in her thin frame and plain countenance. Muriel's spark was her brain, which would prove to be her greatest asset and bring many opportunities to her over the years. But for now she was happy to stay by her mother and play with the books her mother gathered for her.

Elizabeth was seven and a pretty, raven haired child promising of future curves when she would blossom into her teenage years. She was vivacious and curious, and thrived on company and conversation, however childish it might be. She was great friends with one of Lucy-Ann Argument's nieces, a certain Jayne Argument, who had an easy going manner most of the time and loved to be out playing with her friend. They were often pestered by her younger sister, Maria Argument, whom Elizabeth thought was quite sweet and treated as a little pet dog. Jayne would lose her temper with the little girl, her Achilles heel that annoyed her otherwise patient and happy countenance. She would try to sneak out of the house without attracting Maria's attention so that she wouldn't demand to join the two little friends. Maria was an attention-hungry little girl, and if she saw her sister leaving, she was quick to nag her mother in to letting her go. Her mother was keen to hurry Maria out of the house and away from under her feet. She shouted after Jayne to be sure to take her sister with her.

Eleanor was working on the accounts when a peal of childish laughter interrupted her thoughts. It sounded like Elizabeth, so happy even as a baby. She looked out of the window and saw her eldest, Stewart walk by. The boy was only ten years old yet he looked about fifteen. He had been through a growth spurt, and was now long and spindly. Elizabeth and her best friend, Jayne went skipping along after Stewart, calling out some girlish nonsense to the boy. Eleanor smiled to herself, then looked down to the little stool by the fire where Muriel was lost in a book of travel accounts.

"Muriel, sweetheart. It's such a nice day. Are you sure you don't want to go out and play with the others?"

Muriel looked up at her with an expression nearing horror that her mother might have tired of her. And she did try so hard to keep quiet and out of the way when her mother was working. "Must I go?"

"No. You are quite welcome to stay here. Only you are a little girl and little girls should go out to play now and then." Eleanor crouched in front of her daughter. "I am sure Elizabeth would not mind. They often have Maria, Jayne's little sister with them."

"I want to be here."

Eleanor kissed her forehead. "And you are very welcome here. What would I do without my little girl to keep me company?" The girls returned to their work: Eleanor to her bookkeeping and Muriel to the ten year old book of Captain Cook's travels. This particular volume told of explorations to gauge the position and extent of the western seaboard of North America. Captain Cook was a hero of Whitby, now dead, and eaten up by cannibals in the South Seas, so the wide eyed gossips said. Mother and daughter continued in silent yet comfortable contemplation for the following hour, until the peace was broken by Elizabeth stumbling into the house, red-faced from the exertion of running all the way up the hill. Her hair was wild and tousled, and her breathing intensely heavy. Eleanor looked up sharply, and for a moment worried how there was something intensely provocative about Elizabeth, even at this age. It spelt trouble. Her train of thought geared up to the present moment and she stood up from her desk.

"Elizabeth?"

"Mamma," she started, her voice shaking. "They've taken him."

"Taken who? What are you talking about?"

"Stewart!"

"Stewart?" Eleanor felt her heart lurch at the suggestion of trouble for her first born. "What are you talking about, Elizabeth?" She clasped her daughter by the shoulders.

Elizabeth started to cry. "The navy men."

"The press gang? But Stewart's just a little boy!"

"They said he was older than he claimed. That he'd make a good powder monkey."

Elizabeth broke down into floods of tears. Muriel clasped tightly the sides of her book and tried to shrink into the very wall. Eleanor's mind went blank in horror. Her little boy was in trouble. The navy had been causing upset this year throughout the town and across the moorland communities, turning up and rounding up men and boys, forcing them into the navy. But the boys had been teenagers. The children had been left alone. She had never once considered that her little boy was a potential victim. And she had been dealing with the navy, selling them cargos of timber to go to the shipyards to build the fleets.

"They're going to send him to the war!" Elizabeth wailed.

"No." Eleanor let go of her daughter's shoulders and stepped across to the fireplace. She dealt with a lot on her own, and life had not always been simple, but sometimes she felt overwhelmed. Angus left her on her own for so much time during the year. Too much time. What ought she to do about this? Her eyes moved across the fire and the paraphernalia about the place. "I'm going to fetch him," she announced, grimly pulling the fire poker from the stand and marching out of the room.

Elizabeth and Muriel stared at one another.

The navy had set up their press gang office, if one could call it that, in a tavern over the river in the oldest part of town. There was a navy flag hanging outside to declare the building's purpose, as if it were something to be proud of. The everyday folk of the town despised the place, and would spit at the pavement as they passed by. Most folks, not just in Whitby but in the entire Esk Valley, knew someone who had been snatched. All for the honour of serving king and country they said, but it was tantamount to kidnapping and among common folk there was no good will left for the navy. It was quite illegal, not to mention immoral, but most had no voice or power, and the navy was thick skinned and was unperturbed by the slippery film that formed outside the tavern. Those that could have done something, the landed gentry and nobility quietly ignored it. Although they would not admit it out loud, they felt the pressgangs were of benefit for knocking common folk back into their places. The whalers and shipbuilders of Whitby were getting too wealthy and confident for their own good. New wealth was a different race of people to the nobility and needed to be reminded of its place. God forbid something like the nonsense going on in France could happen on good solid British soil.

Eleanor started to see red once she'd crossed the river and started up the narrow cobbled streets to the navy's tavern. Her hand was clenched so tightly around the fire poker that nothing on earth could have separated them. A butcher noticed her single-minded fury walk past, and stepped out of the shop to call and ask what was happening. Eleanor was too angry to even register the sound of his voice. She wanted her boy back. The angry cloud of thunder fizzing over her head started to attract attention, and people stepped out of shop doorways, or paused in their business and watched her pass by. Some even decided that a pause in the day's chores could do no harm, and followed at a safe distance.

Decent women ought not to go into taverns. Eleanor couldn't give a damn about appearances, and marched directly into the building and straight up to the man she assumed was in charge. He was at a table, papers tousled about before him, some kept in position with a tankard of ale. His skin was like tanned leather, his hair scruffy and in need of a cut. He looked up at Eleanor's entrance, and smirked. Pretty woman, would have taken her for a prostitute for boldly marching in the tavern yet her manner of dress suggested a lady of some means.

"I've come for my boy."

"Your boy? I see no boys here."

Eleanor stepped right up to the table and towered over the man. "You have taken my boy. He is just a child. Your pressgangs are illegal at the best of times, but you're taking children now."

"There's no children here."

"Where is my son? Stewart MacCaskill. You have just taken him."

"Get out of here you drunken wench. I'll not waste my time bandying words with a woman."

There was gruff laughter from the other men in the room. The heady scent of ale and tobacco stifled the air. Their manners spoke of amusement as if the taking of an innocent child was just a mere trifle. They regarded her as if she was just a rag doll imbecile. Eleanor stepped back from the table and looked around the room. No one here gave a damn.

"Go get yourself a shag and have another one."

Eleanor swung around with the poker and flung everything off the table, papers like leaves in the wind. Full tankards clattered onto the flagstone floor and a bottle of rum smashed against stone. "Where is my son?" she screamed.

"She's mad!"

"They've all been taken to the ship; they're all gone already."

The man in charge slowly stood up from the table. He was angry, not sure whether it was mostly due to the wasted alcohol or the fact that one woman was causing so much trouble. "Get this silly bitch out of here."

Eleanor lost her senses. Screaming, she started to smash up the tavern, swinging around with both hands grasping the fire poker. She whacked one man on the shin. He roared with pain and staggered backwards, colliding with a table and knocking a stack of papers into the fire. The jovial amusement disappeared from the men's faces as they realised this slender woman was getting the better of them. She was a screaming banshee slicing at the air with the poker. Not easily approached if one wanted to keep the precious teeth one still had. Eventually it took the three of them to get her arms down by her sides, and to drag her kicking out of the tavern door. They unceremoniously lobbed her into the street like an old discarded sack, swearing and throwing general terms of abuse in her direction before returning inside and slamming the door shut.

Sitting in the gutter, Eleanor shouted and waved the fire poker in the air. "You bastards! May your stinking hides rot in hell for what you have done!"

Quite a crowd had gathered in the street by this point. Some were amused to see Mrs MacCaskill lose her dignity, shaking their heads at her ridiculous behaviour. Others were nodding along with her, for she was quite right. It was disgraceful how the navy had treated the communities of this part of northern England. Some muttered and lowered their brows. It was a little shameful that the situation had waited for a woman to take action and tell the navy what people thought. It was all very well spitting in the street, but the situation had escalated and required a little direct action. They ought to show the navy that Whitby would not accept this evil harvest of their young men. Something ought to be done.

Eleanor dragged herself to her feet, brushing her skirts down before looking around at the amassed curious faces. "It's all very well you people laughing at me, but what have you done? You sit back and let them take our sons and brothers. And say nothing." Disgusted and distraught, she gave the tavern one last scream, lobbing the fire poker through one of the windows, before walking back home in tears. Her little boy was lost. She did not know how to get him back. She died inside.

In Whitby town the mutterings and the anger grew until it could not be controlled. Fights broke out, property was destroyed and the tavern hosting the navy was attacked and set afire. The riot was on. The men and boys were not returned, and the ringleaders – men only – were gathered up afterwards and taken to York to be hung, but at least the town had finally spoken.

The following year Clara's daughter was born, and was a beautiful and sweet mannered girl, much to Clara's disgust. Emmerline was the diamond in her father's eyes, and Clara found herself stepping back into second place as the most beautiful in the Mowbray empire. Usurped by a younger model she had been stupid enough to produce.

A lax moment of thoughtlessness she would suffer for the rest of her days. But she was not stupid and did not follow Gillian's mistakes. She made certain she would never fall pregnant again, and for the one babe she had forced out, she would not be a slave. Clara had her nanny and wet nurse lined up and ready before her daughter was out, and as soon as she was, she made sure the bloodied, screaming beast was passed across to her staff. Clara felt dreadful, looked worse and refused to see her husband for the first three days. The baby was taken in a couple of times to meet its disinterested mother. Clara admitted Emmerline looked better now that she had been washed and lost that immediate shocked mole appearance she had been born with. But Clara's eyes kept flicking back to her swollen legs in horror, wondering when her body would go back to normal. Why did women let this happen? It was the ultimate punishment. No wonder Gillian looked as terrible as she did.

She did not send out letters to relatives declaring the new arrival. Most of her family would not have wished to have heard from her, what with her having thrown her mother out only to keep the house empty most of the year. News had its way of spreading regardless, and Emmerline's birth was passed through Andrew Mowbray's circles, through law men, merchants and traders, and eventually made its way to Whitby, where Eleanor learned she had yet another niece, and this time one she would most probably never meet.

Even a year later Emmerline Mowbray was still gossip. Eleanor had been walking back from the blubberhouses when she bumped in to a trader from Leeds who mentioned that he had seen the little girl in an offhand sort of way, having a vague idea that Eleanor might be related to Clara Mowbray. Poor child, Eleanor thought, what a start in life to have with a mother like that.

Opening the front door, she entered her home, hanging up her cloak as she pulled the front door to simultaneously. Lucy-Ann Argument stuck her head out of the kitchen door at the end of the corridor. "Supper's ready in half an hour."

"Very good. Thank you."

"Master's in the sitting room."

They shared a grin. Angus was referred to as the master, this being a man's world, but they both knew who ran and paid for this home. Angus was no whipped and controlled husband, but he certainly knew better than ever to try telling Eleanor about her business. He had returned from London two days ago, envigoured but also tired from the long drove down from Scotland and the agricultural work in the south. Financially he didn't have to do anything. Eleanor could have easily supported him but he had his male pride to think of and the drover's wanderlust in his blood. He was in his forties and the weather had begun to tell on his joints in a way he'd never experienced. Oh to be a young man of twenty again. When he'd arrived at Whitby, travelling alone since the passing of wee Jamie the dog, he'd gone straight to bed and slept for the first day, no energy for his wife despite the pouting, back poking and generally heavy huffing about their bedroom. The second day he'd set things to rights, and now he was in the sitting room, his legs stretched out by the fire, feet resting on a little stool. The fire popped and he wondered if it hadn't been the sound of the bones in his knees shifting.

"You've finally left the bed, I see."

He looked up. He hadn't heard Eleanor return. "You were hardly what I'd call encouraging of me leaving the bed yesterday."

"Yes, yes yes..." she waved it off, feeling irritable as she sat down in the chair opposite him. She settled into the cushioning and enjoyed feeling the heat from the fire. The damp autumn sea fret that crept around the town today was quite chilling.

"Someone been vexing you? You've not heard back from old Catherine already?"

Eleanor gave him a sharp look, but declined to take the bait. Old Catherine, she thought, mentally shaking her head at him. It was hardly respectful of a queen, even if she wasn't their queen. Catherine of Russia had caused trouble for Eleanor's businesses. Or rather, her intention had not been to trouble Eleanor's way of making a living, but in her annexing of the Baltic States. Supplies of raw materials as flax and timber were the blood of Eleanor's trading, had subsequently ceased. They were no longer dealing with the Baltic States, but Russia, and that was a whole new complication. Eleanor hadn't been the only business woman affected, and earlier that year she and Margaret Campion had written to purchase the freedom of the Russian Trading Company in order to trade with Russia. She and Eleanor were hopeful, and saw this as a mere blip in their good work. In the meantime Eleanor found herself with free time, and weavers in Castleton worrying about their future. She tried to distract herself with other things, but in the news it was all talk of the war with France, which only sent her worries in another direction. What was happening to her poor stolen son, Stewart?

The only thing she knew was that as of three months ago he had been alive, for he had written a letter which had reached its destination. After the initial horror of being thrown into the navy life against his will, Stewart had actually taken to the work aboard ship, and was thriving. One of the officers had taken him under his wing, and it seemed there was great potential for the lad. Angus tried to be as hopeful and philosophical as he could about it, despite worrying over his young son, but Eleanor could do nothing but writhe in anxiety. She still spat at the ground when she saw the navy flags, even though technically her son was now part of that machine.

"I was told about Emmerline today. People seem to assume I will have seen her by now."

"This is your witch-sister's child?"

Eleanor pursed her lips and gazed in to the fire. In more heated moments she had referred to her younger sister as a witch, merely as a general term of abuse for all she had done. But Eleanor suspected her of other mischiefs she could neither prove nor completely explain. "An unfortunate child, certainly for its mother."

"Rich children are not raised by their mothers," Angus observed.

"I raise my children!"

"Ah, but you're new wealth," he said. "And besides, Eleanor MacCaskill, you're hardly what I'd call normal."

"I'll take that as a compliment."

"It wasn't meant as one," he teased. "Away with you lass, will you not entertain your man with a few reels on the fiddle? I've not heard you play for a long time."

"Lass!" Eleanor almost shrieked. "I worked it out the other day. I must be thirty-two. Positively an old woman, I'm sure!"

He smiled at her. "Still a lass to me."

"Yes, well, I don't suppose we can all be as old as you."

"I did not come all this way to take such abuse from a woman."

She grinned back at him. "I'm very sure you did."

"Aye well," he sighed, feeling tired again. Now that droving was done for the year he just wanted to stay at home for the winter. He would eventually have to head up to Falkirk to keep up the pretence of his first wife so that she would not cause trouble for him. "Will you not play me something on the fiddle?"

"Maybe later. It's cold out, I've lost the feeling in my fingers just now." She leaned in towards the fire, watching the flames flicker. "So what news is there in London?"

"Mostly the same old nonsense. They are still chattering about the war." Their eyes met. It was a sensitive subject to bring up because of Stewart. Angus hoped something good would come out of it and would be the making of the lad, give him a future of some sorts. "There's some worrying over numbers. I know it was two years ago, but there's still some mention of that riot you started..."

"I did not start it."

"There's none more the grateful than I that they didn't take you for a ringleader, for I heard they hung the instigators in York, but from accounts I have heard, you smashing up the place with the poker didn't exactly calm the mood of the mob that day."

"Yes well," Eleanor avoided his stare. "What's all this worrying over numbers?"

"What with the war with France and the navy press ganging in terror of running low on men, they realised that they have no idea what kind of resources they have in the country. No one knows how many people actually live here. How many potential recruits; how many mouths to feed."

"I don't see that the government needs to know. Everyone looks after themselves and their family. The government is hardly concerned with people's best. Probably only worrying that they could be missing out on some taxation."

"Aye well, that may be possible."

"It's strange though, when I think of these letters we are sending to Russia. It frightens me."

"The Russians frighten you?"

Eleanor smiled slightly. "Not too much. I've met a couple. They're not as grim as their stern demeanour would have you think. But no, the fact that I am doing such things. Writing to a queen of a far off land to continue my business. It feels immense. It's only a moment ago that I was just a girl delivering letters from dale to dale on my donkey. And now..."

"And now you're a woman."

"But where did the time go? It frightens me. Our children are reaching the point in life I felt as though I was still at, but now I realise I am getting old."

Angus burst out laughing. "Don't you be worrying at me about your age, woman. I have a few years on you."

"I'm not a young girl anymore."

"None of us are."

"You never were a young girl."

"Eleanor, you're talking as if you were at your death bed."

"Mamma wrote to me last week. Her husband, Amos Cornforth, died a month back," Eleanor blurted out. She remembered the gentle man from her childhood when he had worked managing the flocks and their estate. It had been his family's own land until his father had drunk away the fortune and Amos, on inheriting debts had been forced to sell everything. Her mother, Maud, had gradually fallen for him and finally, years later and after the death of their son, been able to marry him. Now she was a widow for the second time. Eleanor had written and asked her mother to come and stay with her, but she suspected Maud would want to stay in the land of her own people, up in the west of the county in Haworth. "It just makes me think."

"That you'll be next? I doubt it. None of us know how long we have. It might be a day, a year, perhaps another thirty year. Just remember to enjoy today." He smiled as she met his eye, her face illuminated by the fire as the evening drew on and the room darkened. "Go fetch your fiddle and play us a tune, lassie. We can remember the time we first met and lament that you're no longer a young maid no more."

"All right, then," Eleanor relented, pulling herself out of the armchair. "Because it's you."

Because it's you, because it's you, because it's you, was the annoying little chant that followed Jayne Argument as she headed up to the MacCaskill's house. She was coming to see Elizabeth MacCaskill and spend the day with her friend. As she had been walking out the door her mother had said to take her younger sister, Maria, with her. She was always being lumbered with her stupid little sister. Elizabeth and Jayne were big girls of eleven and they didn't need silly brats toddling along with them whilst they ran about town. It didn't help that Elizabeth thought Maria was cute with her chatty, playful nature, and never tried to scare Maria off. It would have been more fitting to leave her with Muriel who was closer in age. Perhaps Elizabeth dreamed of having a more vivacious sister, for Muriel was a bookish lone wolf. She mostly preferred the company of books, sitting in quiet thought although she would sometimes be seen with that child of the adventurer, William or Bill or whatever he was called. They played some fantasy game called arctic explorers, which was ridiculous both to see Muriel playing – the girl seemed far too serious for such frivolity – but that they would play as though a woman could be an explorer or even be interested in the world. Muriel would be strange as an adult, and Jayne's mother often commented that a daughter of Eleanor MacCaskill's ought to be playing at tea with her dolls and learning to be a lady and a wife. Never mind all that unnecessary reading and running about shouting of harpoons and scientific discovery.

There was a sharp tug on Jayne's skirts. "Are we there yet?"

"You know very well how far it is to go, Maria Argument," Jayne snapped. "And if the walk bores you, you'd better go home."

"Mother doesn't want me there."

"I don't want you here. I don't know why you have to come."

"Because it's you! Because it's you!..."

Jayne grimaced as the chanting started up again.

If she'd hoped that Maria would behave herself when Elizabeth came out, she had been sorely mistaken. The two girls started to walk back down the hill into town. Elizabeth said that she wanted to go to the drapers to look at ribbons. Maria jigged around their skirts, making up silly rhymes to attract Elizabeth's attention and annoy her elder sister.

Down by the river as they approached the bridge, a couple of lads from one of the shipbuilding yards grinned and pulled themselves up from their slouches when they saw the group approach. They were only eleven, but Elizabeth especially looked older than her age, with her figure filling out in a womanly way. She carried a boldness, and would look the lads straight in the eye without shame. Jayne felt herself tilting her head so that her bonnet might shade her blushes. She wished she had Elizabeth's confidence. She was sure Elizabeth would marry such a dashing fine man, and she, Jayne, would probably die an old maid.

"Morning Ladies."

"Looking fine this day..."

"Out for a stroll in this beautiful sunshine?"

The lads brusquely fell into step with them. Jayne was pointedly ignoring their very existence. Elizabeth hadn't said a word, but she was grinning at the taller of the two. Maria just stared at them with the unapologetic fixation of the young child.

"Not as beautiful as you, of course."

"Beautiful girls out for a walk..."

"Well, one is, not sure about t'other. She hides so well. Are you a plain Jane, like?"

Jayne felt her cheeks flush up in an angry hot red as the young men hunched their shoulders and twisted their necks to peer into her bonnet. She felt like a frightened creature in the back of a cave. Maria squealed with laughter, which only made the situation worse.

"Plain Jane!" she shrieked. "Plain Jane. How do you know her name?"

"Oh shut up you little brat!" she snapped, hugging her arms around her body and speeding away from the leering lads, her hysterical sister and a bemused Elizabeth.

Elizabeth paused to give the lads a cheeky wink before she hurried after Jayne, linking arms with her friend. For the moment she ignored Maria who ran after them, almost tripping over the cobbles as they reached the other side of the bridge and headed off into the narrow streets towards the draper Elizabeth favoured. Maria was still laughing, but it was the forced laughter of little children when they believed they were being clever and thought this was the way to gain their elders' attention.

"It was just prattle, you mustn't take it to heart," Elizabeth was consoling Jayne.

"She's a plain Jayne!" Maria shrieked.

"Oh shut up you little beast!" Jayne spun around and glared down into her sister's face. "No one wants you with us anyway."

Maria stuck her tongue out in response. Jayne and Elizabeth continued to walk arm in arm, Elizabeth making a comment over her shoulder for Maria's benefit that Jayne was going to be a very handsome woman. Maria hung back for a moment, wondering if she ought to go home. Her mother would be angry for having her under her feet again and besides, she wasn't sure she wanted to walk all the way home on her own. Stuffing her hands into her pinafore pockets, she trudged along behind the two girls.

They were some time in the drapers as Elizabeth fussed over the selection of pretty ribbons and struggled to pick out one. She repeatedly asked Jayne which would suit her hair best, knowing they all suited her well, until Jayne went outside in exasperation and to scold Maria for kicking pebbles at the shop doorstep. Elizabeth decided to take two ribbons as she could narrow her choice no further, and joined the Arguments outside. A sea fret was thickening in the streets, like wisps of gossamer drifting on the air. The girls pulled their shawls tighter to their bodies and Jayne made noises about wanting to go home. Elizabeth said wouldn't it be fun to get above the mist and see the view of the little port? Without waiting for agreement, she ran off up the street, Maria tearing directly after her.

"Maria, we should go home," Jayne called out feebly, knowing her sister would ignore her. She wrung her cold fingers together and followed the girls into the mist. They moved up through the old town to the hundred odd steps that broke up from the sloped streets and charged to the tops of the cliffs to graveyard and church of Saint Mary. Here, by the open cliff edge one could look out over the whaling port of Whitby and the North Sea beyond.

There were 199 steps up to Saint Mary's church, and Jayne's face was flushed by the time she reached the top. She had been jogging in order to catch up with Elizabeth and Maria, who had seemingly floated up as if it were no effort at all. Maria started giggling when she saw Jayne's sweaty brow. Jayne shouted at her and possessively snatched at Elizabeth's arm, dragging her away.

"Oh Jayne, why do you react so to her?"

"Because she is an annoying little monster."

"She is just a little girl."

"I remain to be convinced."

It was not an argument to be won. Elizabeth wondered if all sisters were meant to be irritated by their younger siblings. She didn't have any particular problem with Muriel. She certainly never chanted nonsense and ran about in the way. She never wanted to come out with Elizabeth anywhere. In truth she was a little dull and unadventurous, always with her nose stuck between the pages of a book.

"Look, it's as though the sea just disappears into the mist." Elizabeth and Jayne stopped at the edge of the graveyard, where the grassy tussocks rolled off to the cliff edge. Beyond was a sheer drop, then the back yards of the houses on the streets below. At their feet there were a number of streets clinging to the decline to the sea.

"It's spooky. I don't like it," Jayne muttered.

Maria's shrill laugh was like that of a banshee. "Scardy-Mary; Scardy- Mary!" she sang out taunting, poking at Jayne's backside with a stick.

"My name is Jayne."

"Plain Jayne got so scared she soiled her dress."

"Shut up Maria."

Maria gave a good hard poke into Jayne's rear end through her skirts, and chortled as she pretended to hear the squish of wet fabric. "She has but soiled herself!" she shrieked.

Jayne turned on her blindly. "Shut up, you horrid little beast." She pushed out at her little sister with both hands, shoving her away roughly. Little Maria stumbled backwards, for a moment wearing a victorious grin that she had won in utterly annoying her sister. Her curls bounced in the motion, her arms flung out and the stick pointed to the sky. Her heels went back onto nothing, then her arms were flapping and the grin melted into a gape of horror. Childish little hands grasped desperately forward, trying to hold on to strands of mist. Then she was gone, as if she had never been there.

There was a crumpled thud, then an awful silence. Neither Jayne nor Elizabeth moved. They looked at nothing, waiting for the moment to stop and normality to return. Waiting for Maria to stand up from the grass and laugh at her own silly trick. The mist continued to curl in from the sea. Jayne blinked back droplets forming on her eyelashes. Elizabeth realised she was holding her breath, and released the air from her lungs. She looked across at her friend, who resembled the mourning angels of the graves of the rich. It had just happened. Cautiously she walked up to the edge, and peered over. She could see Maria's little body lying in one of the yards down below, an empty gaping mouth staring up at the sky. Her limbs were flung about in uncanny positions and she was not moving. She had knocked down some washing that had been drying on the line when the sun had been shining, neglected to be taken in by the maid later on. It now served as a shroud for little Maria, and painfully displayed the blooming red halo that was growing from the little girl's head. Elizabeth had no knowledge of medical matters but even she could see the child was dead. It was so strange. She'd never really had that much to do with death before now. Mamma had fretted that Stewart had died, although correspondence had proved otherwise. But even then it was not something she witnessed. Here one moment Maria was full of life, however irritating she might be, and then like a flame blown out on a candle, she was gone. Life was so fragile. One ought to make the most of every moment.

"Oh no."

She remembered Jayne was with her, and looked across to her friend. Jayne was shaking as if her arms had their own minds.

"No." Jayne wrenched herself away from the cliff edge and fled through the graveyard.

"Jayne!" Elizabeth followed her friend, surprised by how swiftly Jayne could move. They ran past the church and out of the graveyard, over grassland towards the ruins of the old abbey. Jayne ran with her arms flapping wildly, and stumbled up to a low, crumbling wall. Slamming her hands against the top layer as a prop, she pushed against the wall as she threw up into the grass, making unearthly sounds from the pit of her throat as all the bile and terror and stomach acids came racing forth.

Elizabeth caught up and pulled her away just as she finished vomiting. Jayne was shuddering and dreadfully pale. "Oh, Jayne." She took her friend in her arms and hugged her closely.

"Mamma will kill me!" Jayne wailed loudly. The tears poured from her eyes. "I am dead. I am dead."

"She will not. It was a terrible accident."

"I pushed her."

"You did not mean to."

"Oh God. Oh God have mercy on my soul. I will hang for this."

Jayne collapsed into the grass. The shaking was getting worse. Elizabeth dropped to her knees, really not certain what to do with Jayne. She was going into meltdown. She grimaced and gave her friend a good slap around the face. "It was an accident. You will not hang. Your mother will not kill you."

"But I pushed her."

"No you didn't."

Jayne's tormented cries stopped and she looked at Elizabeth, puzzled. "But I..."

"No you didn't. We were playing at the cliffs. Maria was running about. We told her to calm down, but she never listens to what people say. It was a terrible accident."

"But that is a lie," Jayne whispered.

"It's a variation on the truth."

"Maria is... isn't she?" She met Elizabeth's eye. "I mean, she's not... she's..."

"She's dead," Elizabeth spoke the blunt truth. "Yes. That is true. And whatever happens next will not change that fact. Your life should not be ruined as well."

"But I..."

"Jayne." Elizabeth clasped her friend's hands together within the circle of her own palms. "Only you and I know what happened. We can just say Maria was running about and not looking where she was going. It was an accident."

"But I pushed her. No one will marry me now."

"No one is going to know. You have heard what we will say Jayne!" she snapped forcefully when Jayne would not meet her eye. "We know what we shall say, don't we?"

"Yes," Jayne said meekly.

Elizabeth nodded. She did not want to see her friend's life ruined. Although plain Jane was a rhyming joke, Jayne was no beauty. Her one life ambition was to marry, and if she had this hanging over her head, her potential pool of suitors would dry up so that only the really vile would be left.

She stood up, pulling Jayne to her feet. "Come now. Your sister just tumbled over the edge of the cliff whilst playing. We must go find her. And we must go and fetch help."

Mrs Argument broke down when they had returned home with Maria's body. The man at the house where the body had fallen had been kind enough to carry the little girl back to her mother. His wife had initially started screaming about the bloodied sheets and who would pay for the spoiled linen, until her husband had slapped her about the face and sent her inside. Jayne was distraught, convinced this was the end of her life and everyone knew it had not been an accident. Yet a tear-stained Elizabeth told a believable story, and it was automatically accepted. Why look for complications when the simple tale covered this awful tragedy?

Elizabeth had started to shake as she had walked home from the Arguments alleyway dwelling, and by the time she had walked into her own family home she was freezing and barely making sense. Shortly before her arrival home the butcher's boy had been down at the kitchen entrance with a delivery, blabbering about the terrible accident, ignorant to the connection between the little girl Maria and the housekeeper he was gossiping with. When Lucy-Ann had realised who he was talking about, she had sent him packing and run in to the office to beg the time from her mistress, for she must away to her family. Eleanor had given her the next two days off and told Lucy-Ann to let her know if there was anything they could do, whilst helping her into her shawls and cloaks. Lucy-Ann rushed off to her family's aid. Then Elizabeth had returned, and Eleanor realised that she must have been there for she had left with Jayne and Maria earlier in the day. She had bundled her daughter up in blankets and taken her to bed, where she had kept an eye on her all through the night, worrying that the shock might become too much. It must have been an awful thing for the girls to witness. One moment and all was lost. Maria had been a giddy and boisterous little girl and it was not hard to imagine how she could have been running about without paying attention to how close the cliff edge was. One missed step and it was all over.

Elizabeth stayed in her room for two days. Muriel would creep in and silently read her books whilst perched on a stool whenever her Mamma had to go downstairs to deal with business. She was worried that something dreadful might happen if someone wasn't always there to keep an eye on her sister. Eventually Elizabeth felt calm enough to sit up and face the world. Although she felt no qualms over lying about the exact nature of Maria's passing, that moment of horror was on repeat in her mind. That sickening realisation on Maria's face when she had lost her balance and was going over. The desperate, pleading horror of a child wanting it made right.

On the second day a letter arrived for Elizabeth. She was in her own room, taking a little broth, when the letter came. Muriel ran upstairs with it, placing it by the bowl and hesitating for a moment. She decided that Elizabeth was well enough to be left on her own for periods of time now, and ran back downstairs to be with her Mamma.

Elizabeth looked at the envelope and realised that the childish, clunky hand was that of her friend Jayne Argument. Setting her spoon aside, she opened up the piece of paper and read what Jayne felt she could not say to Elizabeth. It was a jumble of guilt-ridden confession and gratitude. It was a confessional to get the horror out of her system. Elizabeth was the only one she could communicate with. She wrote of the same nightmares Elizabeth had dreamt, recalling every moment of Maria's fall. For Jayne's part she was plagued by how she had let the irritation from Maria's taunting grow, and that furious thoughtlessness when she had pushed her sister away and into death. She was terrified it would be the end of her if people knew of her mistake. Her family would disown her and she would be locked up as a murderess. She had not meant to hurt her sister, only to make her quiet. She was indebted to Elizabeth for the rest of her days and if there was every anything she needed, she had only to ask.

It was sweet, if a bit fawning, but Elizabeth couldn't think what she might need from the Arguments. Really, they were of two different social and economic scales, but friends through Lucy-Ann. Still, best friends were best friends. She folded the letter and put it in her treasures box that her father had brought from London for her birthday a couple of years ago. Perhaps not the greatest memento, a note about a little girl's death, but little notes between friends, shells picked up on the beach and pressed flowers were the types of things perfect to fill a treasure box at this age.

The following week the funeral was held. The family hadn't been able to quite put the money together to pay for a proper funeral. The insurances were not fully paid up for Maria. Eleanor had paid the balance, although they said the money came from Lucy-Ann, who had been quite sure that her sister-in-law would have refused the charity unless it had come directly from a family member. Maria was buried in the graveyard of St Mary's, the very place where she had taken a tumble and died. It seemed inappropriate and tragic, yet her mother had been adamant on the place. It rained that day and the wind up on the cliffs was dreadful. The participants were quickly drenched, shivering in thought of the tragic childhood death. So many died in infancy or of childhood disease. Maria had been so healthy and vigorous. That she should be taken by a silly little accident felt particularly cruel.

The following day Elizabeth went to call on the Arguments and speak to Jayne. Mrs Argument was a sullen, silent shadow going about her business and only speaking to her children when she needed them to do something or simply get out of the way. Most had enough sense to keep out of the tracks their mother wore through the home. When Elizabeth arrived she found Jayne's older brother, Horace on the doorstep, hunched over his work. He was apprenticed to one of the jet works, but when at home he would be on the beaches looking for those strange shapes they said were animals captured in stone. There were a lot that looked like curled up headless snakes, but Elizabeth thought they looked like strange snail shells. Some folk said they were the dead petrified snakes killed back in the olden days of St Hilda, who supposedly banished all the snakes with her godliness, or some such miracle. Elizabeth didn't always pay attention to how the tales went. Some of the locals would collect these supposed snakes off the beach to sell to visitors. For amusement, some would even carve snake's heads onto the end, as

Horace was doing now. There was always some gullible type who even thought the head was part of the original.

Elizabeth paused, noting he hadn't noticed her arrival. She leaned forward to peer at his work. He was making a fine job of the snake's head. "I didn't know you had such careful fingers, Horace Argument."

The thin-faced lad of fourteen looked up with a scowl at being spoken to at all, and coloured when he saw that it was Miss Elizabeth. All the local lads who had been lucky enough to have set eyes on her had a thing for the young girl.

"Is Jayne at home?"

"In the kitchen." Horace nodded back over his shoulder, unable to look Elizabeth in the eye. He gathered up his carving implements and rather ungracefully removed himself from the doorstep.

"Why, thank you," Elizabeth beamed at him, very aware of how uncomfortable she was making the lad. "I'll just step right in."

Jayne was ready even before Elizabeth asked to leave the house. Out of formality she asked her mother if it would be all right. Her mother ignored her. Although she knew it had been an accident, and Maria had been a hyper active little girl, she had been in Jayne's care at the time. And she needed someone to blame. Jayne kept her eyes low as she skulked out of the kitchen. She felt like a pariah, shunned by her family. If they had known the truth, they would have thrown her out of the house after a whipping, if not flayed her alive. She could not wait to be old enough to get married and leave home. In the meantime she was considering asking her Aunt Lucy-Ann, if she might not take a job at the MacCaskill's house. Something to get her away from her mother so she might start making her own way in the world. The guilt would gnaw her hollow if she did not escape her childhood home.

The girls linked arms and walked down towards the beach.

"How are you, Jayne?"

"I do not know. My mother hates me, but she does not attack me. I know she would if she knew what had really happened. But the grief in the house..." she caught Elizabeth's eye. "Maria is not the first child she has lost but... she was a favourite. She was so strong. She survived the fever the other year. I think I must take a job or get married or something to get out of that house."

"Oh Jayne, you're too young to get married," Elizabeth giggled. "But as soon as you are old enough, perhaps we can all get married at the same time. I could marry Horace..."

"Horace!" Jayne shrieked. "But he's awful. He's my brother."

Elizabeth grinned. "Maybe, but I saw a smile on your face."

Jayne's smile dropped. "I think my mother wants to punish me forever."

"It was an accident." Elizabeth paused, and they met one another's eyes. "Whichever version you want to talk about. There was never any intention, now was there?"

Jayne didn't say anything in reply. She felt responsible, but she was terrified of what might happen to her if she told the truth. A childish hysteria had come upon her and she now had nightmares and wet the bed, much to the disgust of her two other siblings who had to share the bed. "I need to be out of the house," she whispered. "Do you think I could get a job as a maid?"

"A maid?" Elizabeth sounded disgusted by the idea. As if anyone would catch her being a maid. "I'll speak to my Mamma. She always knows what to do."

Jayne managed a little smile. "I am so glad you are my friend, Elizabeth MacCaskill."

"And I you. Friends forever."

Early in the following year, whilst the winter clung desperately onto its hold over the land, a highly contagious fever spread back up the Esk Valley from Whitby through the villages. It jumped further inland to sink its teeth into the residents of Commondale. Many families were hit with the sweating sickness. Memories ran back to the spate of childhood deaths a few years ago, and parents shared haunted glances that it may happen again. Yet somehow most recovered and most families, bar one, were blessed and avoided the grim reaper's sickle swipe this time around.

For the smithy's family, the multitudes of Longbottoms down near the stream, their run of fertility and good health appeared to be at an end. The oppressive fertility had abruptly stopped for Gillian in her thirtieth year, and there had been no hint of any more pregnancies. Although she was still haggard, overworked and ignored by her husband, her body had chance to breathe again and build up strength. Her final child, Mathias, was five going on six, and she had no babies screaming at her anymore. Her eldest child, Little Will, who had been a scrawny and screaming baby was now a tall strapping lad of fourteen and already living away from home. He was apprenticed as a carpenter over in Egton with Caleb Lyth. The only way they had been able to arrange and afford an apprenticeship for the lad had been the family connection, for Caleb had married Ellen Withers. The lad was now lodging with the couple. Gillian's second eldest, Jeremiah, who was now thirteen, would often go out helping his father with his work, but on this trip across the moors William had left their son had home without giving any convincing reason. Gillian was alone in their little cottage with eight growing children. The harsh winter kept them all in close quarters. Tempers were easily frayed.

It all started when the twins, Harriet and Agnes, had been away playing with Gilly Beecroft's youngest children. They came home with particularly red and rosy faces, the heat coming off them as if they were formed of hot coals. Gillian put them straight to bed, where they sweated and drenched the sheets, giving their bedfellows no peace and Gillian a pile of laundry for the following morning. Their breathing became strained and painful just as Montague and Albert's little cheeks were beginning to glow.

That night the twins died.

Gillian could not cope when she woke up in the early morning and found the two cold, slack little bodies curled up together. She picked up Agnes, trying to shake a reaction out of her. Part of her understood the girls were dead, but her consciousness could not accept it. She ran out of the house barefoot, clutching Agnes, screaming gibberish and looking for someone to help. Her eldest daughter, Mariah, who was only eleven at the time, had to wipe up her tears and try to be a brave girl. She got the other children out of the room and tried to care as best as she could for Montague and Albert, whose conditions were rapidly deteriorating. By that night they were also dead.

Gillian sat in the corner of the kitchen and stared at nothing as if she were quite mad. Her eyes were unable to focus, her ears unable to comprehend words. Her mother-in-law, Ann Longbottom, moved into the house temporarily as Mariah was struggling to cope, and soon went down with the fever herself. Ann sat with Mariah, wiping off the sweat from her brow and sharing a worried look with Gilly who had come by with a stew and other provisions. They could hear Gillian muttering about God and curses by the kitchen fire. The sound of children either coughing or crying permeated the walls, yet Gillian did not move. Gillian wouldn't or couldn't respond to questions or requests. No one knew where William, the husband was. Jeremiah, the second eldest had been sent out with word of the four deaths and that his father was needed at home. They hoped that as the bad news was passed along, the message would eventually reach him, wherever he was. Having helped his father, Jeremiah had a better idea of the places William worked, and would find him quicker than leaving it all to chance.

What was happening to the Longbottoms was quite incomprehensible. Gillian's brood of children had always been so hearty and healthy. When scarlet fever had decimated Commondale's young population of children, Gillian's family had been untouched.

"There's talk in the village," Gilly had muttered ominously one morning after delivering a basket of bread. She took her mother's arm and led her outside for some air. Ann was nursing three children: Mariah, Joseph and the youngest, Matthias. The four dead children were due to be buried over at Danby although Gillian couldn't afford the burials, and everyone was lingering over the plans in the unspoken worry that there could be more bodies to go into the family grave yet.

Ann wrung her hands together and took a deep breath, watching her exhalations steam out through the crisp winter morning. She was too old and too tired for this.

"It is uncanny how this fever spreads and yet is contained," Gilly continued. "These children put the touch of death on one another, yet we are not affected, and all the other families..."

"Gilly," Ann said as a warning.

"I told you, there's talk in the village. There's always been something odd about the family. William's never here, and Gillian is always right off with folk. And when that scarlet fever took my Harold, every family had a tragedy expect this lot. And now look at them. Folk are saying..."

"I don't think we ought to mind what folk are saying."

"Mother, you'd do best to mind it. Folk are saying that they've heard Gillian cursing her children before now. She did not want anymore and thought them a burden. It was all of a sudden she stopped being able to be with child. And now these burdensome children are dropping like flies."

"Gilly!" Ann exclaimed. "You should not join in with gossip and slander."

"There may be some truth in it. There's much in this world we do best not to understand or meddle in. And you remember how Old Marsden used to take an interest in that family when she was alive? And Gillian's father; he was not right, and then him just disappearing..."

"I think the fever of a loose tongue has caught you."

"It's true. Don't look at me like that, mother. Don't tell me you'll all wise and above all of that, for I know you wouldn't let anyone take that witchpost out of your kitchen."

"It's just old superstition and nonsense."

"Something's not right here. Look at her, talking nonsense by the bubbling pot and making no effort to care for the children who are still alive."

"Gillian is grieving. Four of her children have died and I suspect three more are soon to go the same way. Show a little compassion."

"She's cursed them," Gilly hissed. "There's been nothing but trouble ever since she married him. He should have married Megan Hammond."

Ann pursed her lips but didn't contradict her daughter on that point. The obsession of having children had driven more than one person a little beyond their senses.

"You have to wonder about her accident as well. A little convenient."

"Gilly..."

"They say he's over in Osmotherley, you know."

"Who?"

"William."

"Well, he does travel about for his work. Hopefully word will reach him soon."

Gilly rolled her eyes in exasperation. Why did her mother have to be so dense at times? "She still lives there, you know. Never did marry."

"You should not say such wicked things about your own brother. Show some respect. I know you are a married woman now, but I still feel a mind to put you over my knee and slap some sense in to you."

"Why do you want to slap Aunt Gilly?"

The women jumped and turned to see little Prudence, only eight years old, loitering at the door. She was still fit and healthy as of yet, and had been helping Ann by fetching water throughout the day.

"Prudence." Gilly was the first to find her voice. "How would you like to come and stay with me for a few days?"

Ann's eyes widened. "Would you risk taking the fever back to your home again? So soon after your children have recovered."

"Prudence is quite well as of yet. Besides, it's this house." Gilly's eyes narrowed. "It's her," she added low so that Prudence hopefully wouldn't hear. "Best place for her is away from all this death." She let her voice return to normal levels. "Come along, Prudence, fetch your cloak and you shall stay with me for a few days."

"I don't have a cloak."

Of course they didn't. There were too many children, not enough money, an absent father and a mother who wasn't quite fit for purpose in Gilly's eyes. "Well, come along anyway. We'll see if we don't have something at home to sort you out with."

Prudence's grubby little face broke out into a delighted grin and she skipped through the icy frosted ground to grab at her aunt's hand.

By the end of the week the fever had run its course. As abruptly as it had arrived in Commondale, it was done with the village. Six of Gillian's nine children were dead. It was not until the final death of little Mathias that William Longbottom, a guilt-ridden shadow of himself, returned home. His appearance, that with what had happened in the household that past week, was noted and remarked quietly upon by the locals. Not least the fact that the only children to have survived, Little Will, Jeremiah and Prudence, had all been away from the Longbottom home. It left a sense of unease in the community that did not melt away as spring arrived.

The surviving children did not return home. No sooner had the head of the house, William returned than he was taking to the road, certain to take Jeremiah with him. Little Will remained at Egton and Prudence stayed at Gilly's home, never receiving word from her mother that she would like her daughter back at home. One of her maternal aunts, Eleanor MacCaskill, arrived soon after she'd received word of the awful tragedy, with new clothes and toys for the little girl. Her daughter Muriel had come with her. Eleanor had left her to play with Prudence at Gilly's property, whilst she sought out her own twin sister. What she found horrified her.

They had started out at birth as identical twins. A matching pair of sweet little girls. Now it was hard to state whether they were even related. Time and circumstance could affect a body. They were in their mid thirties and their looks had changed, but the difference ought not to be so drastic. Eleanor looked healthy. Her hair was still glossy and predominately dark with only a few white strands. Gillian's hair was completely grey. Perhaps it had been so for a long time, but she usually had an ugly mop cap bonnet primly on her head. The only positive Eleanor could pull from their meeting was that it appeared that the cap was lost. The long, ragged grey hair was on full view, tattered and tangled like an old uprooted tree. It clung regretfully around Gillian's wan and wrinkled thin face. Her eyes seemed to be vacant. She hobbled about on pin-thin legs, and old witch-bony fingers fussed with the raggedy edges of her shawl. She looked and smelled as though she hadn't washed herself or her clothes in months, and there were some suspect stains on her skirts that Eleanor didn't want to give any closer inspection. The entire wardrobe wanted burning, Gillian throwing in a tub of hot water and everything starting again from scratch. There was so little to behold, one wondered if there would be anything of Gillian left after such a cleaning.

Tears pricked at Eleanor's eyes as she approached the little house. The fire was obviously out, and it looked colder inside than out. There had always been so much noise with Gillian's hoards of children but now a miserable silence filled the place. Gillian sat on a little stool outside the door and swung her cradled arms.

"Sister," Eleanor whispered as she approached. "What has happened to you?"

Gillian did not respond.

Gilly had told Eleanor that rumours were flying about the dale regarding William. He had abandoned his wife completely now she was no more use to him. There were no more children to be had, and that had been the only reason he had taken up with her in the first place. He was consorting with the unmarried Megan Hammond, and apparently it had been going on for years. The gossip was open wildfire and if Gillian hadn't known earlier on, it would be impossible for her not to have heard by now. The village thought Gillian quite mad. There were other tales, Gilly had added, clutching on to Eleanor's wrist. About Gillian's madness and the strange circumstances of her children dying. She had looked meaningfully at Eleanor, then pulled away when her mother had turned up at the back door.

"Where is William?" Eleanor asked Gillian.

It was disgusting that he had abandoned her at such a traumatic time. The great condescending Christian was a little lacking in his human kindness when true need called. He had been back for the children's funerals and would have at least seen his wife. He could not have knowingly left Gillian in this state had he really cared for her. Eleanor wiped at her eyes as she thought back to her childhood, when they had been little girls, pretty and healthy, and ideas of marriage and children had been so far off in the future as to be notions of a foreign country. Now look at her sister: she was utterly ruined. Maud had written as best she could to Eleanor asking her to tell everything and let her know if she ought to come. Their mother had problems of her own. Her deceased husband, Amos Cornforth, a tenant farmer, had essentially left her with nothing. Necessity had forced her to go back into service in her early fifties in order to keep a roof over her head. Between the impassable roads when Gillian's children had died and the delays in the post Maud hadn't heard of the dreadful news until it was all over and the children were in the ground. Commondale was a long way from Haworth. Even for Eleanor's part she hadn't been able to get up here until now.

"Gillian!" Eleanor shouted, taking her sister's shoulders to shake out her attention. She was shocked by how bony and fleshless her sister's frame felt. It was like shaking a bag of dry, distressed twigs. She could not stay here on her own. She would have to take her back to Whitby and nurse her back to health. If she was left here and continued to deteriorate, she'd end up in the workhouse or the madhouse. "You must quit this place and come away with me."

Finally she reacted to Eleanor's presence. Gillian looked up at her sister. "I will not. I must stay here. For my children."

"Your children are not here. Will is away at Egton, Prudence is staying with Gilly and Jeremiah is with his father. The other's are ..."

Gillian glared at her.

"Just look at the state of you. You can't stay here. Please come home with me."

Gillian's lips curled and wrinkled in distaste. "Slut," she said quite firmly. "Whore."

I want to hit you, Eleanor thought, but I must be patient. "Gillian, please."

"You stay away from me. You and your wicked ways." Gillian jumped up and pushed Eleanor away with surprising strength. "You're going to hell, Eleanor Hurst, and you'll not drag me down with you." And with that final damnation, she ran away into the woodland. Eleanor started to run after her, but tripped over a fallen log. When she got up, she could hear Gillian cackling in the distance but could not see her. She was gone. In every sense. Eleanor set herself down on the log and cried her heart out for the terrible mess of her family. Her little brother long dead, her twin sister's life wasted and ruined, and a final sister who was a money-grubbing soulless beast. How could a sweet innocent childhood end up like this?

She stayed with Gilly for two days, but Gillian's house remained hollow and empty. She couldn't wait forever and eventually accepted that for now she would have to go home without her sister. She and Muriel set off back to Whitby, with promises from Gilly that she would write with any news of Gillian. Promises that were easily forgotten and by the time Gilly thought about contacting Eleanor, it was all too late.

Early summer saw the return of the Mowbrays to Pines Lodge at the edge of Commondale. Emmerline was now a little girl of four, and a more radiant, happy little beauty there had never been. She had all the best dresses, shoes and toys and was the apple of her father's eye. His only sadness was that he and his wife had not been able to increase their family with any more fine looking children, provide Emmerline with some siblings and himself with a male heir. There was still time, for Clara was only twenty-nine. He had spoken to a reputable doctor on the matter, who had assured him that all was not lost and suggested some things to try. As yet Clara was still blissfully ignorant of all of this, happy in her shopping for new fabrics for the Commondale house, and in secret making up new scams with Mary Bateman.

Clara had sent the nursery maid out with Emmerline, for the child was shrieking so and becoming quite annoying. Inside the housekeeper was unpacking the trunk with the new curtains Clara had arranged to have made in Leeds. The housekeeper held one curtain up against the far parlour window and Clara considered it and wondered if the curtains she had planned for the master bedroom might not be better here.

"Goodness, wife," Andrew exclaimed as he stepped in the doorway. "You have a very strange taste in curtains. Why must we have new ones when the ones already hanging are perfectly adequate?"

Clara, still with her back to her husband, raised her eyes to the ceiling. Spoken like a true Yorkshireman. "Do not trouble your mind, dear husband," she trilled. "I only fritter my money on these things."

She could hear Andrew smirk. "Your money? I think it is I who am the well respected lawyer in Leeds."

"Yes, but I do have my own money," Clara turned around. "My inheritance from my father."

"Sweet lady, everything goes into the husband's name. You know women can't be trusted to manage their own finances." He gave the curtains another look. "Especially if they will fritter their fortunes on this," he quipped before striding back out of the parlour.

Clara felt a chill when he left, and lost all interest in the curtains. It was true enough and not a revelation to her, only that she had never really thought about the law in regards to her own position. When it was stated that all money and property of a woman's became her husband's property upon marriage, she had always thought of those wives as silly creatures who struggled enough to decide what they might have for breakfast. She had never associated herself as being in the same category. Truth be known, although she had considered herself a wealthy woman, technically she was penniless and living off her husband. All her Pappa's fortunes, left to her in his will, were legally the property of her husband. The thought made her furious.

The housekeeper, married to the estate manager and not concerned with Pines Lodge most of the year, noted the flicker of expression on Clara's face. "Shall I come back later, madam?"

"We'll leave the curtains for now," Clara said. "Tell me, what news of Commondale these days?"

The older woman shrugged. "Aside from the sad story of your sister, there's not much happening."

"My sister?"

"Well, yes. Since her tragedy..." she faltered, realising Clara had no idea what she was talking about. They said Clara Mowbray had no contact with her family. It had been the gossip of the village at one time, how everything had been left to Miss Clara Hurst, and she had thrown her poor mother out of the house, her other sister ejected from the family business, and given Gillian, who was clearly struggling, nothing. Why would the family wish to have anything more to do with her? "I do not like to gossip," she unconvincingly proclaimed, and busied herself with folding the new curtains.

"Oh pish, posh," Clara sniffed. "Are you talking about Eleanor or Gillian? It must be Gillian. Is she still living down by the stream?"

"No one is sure where she is living. She is seen now and then in the village, but then she disappears back into the wild."

"Has she gone mad?" Clara sounded delighted.

"Er, no, madam. She is very sad. Six of her children died earlier this year, of the fever."

"Six you say?" She nodded to herself. That sounded about right. Perhaps it was time to set the final wheels in motion and bring this all to closure. "That must have been a great shock for everyone."

"It was, madam. Your nephew Will is still over in Egton, and Jeremiah is out working with his father..." she stumbled upon her words, having almost said something about Megan Hammond. It was common knowledge now that William Longbottom visited his first sweetheart most weeks. His mother was furious with him. But William Longbottom did not appear to care, having washed his hands of his wife and all her troubles. "And little Prudence stays with her Aunt, Mrs Beecroft, in the village."

"Does she now. Perhaps I shall take a stroll down the hill to the village."

Whilst Clara was pondering over curtains, revenge and the disgrace of a husband owning that which was not really his, Gillian had found her way back in to the village. Last night, whilst sleeping in the woods, something had broken in her mind, like a great damn bursting, and she had woken herself again. She was fully conscious of all the pain and regret of her life. It was incredibly hopeless, yet her brain would not allow herself to hide behind the tragedy anymore.

Straightening her bonnet and trying to neaten the grubby neckerchief around her neck, she brushed down her skirts and headed towards Commondale. As she approached drystone walls, some of the cows in the field were stood at the boundary, peering across at the ragged woman limping towards them. She stopped in a patch of buttercups and met the beast's eyes. It was as if an eternity of knowledge swilled around in those big black eyes. She reached up and stroked the creature between its eyes.

"Oi, you, you let my cows be!"

The farmer was suddenly upon her. Gillian was so surprised by the intrusion, having been in a trance-like state staring at the cow, that she stumbled in surprise, and would have lost her balance had she not grabbed on to the farmer's wrist.

"Get your filthy paws off me, vagrant." He roughly shoved her away and to the ground. As she landed on her bony rump with a sigh, he peered forward. "Gillian Longbottom? By god, is that you?"

Gillian scrambled up, muttering something about needing to get on, and hurried away.

It was midday, as Clara sauntered into the village, that the gossip about the dead cows was rife like fire. The beasts had been fine that morning, then they had just laid down in the field and died. One after the other, until there were three dead beasts. No one would want to touch that cursed meat. The farmer stood outside of the inn, showing anyone who would look the dreadful boil upon his arm.

"It's a swelling like the plague. First she was patting my cows like they were cats, and then she grabbed my arm."

"Not got long left to live then, have you?" someone joked.

"You mark my words, everything was well until Gillian Longbottom turned up."

"I always thought it was strange, her children dying like that."

"She used to curse the day she had them you know."

"Her husband won't have anything to do with her now."

The barmaid, with a jug of beer, came out of the door and paused to take part in the gossip. Clara wandered by, brushing past the jug and eyeing the tankards that were set out on the bench. "A hundred years ago, such things got a woman hanged."

The farmer with the boil eyed her. "What nonsense is this now?"

"I'm quite sure you have a witch post in the farmhouse, by the fire."

"Superstition and nonsense."

"But there's something not right about it," the barmaid said. "Cows don't just drop dead like that, and will you look at your arm? That the place she touched you? It's not natural. And what about that fever? Everyone recovered apart from the children of Gillian Longbottom. The only ones survived were well away from the house. There's plenty folk who have heard her curse about her ruined life. How she wishes she didn't have the kids. What kind of a woman says such a thing?"

"Back in the day she would have been accused."

"We've got a bit more order and sense now."

"These things happen. They'll happen more if someone doesn't do anything."

The barmaid decanted the jug's contents to the tankards she could see. The farmer took a deep slug of beer. The light from the sun pounded down on his scalp. He felt sweat trickle down his forehead. The very air along the street seemed to waver. Something lurched through his senses.

"They used to hang witches..."

He found himself staring at a tree just down the road.

"The magistrate would never entertain such nonsense."

"It'll only get worse. The family's done, children dead, husband gone. The poison will leach out across the village."

"I don't feel quite right," one of the other drinkers complained. "What did you put in that ale?"

Clara smiled to herself and sauntered on, twirling her parasol in her hand and humming a little idle tune. "First the cows and then your arm. Your crops will fail and your children will starve. There'll be graves to be dug. But who will pay?"

The heat and the beer started to jumble people's thoughts. Their vision felt wavy. Another farmer turned up, carrying a rope in his hands and complaining about a sick cow he had just put out of its misery. Its coordination had failed and it could not control its hind quarters. Like a mad thing it had juddered about on the ground. Another sick cow, people had whispered. It is a curse. Our livestock will die, our crops will fail and we will starve this winter. She sacrificed her children for this power. People jumped to their feet and started shouting. They felt possessed, their heads throbbing with demons. How to rob themselves of this curse? Gillian Longbottom had the misfortune to stumble onto the road through the village.

Across the moors and to the coast, Eleanor MacCaskill was in her office working on the books. She felt an itch in her throat, and set down her quill to give a little cough before continuing with the accounts. As she reached for the quill again her throat seized up as if suddenly swelling and she found herself wretching for breath. She lost her balance and fell from her chair, dropping to her hands and knees. Somewhere she heard her youngest daughter screaming. Muriel threw her book to the floor and ran to her Mamma's side. Tears streamed down her face. She wanted so desperately to help but she did not know what to do. Lucy-Ann, who was in the parlour setting out fresh flowers, heard the commotion and ran through to the office. Eleanor was now sprawled out on the rug, her face crimson and her head resting in Muriel's lap.

Lucy-Ann had no better idea of what to do than Muriel. She acted automatically, pulling Eleanor up and letting her hang her head over Lucy's shoulder as if she were a mere babe. Lucy hit her sharply between the shoulder blades once, twice, and on the third hit something happened and Eleanor took a deep rasping breath of air.

"Mamma!" Muriel wrapped herself around her mother's waist.

Tears were streaming down Eleanor's face. Her brow was red and sticky with sweat. She sat back on her haunches, still shaking.

"What on earth happened?" Lucy-Ann asked.

Eleanor coughed again to be certain her airways were clear, then wiped at her eyes. "I do not know," she confessed. "I was writing and suddenly it felt as though my throat had been pressed into oblivion." She looked to the window and felt as though her world had just ended. "There is something very wrong, but I do not know what."

Clara had strolled back up the hill to Pines Lodge before the mass hysteria had grown too great. It wouldn't do to accidentally get caught in the cross fight. She spent a pleasant afternoon lazily reading a novel. She was just instructing the governess as to what Emmerline ought to be taught the following day when her husband came marching into the parlour in a fluster.

"There is a dead woman in the village!"

The governess paled as if she might feint.

Clara let out a sigh. "These things happen, husband dear. People cannot live forever..."

"She did not die of natural causes," Andrew interrupted furiously. "She has been hung."

"Hung? But the magistrate would not pass judgement to be enacted here."

"Exactly. And I cannot even ascertain as to what this woman has done. No one seems to be know. At least they're not admitting to it. But there is a guilty, shifty look about the village."

"Oh dear," the governess moaned. "Are we quite safe to be here?"

"Of course we are, don't be so stupid," Clara snapped. She looked back to her husband. "Did they say who she was?"

"Yes, she's..." Andrew faltered as he realised the connection. He'd been so angry for the blatant disregard of law and order that he'd quite forgotten the fact that it had been Clara's older sister hanging by the neck. The awful empty creak of the rope as the body seemed to swing back and forth ever so slightly in perpetual motion. "I... er, I say, my dear, you ought to sit down."

The next day Andrew Mowbray rode out to see the magistrate and what ought to be done about this illegal execution. Although the matter was looked in to, no ringleader or in fact any participant could be found. No one seemed to know anything, even though it was quite impossible that a woman could be hung in Commondale in the middle of the day without anyone seeing anything. But the entire village could not be arrested.

Up at Pines Lodge Clara smiled to herself as the sunshine streamed through the window. Justice had been done, and now everyone involved had paid for involving themselves in her poor Pappa's death. Some sort of memorial was required to mark the end of this venture. She sent the farm boy off to the nearest stone mason's shop, who sent back one of his elder apprentices to see what the matter was.

Clara explained that she wished to purchase two pieces of stone, of a height similar to herself. They were to be erected on two cairns, which she would take the lad to see. She wished to have some words hewn into the rock as well. One would be called Hob's Cross, and the other Hob on The Hill. Although she could not admit to it in private even, she was not quite sure where her father was buried, and was covering all bases by marking both spots. Not that she would admit to anyone that she knew her father was dead.

"Yes, those are the words I want, and I also want the year marking on both."

"The year, madam?"

"Yes, this year. 1798."

The lad looked a little worried. "Begging your pardon, madam, but I think I know the places you mean, and I don't think it would be too clever to go interfering with them."

Clara peered closely at him. "But they're on my land. Whatever could you mean?"

"Well, they'll be hob mounds, won't they?"

She scoffed at him. "You'll do as I ask and I'll pay a good sum for the work. Now away to your master with my request."

The rough stones were hewn from a local quarry, engraved as per order and transported up to Commondale on horse and cart. They were then carried by eight men across the moors to where Clara wished them to be erected. Her husband thought she was quite mad, but humoured her and let her get on with her little whimsical scheme, for of course he knew nothing of the real reason for Clara's memorial stones. And so the markers were placed on the two hob mounds out on Commondale moor. Atheleys watched furiously from a distance as the markers were placed in such sacred places. The blonde woman overseeing the activity obviously knew that the old hob's bones were under one of those mounds. She made out that it was the whimsy of a rich, bored woman, but Atheleys could sense the uncanny about her. At least she had not gone digging to disturb the dead and to bother the living with yet more revelations. Clara on the other hand was supremely satisfied and felt that her father's spirit had been laid to rest. All was well in the world.

"It takes many hours to kill a whale."

"I thought it was just one shot."

The eleven year old boy chortled at the notion, even though he had no experience either. All his knowledge was gleaned from his father's tales and what he had read in books. But how he loved to talk and advise, even at the age he was, and enlighten others to the knowledge he was amassing. Even if his audience was just girls.

"The first shot with the harpoon is to weaken the whale. When they first see it, and are close enough, they throw the harpoon. This usually makes the whale dive. The whalers have to wait until it resurfaces."

"But surely the whale would not be so stupid as to come back up where the men are." Muriel was sitting cross legged on a cushion in the parlour, her eyes as bright and wide as shiny new buttons.

"They can guess where it will surface."

"But how can they know?"

"Experience. When it resurfaces the men in two boats throw more harpoons at the beast in order to kill it. They go for the vital organs. They are massive creatures and it takes some effort to kill one. Even when they are dead they are too large to bring aboard the ship for butchering so they must do that at sea, with the whale fast to the side of the ship. The men use flensing spades so they can slice off sections of blubber..."

"William Scoresby!" Jayne Argument shrieked. "I do declare, you are the most revolting little boy."

The two children on the carpet looked up sharply at the wail of disapproval. They had forgotten that the two older girls, Elizabeth and Jayne, were at the table supposedly working on their German grammar as set by the governess. In reality they were more likely giggling over the smart young men they had last seen. Mamma was really wasting her money trying to educate those two. They simply did not see the magic of discovering new things. Muriel sat in on the German lessons, wishing they could learn French as well, but whilst England was at war with France, the governess refused to utter a word of the language. So German it was, and picking up Estonian and Russian from the traders. Some were amused by her fascination for languages, and would bring her little books in their languages. Elizabeth turned her nose up at the weather-beaten, bearded foreigners. Of all the men in the world, surely better examples could be found to converse with.

Jayne and Elizabeth bemused William Scoresby. They had so many opportunities and yet they had little interest in anything. Plain Jayne Argument had been living with the MacCaskills for three years, in an odd act of charity on Eleanor's part. Getting her ready for marriage so that she could go and live off someone else, but it was true enough that her prospects had improved since the move. Her mother didn't miss her; looking at Jayne only reminded her of darling little Maria, these three years dead in an accident. Besides, it was one less mouth to feed, which had become more and more of a blessing. Food prices were forever rushing up, and the ongoing war with France was not helping.

Jayne closed the book she had not been reading. "It is vile to talk so joyfully of killing an animal."

"Killing such animals is keeping you in dresses and food, for Mrs MacCaskill must pay for her charity somehow."

Jayne narrowed her eyes. She didn't like to be reminded that she was a charity case.

William was not usually a cruel boy, in truth his mind was usually focused on discoveries and adventure, science and learning. He let petty bickering pass him by. But over the years he had seen Jayne assume her place as if she was one of the MacCaskill daughters, and somehow more important than Muriel. She could be quite mean at times. It did not hurt to remind her of her place now and then.

"Mamma has some shares in a blubberhouse," Muriel said. "But it is mainly the flax and timber we deal in."

"She has dealings with the mill at Castleton?"

"Yes."

"I wonder how long the mill will survive. The cloth industry in the west of the county is rocketing, and the output far greater than what Castleton can manage."

"Then Mamma will deal with another mill. Mamma always fixes it," Muriel countered.

"Your mother is very special. It is not normal for a woman to have such a head for business."

"Those are brave words from a boy in a room with three women." It was the first time Elizabeth had spoken. "Besides there are lots of women in Whitby who manage the family business and finances."

"Only because the husbands are away at sea. They are keeping things running. Your mother is the driving force. I heard it's in her blood, that her father was a very canny businessman. He used to have offices at Whitby as well. Did you ever meet him?"

Elizabeth glanced at Muriel then back to William. "No. He died before we were born." Their grandfather was not a subject their mother liked to speak of. Occasionally she muttered of a hob and his cursed seed, but that was all she would say, and their grandmother, whom they saw infrequently, was quite vague about the past. Really,

Maud was the only grandparent they had met, or even were allowed to know anything of. They'd never met any of their father's relations aside from a cousin who was also on the droving road, and he they'd only meet when he came to them. The girls had never been out of the county. Relatives seemed to be a luxury, whereas families in Whitby were spilling over with complex family histories. On their father's side they did not know if they had aunts and uncles, and on their mother's side such people were either dead or not to be spoken of. There had been an uncle, Stephen, who was now dead a good ten years, and Gillian, Mamma's twin sister who had died two years ago. Mamma would rarely speak of it, and the girls didn't really know what happened. Only that Gillian had died, along with several of their cousins from Commondale, and they weren't to speak of it anymore. Clara – and Elizabeth only knew the name from eavesdropping on one of her parents' conversations – was the black sheep of the family and Eleanor would have nothing to do with her since some terrible thing she had done to their grandmother.

"I am going away to sea," William announced, looking back to Muriel for approval.

"To sea? Whatever do you mean? But you must be too young. Your father wouldn't allow it."

"No, he won't," William admitted. "But I won't let that stop me. I'll sneak aboard a ship..."

Elizabeth laughed. "Sneak aboard a ship? And where are you wanting to go to?"

"I'm going on one of those whalers."

"To see whales being killed?" Jayne was disgusted. "What a revolting little boy."

"I think it's dreadfully exciting," Muriel said, ignoring the older girls. How she would love to travel on a ship somewhere. Learn new things. Explore the world. "Can I come with you?"

"Don't be silly!" William laughed. "Girls can't go whaling. Their bodies are too weak and their minds too feeble."

"There's nothing feeble about my sister's mind," Elizabeth interrupted. "Do you know how many languages she speaks? She can talk to all the traders that come here."

"Women are made for minding the home and looking after children," William spouted out a line he had heard an adult say.

"Now finally some sense from the little boy," Jayne agreed. She could not wait to be married and have a home of her own. She had managed to get away from her siblings. Although on some level she was grateful for the kindness Eleanor had shown her, she was conscious that she was a ward of the MacCaskills in all but name and that did not suit her so well either. She was still only fourteen, but the day would come, and then she would be free.

Elizabeth and Muriel caught one another's eyes. They did not have their futures planned out at all, only that they knew they wanted more out of life than just getting married and having children. They were going to have adventures.

Whilst Muriel's aspirations were still vague, and not fully formed beyond fantastical ideas of sneaking away to sea with her little friend, William; Elizabeth was moving on to the start of her adult life. She had plans and hopes, and before speaking to her Mamma about them, had already set things in motion. There was an old woman, by the name of Margaret Gaskin who was a distant relative of the Gaskins of Whitby. She had retired to Scarborough to live out her days with the refreshing sea air and elegant life that Scarborough was starting to offer its more well off residents. She was an old maid with no direct descendants, and was in want of company. There was a maid and cook at her apartments, but she required a companion. It was the sort of position on a level with governess, probably better for a middle aged spinster in desperate need of an income and home. Yet the position had appealed to Elizabeth and she had already written to the woman. She said she intended to continue her studies from books, and could read to the old lady and bring a youthful spark to the household. On a personal level and not noted in any letter was Elizabeth's eagerness to get out and explore more of the world. They hadn't really travelled very much except a couple of trips inland up the valley to Commondale. They had never even been across to Haworth to visit their grandmother, who much preferred to come to visit Whitby to see the family. Her father was a drover and had been up and down the length of the kingdom more times than he could remember. The curiosity of new places was in her blood, and going away to live in Scarborough sounded so exotic and exciting, she could barely contain herself.

Eleanor was not convinced. Elizabeth was still very young and naive, coupled with an exuberance and enjoyment of attention, particularly from men, that could get her in to trouble. It did not help that she was rapidly blossoming, and although she was only fourteen, she looked older. Eleanor had no doubt that Margaret Gaskin was highly respectable and able to advise Elizabeth in proper behaviour for a lady, yet due to her age she would not be able to watch and control Elizabeth all the time. Which was probably one of the reasons Elizabeth was so keen to get over there.

"You are still too young," Eleanor finished that evening having listened to Elizabeth's rather long and detailed description of the position and why she ought to go.

"That is not fair. When you were my age you were walking about all over the moors with that donkey of yours."

"The countryside is one thing, but town life brings other dangers with it."

"And you were earning your own money with deliveries. Would it not be good for me to earn my own money, learn how to..."

"We are not in want of funds, Elizabeth."

"But it would be my money. Or do you think I should just sit at home and wait to get married so a man might look after me."

Eleanor pursed her lips and watched her daughter out of the corner of her eye. She was very pretty illuminated by candlelight. She ought to be in bed now, and was dressed in her night clothes, but had snuck down to bother her mother with this scheme. She was not stupid and was playing to Eleanor's eccentric notions of what women were able to do. There were many in Whitby who thought she was very strange, despite the fact that women there managed much more than the average woman these days. Eleanor was quite certain women, especially her girls, were capable of more than just getting married. Yet she was not altogether sure what she wanted for her children. She didn't necessarily want them to be spinsters to prove a point, but did she want them to be businesswomen like herself? For then they would need to stay in Whitby. Other places in the country were not quite as accommodating towards enterprising and reasonably wealthy women.

"No," she finally decided. "You're too young and still have your education to complete."

"But Mamma!"

"And I do not think you are mature enough yet to leave my care."

"Mamma, I am fourteen. Aunt Gillian was married by this age!" Elizabeth's voice faltered slightly as she brought Gillian into the discussion without thinking. It had been two years since Gillian had been lynched in Commondale, but it was still an upsetting subject for Eleanor. The strange death of her younger brother many years ago was still a sadness, but the loss of a twin was like the loss of a limb. It was different to losing a sibling and difficult to explain. She and Gillian had been estranged for many years and yet she had always deeply cared for her sister. It was like having a hole in her chest that she could never quite mend.

No one really knew what had happened to Gillian. Or rather, if people did know, they had made a pact of silence. The local magistrate had tried to investigate, but the population of Commondale were keeping together and holding their tongues. From a mad hysteria came a distinct calm reserve. But Gillian had not hung herself from that tree, and there was a person or persons responsible for her death. It looked like an execution, but there had been no trial, no procedure and no chance of defence. Eleanor wasn't even sure what the charge might have been. Even now there was no spoken accusation. What had the woman done to warrant such treatment? Six of her children had died earlier that year. Surely she had deserved their deepest sympathy and nothing less.

William Longbottom had returned to Commondale with his son, Jeremiah two days after Gillian's death. He had taken Prudence back into the family home from the care of his sister, and had managed as best he could. He had waited a few months, more than some people had thought he would manage, and then had married again. Megan Hammond of Osmotherley become Megan Longbottom of Commondale, and walked in to a ready made home and neat little family. Jeremiah already knew her and did not mind her too much. Prudence was more uncertain, although her Mamma had always been so busy with so many children that she had never had much time to dedicate to any one child. As the months went by, Prudence's memories of her mother, sparse as they were, faded, and she enjoyed the attention Megan gave her. And as much as the villagers wanted to disapprove of the new wife, who, rumours to be believed, had been the lover whilst the first wife had been alive, they were keen to put Gillian's memory to the mists of the past, and accepted Megan into the community.

In Whitby, Eleanor would not be persuaded and sent Elizabeth to bed with strict instructions not to raise the subject again. Eleanor went to sit in the kitchen, a hot drink in front of her, a candle burning on the table and a fire in the range. It was not really the proper place for the lady of the house to relax, but in the quiet hours of the night, she found it comforting to sit in the kitchen, reminiscing of her childhood and the time spent in the kitchen with her Mamma, Ellen Withers and her dear sister, Gillian.

At some point in the small hours of the morning someone knocked at the door. With no man in the house Eleanor ought to have ignored it, but instead she went to the door and was rewarded with the sight of Angus' second cousin, Allan MacCaskill, originally of Shetland. He was an old man now, and she was somewhat surprised that he was still on the droving road.

It was raining outside, and she ushered him into the warmth of the house and down to the kitchen. She asked after her husband, a little surprised that he was not yet back. Allan said Angus had some business to complete in London, and would probably have set off north a couple of days after him. Allan was thinking that this was perhaps his last drove, finding it all too tiring, and had headed off promptly on the journey home. He had not planned on coming to Whitby, but a stop off in Wetherby had changed his mind.

Eleanor had given him a bemused glance before sorting out some broth Lucy-Ann had left before retiring for the night. She set a bowl and a hunk of bread before sitting down herself. Why should

Wetherby upset him? She'd never been there, but knew of the little market town. It was a good distance away from Whitby, far inland, further than the moors, and even the city of York. If he had been at Wetherby, Whitby would certainly not have been on his route home.

"I have not heard of any trouble in Wetherby. Why should it have upset you?"

"It's not me that should be upset. Heaven knows I am surprised this did not happen years ago, but happened it eventually has. I saw Anna asking questions on Scott Lane. It's known that droving folk tend to gather round there, so it was the place for her to be asking."

"Anna? Who is this? Ought I to know her?"

"Anna MacCaskill. The wife. You ken who I mean, lassie? The first wife."

Eleanor's colour dropped. "Oh."

"I made myself scarce but Angus is well known. I'm surprised she's not found out before now, but she knows now."

"She knows my name?"

"Not when I heard her talking but I suspect it's only a matter of time. Mrs MacCaskill of Whitby is known quite far, given her trading."

"But I could be any MacCaskill."

"Aye, but when she tracks down Angus..." Allan drew in a breath between his teeth. "Take care, for if this woman finds her way to your door, it'll be ruin for you. If folk here find out you're not a married woman, not in the eyes of God."

"I was married in a church."

"Aye, and both you and Angus fully knowing he was already wed."

Eleanor lowered her eyes. They had been foolish. They should have given one another up, but it had been impossible. The thought of not having him in her life made her think there was not much use with life. And it had worked so well. All these years. It was not perfect for he was not always at home, but their arrangement had worked and she was happy.

"Folk will know your children are bastards."

Her eyes snapped open wide. "My children are not bastards. They knew full well who their father is, and..."

"Technically you're not married. Not only that, but Angus could be prosecuted for bigamy."

Eleanor dropped her face in to her hands. "Oh god," she moaned.

Allan petted her hand. "I've come to warn you. She didn't know the particulars from what I overheard. But it is better to be forewarned."

"Yes, of course." She did not know what to think. This could destroy everything. If that woman found out names and addresses, she could turn up at her door screaming for her husband, taking claim of him because she had been first. First was not the same as true. "It is late," she said, suddenly feeling very weary. "I must away to sleep. Shall I make up a bed for you?"

"The kitchen will be fine for me. I'll warm myself here and get some hours sleep upon this bench. I want to be away early."

"Very well. Good luck to you if you are away before I am up."

"You too."

Picking up her candle, Eleanor left the kitchen and headed up the hallway to the staircase. As she set her foot upon the first step she heard a scuttling above her and realised she was not the only one still awake. Not only that, but she suspected someone had been eavesdropping. Just how much had been overheard?

She did not have to wait long to discover the answer to that question. On reaching her bedroom door, her eldest daughter, Elizabeth appeared from the shadows.

"Mamma, I want to go to Scarborough."

"Elizabeth!" Eleanor exclaimed, surprised by her appearance. "Not this again. I have given you my answer. Away to bed with you."

Elizabeth did not move. She was a flickering statue in the gloom, staring at her mother with piercing eyes. Suddenly her mother had a past, a life and secrets. She deepened and grew complex. "I heard."

"You heard what?"

"You and Mr MacCaskill in the kitchen."

"Elizabeth MacCaskill, it is a bad habit to eavesdrop and you'd be best..."

"I heard it all," she interrupted. "That we are bastards."

"You are not..."

"He said that papa was already married when he married you."

Eleanor felt her skin chill. It was breaking apart. "You do not need to worry. No one here knows..."

"I could tell people."

"Why would you do such a thing? Ruin your own reputation."

"I want to go to Scarborough."

Eleanor met the intense stare of her daughter. She was genuinely shocked. "You would blackmail your own mother?"

"I would not call it such."

"I would. Elizabeth, I am thinking of your best."

"So am I. If you are worried about my education, we can hire a tutor there. But I am going to Scarborough."

It was no longer a request, but a statement of fact. Eleanor was too shocked and tired to argue convincingly. She had all her children to consider. She could not understand how Elizabeth thought she would manage if such a scandal should come out. But it would be dreadful for Muriel. How would such a dear little heart deal with the gossip and the jeers? Elizabeth was prepared to risk all of that for one of her little whims? Perhaps Eleanor ought to call her bluff.

Elizabeth's mind was made up and as far as she was concerned, the battle was already won. "I'll leave at the end of the week."

The first year of the new century had been a trial on Eleanor's family. When the year was over, most issues appeared to be resolved, if only on the surface, yet Eleanor remained uneasy. Elizabeth was settled at Scarborough, saw a tutor four afternoons a week, and from the letters sent from her and old Miss Gaskin, was said to be blossoming and becoming quite the conversationalist. This was all supposed to calm her mother, but Eleanor saw more to worry about. Elizabeth's ego was too keen for compliments and winning smiles from the opposite sex. She had not yet developed any sense to know when she was being used, or when she could lead herself into trouble.

When Angus had returned home and heard from Eleanor that Anna had been seen in Wetherby asking questions and looking for him, he only stayed two nights before continuing his journey north to Falkirk. She did not see him for another three months. When he did return, he said that there had been no dissuading Anna of the notion that there was another woman. But regardless of how many women, affairs or lies there could possibly have been, one thing was certain. The amicable marriage of convenience was over. They could not stand to be in one another's company which only made Angus wonder why she was so angry. Anna was quite used to living her life without his presence. Why should it matter? Eleanor had just scoffed at him when he had told her about this later on and told him despite having two wives, he really knew nothing about women.

"I'm fifty," he retorted. "I'm far too old for all this nonsense."

After the argument with Anna, he had left, telling her she could do what she liked with the marital home. She'd never see him again. The house and the original wife had served their purposes for the droving life and he had no need of them now. Anna swore she never wanted to see him again, so it all suited her fine. But he knew she had followed him out of the village. She was still convinced there was another woman. What was she thinking, following him on foot as if the other woman lived down the lane? Anna wouldn't have the energy to walk to Edinburgh, let alone all the way down to Yorkshire. Foolish woman. Regardless of his confidence, he had soon double backed and lost his wife, before setting south for Yorkshire and England.

He arrived in Whitby full of complacence and certainty it was all over. Anna was too stupid and lazy to find them, and besides, once she had calmed down she would not rightly care where Angus had got to. Eleanor didn't know the woman, in truth she did not care to think of her, but was not convinced it would be the last they heard of her. She stood at the parlour window, gazing out onto the midmorning. There was a man loitering across the street. When she met his eye, he unbent from his nonchalance and sauntered off down the street. Eleanor felt unnerved.

"You shouldn't be so casual about all this. There are severe punishments for bigamy."

"Ah, you worry too much, wife. We'll soon have been married twenty years past."

"I do wonder about her. It's strange that she accepted so little."

"She has done well enough out of the arrangement."

"But to live alone in a house, a husband she has barely seen the entire marriage, even with the droving accounted for. Much like a spinster: no man, no child..." Eleanor paused, expecting Angus to come back with some light hearted quip, but there was only an awkward silence. She turned to find him staring at his boots. "As I said, no child." Eleanor moved across the room. "Why am I suddenly uneasy? I said there were to be no children up there if you and I were to..."

Angus looked surly.

"Angus?"

"We had to keep up appearances."

"What?"

"There's only the one."

It felt as though a stone was stuck part way down her throat. What was he saying to her? After all this time, almost twenty years as he had just recently pointed out, he was admitting to something that should have been spoken of a long time ago. "Angus, what are you telling me? You have another son?"

"A girl."

"A girl? Is this in jest? I thought we told each other everything?"

"We do."

"Clearly we do not. How old is she?"

"Eleanor, what does this matter?"

She folded her arms.

"Eleanor!" he sighed, realising he wasn't getting away with this. "Very well, she is fifteen."

"The same as Elizabeth. But then you must have... with her..."

"That is the way."

"How could you?"

"Eleanor, please..."

She pushed him away, hurrying out of the room. "I need to be alone. Don't follow me." Pulling a shawl from the hook, she rushed out of the front door, her mind a blur and her eyes watering. She felt betrayed. The deed was over fifteen years old and yet it hurt as if he had just sliced open her fingertips. She had always known he was married to another. She had known he had to continue with the first marriage to save face up north, to keep the droving licence and keep out of trouble. She had tried not to think too much about what went on up in Scotland but had always just assumed it had been platonic. And certainly not that he had done anything years into their own partnership.

She needed to walk and clear her mind. She needed the sea air, the violent winds of the North Sea, and the sharp high cliffs of the coast. She walked down to the river in a daze, paid the toll over the bridge and then wound her way through the narrow little cobbled streets up the steps to the top of the cliffs. It was only as she was entering the graveyard of St Marys, that she realised the figure in the corner of her eye had been following her all this time. She remembered the strange little man on the street, but when she paused to turn and face him straight on she was surprised to find an old woman leering up at her.

Old was perhaps not quite the word. Middle aged suited better. The woman looked to be in her fifties, so whilst whatever beauty she might have possessed had been taken by the weather and hard work, she was still relatively nimble in her body and could move quickly enough. She was not a local, for Eleanor had never seen her before, but the wind and the chill clearly did not worry her.

The woman smiled, but it was not friendly. "Mrs MacCaskill?"

She didn't have time for nonsense. "Who are you? What do you want?"

"Mrs MacCaskill."

"Yes, that is my name," Eleanor snapped irritably. She opened her mouth to send the woman off, before she realised that she had been answering the question, not asking.

"I just had to come and see the little whore he's been with all these years."

Eleanor was so taken aback to find herself face to face with Anna MacCaskill that she could not think of a thing to say.

"You're a pretty thing, I suppose, for a *sassenach*. Not short of a bit of money either, from what he tells me."

"He?"

"My man I hired to find you."

The man on the street. Angus wasn't quite as clever as he liked to think. Anna might not have followed him, but someone had.

"I just wonder if you knew when you took him on, or if he lied to you. Like he's been lying to me all these years. But I'm the first one, I know that for a fact. So that just makes you his wee whore and mother to three bastards."

Eleanor slapped her face.

The attack only seemed to energize her further. "This comes out, it'll be trouble for him. Prison. Your reputation will be in tatters when folk know the truth about you. I don't rate your children's futures either."

"Is there some problem here?"

The women's brewing fight was interrupted by the appearance of the pastor. He stood in the doorway to the church like a schoolmaster checking naughty girls in the yard. Both women stopped and looked to him. A balding, thin and shrewd man. He had only been here a few years, not as kind as the previous man who had married Eleanor and Angus. Eleanor was bewildered. There had been no malice in her, yet here she was a criminal and all the truth and right was on Anna's side. She could destroy them all.

"I'm Mrs MacCaskill," Anna told him proudly.

"It's a pleasure to meet you."

"She's not." She pointed at Eleanor.

He glanced from Anna to Eleanor. Although Eleanor showed her face at church, she was not what he considered his most diligent of parishioners.

"I'm Mrs MacCaskill before she started calling herself such a thing, if you ken what I mean. You look in your books and you'll see they were married here. But it's not legal for he was already married to me."

"And you can support these claims?"

"Oh yes."

Eleanor stared at the players in silence, utterly inept. She had dealt with businesses and tradesmen across the country, petitioned for the freedom of Russia to continue trading with the Baltic. She had three living children, one that died. She had survived the grief of the death of two siblings. She had helped to cover up the death of her father. Nearing forty and surely she was supposed to be competent and handle any situation that life might throw at her. Yet here she stood at God's door, with the truth blazing and she did not know what to do or say.

"You'll be the person I ought to report it to," Anna continued. "So the right can be done."

The pastor stood and considered the situation for a moment before coming to some silent conclusion. "Away with you woman, you've said your piece and I shall do the necessary."

"Make sure you do. I want him to suffer."

Eleanor remained rooted in place, unable to look at Anna. The Scotswoman snarled in her general direction before heading back down the steps. It was starting to drizzle with rain. She stared at the pastor, feeling utterly hopeless. "What will you do?" She finally managed to wheeze out.

"Go home, Mrs MacCaskill," he told her. "I have a sermon to write."

If Eleanor had been foolish enough to think that might be the end of the matter, she was soon set right. If she had expected a pastor to be forgiving or keen to hold forth on justice and righteousness, she was to be very surprised.

The pastor appeared at their door one morning in May, clutching a sheaf of papers, and requested Mrs MacCaskill's audience immediately. Eleanor did not have any visitors that morning and so took him into the office, a little bewildered as to what he might require from her trading businesses.

The pastor entered the room and gave Muriel a distaining look. "The child is in here every day?"

I don't think I need advice from you on child rearing, Eleanor thought sourly, but kept the insincere smile on her face. "Muriel, perhaps you should continue your reading in the nursery."

"But Mamma, I..."

"Go and see what Jayne is occupying herself with."

"Yes Mamma." Muriel slumped out of the room.

"Well, now," the pastor spoke, settling himself down in one of the armchairs uninvited. "Now that we can speak freely, I come with various pieces of news."

Eleanor felt as though she was being toyed with. She managed most things in life on her own, but she really wished Angus was here now. This was a mess of his creating. Holding her nerves together, she was the picture of calm serenity, even if she did not feel it. She slowly stepped across the room and sat down in front of the pastor.

"I'm sure you'll need no reminding of the Scottish lady who made certain accusations outside of my church two months back."

Eleanor felt nauseous.

"She did return to me and left me evidence. It leaves me in no doubt of the fact of bigamy, nor the sad truth that your marriage was a sham. I do not know whether you were aware of the facts at the time, but now you are in full receipt of these truths. Your own potential guilt in the crime aside, the question of your husband's... or rather the man acting as your husband... guilt is not in any doubt whatsoever."

He will destroy us. This town's snobbery and hypocrisy will judge us. There are plenty of children sired by other men who are brought up by their legal fathers; other children malnourished, beaten or neglected; fallen woman rotting in the gutter or forced to the street trade and gin, yet we will be torn to shreds for a technicality. Inside Eleanor was evaporating into misery. Outside she remained cool. In negotiations one ought to keep one's true emotions and opinions hidden. "Have you reported this?"

His reply surprised her: "Not yet."

"I do not understand what..."

The pastor raised the collection of papers he had brought with him and passed them to Eleanor. "I find myself with too much work, and yet if I get this completed, I will find myself one shilling and six pence better off. It must be completed as of tomorrow, on how we find the state of things as of tomorrow, if you catch my meaning."

Eleanor did not.

"You may find the question on number of marriages performed of particular interest." He stood up, his business complete. "I would be grateful to have all the relevant papers returned the day after next. A grateful mind brings forth a silent tongue. Good Morning to you, Mrs MacCaskill."

She was left alone in the office, utterly confused and yet quite sure she was being blackmailed. It was not how one expected blackmail to be performed, for only a shilling and sixpence had been mentioned and from what she understood, she would not be providing the coin. She looked down at the papers. Forms. A request for notation of the town, city or parish, and then six questions pertaining to said place.

As she read on, Eleanor's horror grew. She was supposed to collate all this information in one day? And really, what right did anyone have to gather such details on other people? She flicked through the papers, realising this was a request sent out from central government in London. Damn them for expecting to poke into people's private lives. Terrified they had missed six pence in tax. And due to a shameful secret, the pastor had absolved himself of the work, if not the payment, and lumped the burden onto Eleanor. He expected her to go about the town asking such questions and sticking her nose in where it was not wanted. This was that damned census she recalled Angus speaking of.

The forms wished to know how many inhabited and uninhabited houses there were, and how many families lived in said buildings. On the day, tomorrow, how many people were to be found within her town – was she supposed to run about the streets counting heads and knocking on doors? Not only that, but split the figure down the male-female divide. Don't count anyone currently out serving in His Majesty's Forces. How many people are employed in agriculture, trade, manufacture, handicraft and how many in non of the above? How many baptisms and burials every ten years from 1700 to 1780 and every year there from up to 1800. How many marriages from 1754 to 1800? Eleanor's stare darkened. Was the pastor wondering if she would count her own marriage in that figure? She couldn't be the only one. There would be lots of people in this situation. Men who abandoned families and set up a new life elsewhere. There would be so many such second families that were never discovered. To complete this work she would have to sit and look at the parish records at St Marys. And if she didn't, Angus would be arrested and sentenced to seven years hard labour and she would become a pariah and her children...

The door creaked open and Muriel's tentative face peered into the room. "Mamma?"

Eleanor looked up from the papers. She was not so naive as to think if she did this work, it would be the end of the matter. But what else could she do? She wished Angus was here. She needed someone to talk this over with.

"Mamma, may I come back in? The pastor has gone now."

Eleanor let go a sigh and set the papers on her lap. "Muriel, my sweet. You like your books, don't you? How about a little mathematical challenge for you to do tomorrow?"

Muriel's face lit up and she hurried to her mother's side.

"You will have to go up to St Mary's, so take Jayne with you. I need you to work out some numbers of people for me, so you will have to look at the church records."

Muriel's brightness dropped a little. She found the pastor a little creepy and did not want to have to go up to the church. "Will you not come with me?"

"No. I will be walking about town asking questions," Eleanor muttered glumly. "Taking a survey, lock, stock and barrel of the town. There is simply not enough time, which is why I need your help. Perhaps you could get Jayne to go through some of the records with you."

"Jayne does not like maths."

"No." There wasn't that much that Jayne did like, Eleanor thought. Since Elizabeth had gone to Scarborough, Jayne had lingered on. There was a panic stricken look about her, terrified she would have to return home. Yet her mother never asked for her, and from what Lucy-Ann told her, it did not sound as though the girl was wanted. Eleanor didn't have the heart to send her back, so kept her as company for Muriel in the schoolroom, although from what the tutors told her, Jayne had neither the diligence nor the ability to excel at her studies. Jayne was waiting to be old enough to marry, and staying at the MacCaskills improved her prospects greatly. Eleanor knew she was particularly taken with one of the younger sons from one of the Gaskin family branches. The lad had no prospect of inheriting and so must take a profession to support himself. He had been down at Oxford and she believed he was planning to take orders soon.

Muriel took her mother's hand, assuming the line of worry on her brow was purely from the thought of all the maths she would have to do tomorrow. "Don't worry Mamma, I will do the sums from St Mary's."

The day of the first census in the United Kingdom, which coincided with the first year of the United Kingdom itself what with the Act of Union that January, saw Muriel trotting up the 199 steps to St Marys with Jayne. They would be counting up the marriages, births and deaths for her mother, whilst Eleanor turned her sinking heart to the streets of Whitby. Males and females to each occupied house. What sector were they employed in? As if she had any right to go asking people about their private business.

She started early, taking a book of papers with her so that she might record the answers. Eleanor had lived in the town a good number of years, and was acquainted with a number of families. If she already knew who lived there and what they did, she did not bother to knock on the door and confirm the details, both to save time and out of simple embarrassment. Only when it was strictly necessary she would knock on the door, wondering why on earth she was doing this. To keep Angus out of prison, of course, but then she didn't have to take this survey so scrupulously. Would the pastor actually know if she cheated a little?

Whether she cheated or not, the results would not be the definite answer. Some households asked her what business it was of hers before slamming the door in her face. Others waited a little longer to share their opinions of such a survey and the government. Just a reason to squeeze more taxes out of folk, or perhaps it was sniffing around for more men to drag into the navy. They were surprised someone such as Mrs MacCaskill would join in with such endeavours, given what had happened to her own son. Some duly answered the questions, only to ask themselves at the end what they would be paid for having done their civic duty. One old gentleman took the questions far too seriously. Having given the matter some thought he informed Eleanor that there was himself, a parrot, two cats and a great number of mice although he did not know how many, on account of her not having given him any warning to take stock of his house. He was not being flippant, and went on to say that he was retired, but as the cats chased the mice and the mice ate the food, perhaps they could be classed as some kind of agriculture? Certainly the cats were hunters.

I will be the laughing stock of Whitby, Eleanor thought miserably as she forced herself up another steep ally to clear another section of town from her list. No wonder the pastor was keen to get this awful task passed to some other fool. The letter with the survey had stated that it was their legal obligation to complete the survey, for the good of the country. As time would tell, there were a great many parishes that did not even bother to send back any kind of figures, news that Eleanor heard months later with a curse in the back of her mouth. Late that night, after Muriel had retired to bed, Eleanor sat and added up all the figures. Writing out the compiled data for the original survey, she looked at the seemingly simplistic set of numbers to be returned to central government and felt the indignant throb of her feet. Would anyone really care about these figures for Whitby?

More worryingly was what she had started in accepting the task. For it was true, once a blackmailer, always a blackmailer, and in such underhand endeavours, there was never such a thing as paid debt. The visits were not so regular as to draw too much attention to the matter, drain Eleanor's finances dry or infuriate her too much, just as they were well timed to be certain that Angus was not at home, for he would have most probably thrown the pastor out on his rear end. Yet the longer it went on, the less Eleanor felt she could bring a stop to it, and the more embarrassed she felt that she had been stupid enough to start on this road in the first place. There would be a visit and a casual mention that a bottle of port would be nice to have in one's cupboard. Or a little money to update a particular item in the wardrobe. Or that the church was in need of this or that. Then the church roof needed repairs.

Two years had passed since she had first been dragged into this mess. Two years she had hidden this from her husband, who was under the impression that Anna had never found the location of his other family. Two years of paying for the pastor's lifestyle. He had become a heavy outlay and the most recent request was the heaviest yet. "He will ruin us," she whispered to the flickering candle as she hunched over her writing desk. "And when he has utterly ruined us financially, he will broadcast the truth about my marriage and I will have nothing." She should have stopped this a long time ago, even if she had been dumb enough to take on the census work. She should have never have parted with hard cash. Costs were rising, food was more expensive and there was talk that this was only going to get worse. They were not at war with France anymore but there was so much worrying news coming out of the country about this little man Napoleon and his ambitions. Many folk said it was only a matter of time. Then the troubles with the navy would start all over again and food prices would rocket. Against all this, business was getting harder. Whitby as a trading port was suffering as many now preferred the mighty port of Hull, further south on the east coast.

It was getting tighter with money, and although the family did not suffer anywhere near as much as others in Whitby, Eleanor was having to increasingly put restrictions on what meat they might eat. Elizabeth was still working as a lady's companion to old Mrs Gaskin, which meant one less mouth to feed, but in her place they still had Jayne Argument, who quite considered herself the eldest daughter of the household, and with the comfort of the passing years, had grown complacent in her rights. Only last week Eleanor had come across her scolding and bullying Muriel as if she were an inferior little sister and not important in the pecking order of offspring in the household. Little Muriel had been so excited for her childhood friend, William Scoresby, was back in town and school having had his adventures at sea with his father on the whaling ship. Muriel had come running into the house, bubbling forth with the stories she had been told and Jayne had turned on her, sneering as though she spoke only nonsense and scolding her for trying to take attention away from her future marriage. Eleanor had been lenient with the girl all this time, for she had suffered such a tragedy in the untimely death of her little sister and the subsequent loss of her mother's love, but this was too much. Eleanor had stern words and scoldings of her own, which had sent Jayne off running in floods of tears to her aunt, Lucy-Ann, who had been even less sympathetic. Lucy-Ann had been increasingly mortified by Jayne's leeching on the family, which she knew to be a burden Eleanor was too kind hearted to rid herself of. Household money was shrinking, as was the business, and the pastor seemed to have some strange hold over the lady of the house. Eleanor believed she was keeping this from her trusted housekeeper, but Lucy-Ann was no fool. The worst embarrassment for Lucy-Ann was when Jayne started speaking of her trousseau, her wedding and all the clothes that would be bought for her. It was an accepted assumption that the MacCaskill's would pay for everything. Jayne was a little irritated that the money had not yet been spent on her. It had now been two months since Edward Gaskin had proposed and she had accepted, and yet Eleanor had not said one word to her about the money and the clothes that would be coming her way.

This was as much arrogance as Lucy-Ann could take and after scolding her niece severely she went through to inform Eleanor that the family were eternally indebted for all the time and care Jayne had received, but for the last month of her unmarried life, Jayne and her mother both wished to spend the time together. After Jayne and Edward Gaskin were wed, they would be moving to Lincolnshire where Edward had secured an income as a parish priest. Eleanor had barely acknowledged the news as she was at that moment worrying over a letter from her daughter, Elizabeth. Lucy-Ann then took a sobbing Jayne directly home, reminding her the entire way that she ought to be ashamed of herself after everything Mrs MacCaskill had done for her, and marched her straight through her sister-in-law's door. It was time she took responsibility for her own daughter and stopped blaming her for little Maria's death. It had been a terrible accident and they could not keep avoiding each other like this. The mother of the household had glanced at Jayne, who had become a refined stranger with ideas above her station. She agreed that she might as well take Jayne back for the time being, considering she would soon be married and then would be no one's problem but her husband's, and thankfully a long way from Whitby. She added a cutting remark as Lucy-Ann was leaving that she wouldn't understand really, what with her never having married or had children. Given the age and shape she was, she probably never would now.

Whilst the bad feeling and sulking brewed around the Argument's households, Eleanor sat back the window in the parlour and fretted over Elizabeth's letter. In isolation there was nothing in particular that could cause distress, only that it was part of a worrying trend. Elizabeth wrote much of her life, her duties and the people she met in Scarborough. Miss Gaskin led a refined but calm life, being the age she was, but she did entertain visitors on afternoons, and from these afternoons Elizabeth had gotten to know a diverse array of characters. She told her Mamma of how impressed people were by her wit and conversation, especially as she was only seventeen. In her letters she wrote of the compliments and dazzling stories she was given and told. Details of her studies and tutors grew less and less as the months went by.

All because I gave in to another blackmailer, Eleanor thought sadly. Although Elizabeth had never asked for anything more, which was a plus, but hardly sufficient for the troubles Eleanor had gone through these past years.

There was one particular name that cropped up all the more frequently as she wrote. It was not just the increasing frequency of the visits that Elizabeth wrote of, but lengthier passages about him and the details of his stories and his work. One might have assumed that Elizabeth had her own fiancé lined up, just as Jayne had managed, and certainly Elizabeth's object was a known name, well to do and very well heeled. Yet there was an insurmountable problem with the man, and that was simply that he was already married.

That didn't stop you, Eleanor thought miserably, reading on through the letter. Elizabeth's emotions were so transparent in her girlish chattering. Elizabeth was seventeen and Mr Percival Farrow was forty, married and had three children – jabbering little beasts who had neither the charm nor sophistication that Elizabeth had in abundance. Forty, Eleanor read with worry. He is the same age as I. *Dear Percy* – dear Percy! Eleanor's mind echoed in horror – was of the landed gentry, with estates over Snaiton way, inland directly west from Scarborough. He had financial interests in shipping, mostly based in Hull. He was an energetic and positive man, with a fine head of curly hair, the most becoming moustaches and had the most engaging of all conversation in all of Scarborough. He came in to town now and then for business or to visit friends, but had confessed that these past six months he had been coming into town all the more regularly as the company was quite simply scintillating. And these are his very words, Mamma, Elizabeth wrote. I am exaggerating nothing. Despite his great age, he does not look so old and his manner is very youthful. He has an interest in all the latest novels and plays and keeps himself very up to date. Eleanor shook her head. The way Elizabeth wrote about forty year olds, one would think they were as old as the earth. She probably had no inkling of how old her own mother was.

She was pulled out of the letter by a heavy repetitive knock on the front door. Eleanor waited for that reliable tred of Lucy-Ann's towards the door, then remembered that Lucy-Ann had just taken her niece back home to her mother. Sighing, Eleanor folded up her daughter's letter and rose from the chair.

A tall young man waited at the door. He wore a straw hat, navy blue jacket with shirt and waistcoat underneath, along with once-white trousers that were now grubby and not in full use given that one of his legs was missing just above the knee. His face was flushed with fever, yet the burning in his eyes was also from a thrill to be on this very doorstep. His grin widened as Eleanor gawped at him.

"Petty Officer Coxswain..." He did not manage to finish the introductions for Eleanor had flung her arms around him, stretched up on her very tip toes so that she might get her arms around his neck. Her eyes filled up with tears. So much was falling apart in her life just now, and then this should happen.

The young man laughed, feeling equally relieved to find himself here again. It had been many long years since he had last been in Whitby. He had never wanted to leave, but had not been given the choice. Bundled off by the press gang and sent to fight in a war with France. A war, that quite frankly had nothing to do with him.

"Stewart," Eleanor finally managed to speak. "I did not think I would see you again."

"Did you not get my letters?"

"Some, yes, but..." She stepped back from him to reassess his situation. The missing leg was a heartbreaking void and yet it had not immediately registered with her. He was only twenty years old and already he was damaged. "Oh, my boy," she sighed, feeling her voice break as she took in the changes in her son. He was her first born baby, who she had wanted to protect from all the ills of the world. She had failed so miserably in that duty. He had grown tall, and broadened out since she had last seen him. More and more like his father. His trouser leg was rolled up and tucked around what would have been the stump of the leg. The stump and trouser fabric cushioned against the prosthetic wooden leg he was strapped into. "You must come inside," she said, ushering him into the house. "Sit down."

"I have been travelling a long way." Stewart dropped his bag in the hall way then hobbled through to the parlour.

Eleanor bit back on a sob threatening to break through. Crying would take hours to dissipate once started. She brushed a hand at her forehead and then wondered if she had already been crying without realising for her cheek was wet and clammy. She wiped at her face with the back of her hand, feeling the sticky sweat. It wasn't her, it was her son. She walked through to the parlour and looked at him again, in the chair and hot and red as if it were the hottest of summer days and he was beside a blazing fire.

"What has happened to you?"

"I have been discharged. Medical grounds."

They both looked to his wooden leg.

Eleanor hurried across to him and put a hand to his forehead. His skin burned under her touch. "You have a fever."

"I'm just settling down." Stewart lent back into the chair and closed his eyes. "It was shrapnel. They tried to save my leg, but..." his voice wavered. The fighting, the rough life at sea. The blood and gore and death. It had made him grow up and harden very quickly, and still somewhere inside there remained the little boy. "They tried but they couldn't, so they had to cut it off."

"Stewart," Eleanor whispered, wrapping her arms around him.

"Mother, don't fret so. I am lucky. So many die when the surgeon starts on amputations..."

"By my life, is that Stewart MacCaskill back home?"

Eleanor looked up to see Lucy-Ann Argument in the doorway, returned from trying to talk sense into her sister-in-law and Jayne. "He has arrived just in the last few minutes."

Lucy-Ann stepped into the room, her brow lowering in concern. "He looks feverish."

"He is not well. We must get him to bed."

"Mother, do not fuss."

Lucy-Ann walked across the room as Eleanor started to get her son out of the chair. The energy seemed to have poured out of him since he had first arrived, and he would need the help of both women to get to bed. Lucy-Ann faltered when she realised he was missing a leg. As she grew even closer, she noted the sickly rotting smell and could not look Eleanor in the eye. They got Stewart in to bed, then without needing to be asked, Lucy-Ann told Eleanor that she would go and fetch the doctor immediately. She did not like the smell, the colour of Stewart's face, the temperature of his body nor the fact that he now seemed to be drifting out of consciousness.

The doctor was duly summoned and returned directly to the house with Lucy-Ann, who prepared hot water and towels. Eleanor loitered in the background of the room as the doctor came upstairs. He immediately went to the leg; a quick glance at the patient was enough to tell him what was happening and where the source of the trouble was. He got the prosthetic limb off and unrolled the trouser leg, now wet and soiled with seepage and blood, to reveal the newly stitched stump. Eleanor gasped when she saw the bloated, weeping mess that was all that remained of her son's left leg. The flesh was blackening, rimmed with vivid red. The smell was unpleasant and penetrating, suddenly released as the fabric was removed. Lucy-Ann held Eleanor's hand and felt the shaking from the woman's body.

"Can you feel this?" The doctor asked as he prodded at some sections of the leg.

"No," Stewart mumbled, a strange smile on his face. "My leg has no pain at all."

The doctor looked grim. He stood up, knowing what needed to be done, but waiting to find the courage to go forth with this. "Just rest easy a moment, my boy. I must speak to your mother."

Stewart did not look particularly concerned, his eyelids fluttering down. The doctor ushered the women out of the room. Lucy-Ann felt sick. She'd seen a couple of amputations and maiming, and of folk that couldn't always afford the medical treatment to help them through the injury. The odds of men surviving this kind of thing were not good.

Eleanor was staring pleadingly at the doctor.

"Whoever performed the original operation has not made a good job of the procedure. Sepsis is setting in. There is gangrene. The leg, it is dying."

"But you can make him better?" Eleanor wrung her hands together.

The doctor looked hopelessly back at the door. The lad was in a mess. He didn't rate his chances of seeing the night out. "The leg will have to come off. I mean, more of the leg, the thigh."

Eleanor shut her eyes.

"I will send for an assistant. I can't perform an amputation on my own." He stopped, stepping forward as Eleanor seemed to waver as if about to feint. "Perhaps you need to lay down yourself, Mrs MacCaskill?"

"No, I must..."

"There is nothing you can do. I will fetch my assistant and my instruments, and we will start immediately. But I must warn you that there is a chance..."

A sheet was placed over Stewart's leg whilst they waited for the doctor. Eleanor sat with her son, bathing his forehead with a cold flannel, tears running down her face as she watched in horror at how quickly he was deteriorating. He was no longer lucid, but feverish and trapped in a mental nightmare. The doctor returned with his assistant, both carrying bags of instruments, aprons, sheets and other essentials. Eleanor had to retreat to the corridor, unable to watch. She had been through some bloody and intense experiences. She'd given birth to four children, three born alive. It was not as though she was unused to the realities of life, but she was not prepared to see such gore and suffering on her adult child. Lucy-Ann waited on the doctors, fetching hot water, taking away bloodied clothes and running errands as requested.

The dead part of the leg was duly removed, the skin stitched around the new stump and bandaged and dressed. Clean sheets were brought into the room to make the scene as civilised as possible, but Stewart was fading fast. He burned hot as hell yet he was growing pale from the blood loss. Internally he was fighting a battle fiercer than anything he had seen at sea, and if the fever did not break that night, then the doctor feared the worst. Eleanor returned to the sick room and sat beside her son's bed, clutching his hand and praying. Muriel, who had been out during the day, had been ushered to her bedroom by Lucy-Ann to stay away from the horror, did not sleep that night. She was huddled in bed with her dollies, praying for Stewart's life. She had been told that he had returned, and yet she was not allowed to see him. He was sick and the doctor had been called. She wanted so to help the doctor, to see what the problem was and what she might do for her brother, but was sternly told that little girls didn't get involved in such things and she was to stay in her room.

Stewart died in the early hours of the morning. The doctor had remained to see out the case, having not held out much hope for the lad's survival, but remaining to do all he could for the sake of his poor mother. Eleanor dumbly sat and clung on to her son's cold hand, unable to comprehend what the doctor had just told her. Her mind flittered back twenty years to the night he had been born. He was her second child, but the first live birth. So long, scrawny and with such long, wriggling limbs and a screaming little face, furious to have been plucked from his warm bed. There had been such innocence and so much potential. A great life ahead of him. He would live to see all kinds of miracles, Angus had declared when he had first held the bundled new born infant. Her sweet boy. Yet she had only been able to enjoy ten years with him, watching him rocket in height, before the press gang had stolen him away to the navy life. She had gone to the press gang office, smashing the place with a fire poker. She should have tried harder, fought more, and she would have had him back. He would never have been in the battles. His leg would not have been torn apart by shrapnel and he would still be alive now. Who knew what he might have done with his life had things been different.

The pastor turned up at the house the following day with another request for financial help with the roof. The words died in his mouth as he learned of the death of Stewart MacCaskill. He had not realised that the lad had even been back in the town. He arranged the funeral, and let the requests lie for a few weeks whilst the family grieved. Immoral they might be, but this was the death of a child and he was not a monster.

Autumn came, winter passed and still the money for the roof had not appeared. He returned to the house, feeling that more than ample time had been allowed for grief. He was growing frustrated and thoughtlessly demanded his due in the parlour. He had not considered the time of year nor the fact that the bigamous husband was at home. At first the pastor thought that it was opportune timing, for Eleanor MacCaskill was a saddened creature these days. She may not care quite as much whether her husband should be taken into prison. The husband on the other hand, would feel the fear a little closer to home, and might be persuaded to get the issue of the church roof resolved soon.

Things did not work out as he had hoped. Angus did not realise what was happening to begin with – obviously he had been kept in the dark about the blackmailing. When he understood where the pastor was going with his requests for money, he stood up and told the man to get out and never darken his door again. The pastor remarked that Mrs MacCaskill had always been very amenable on previous visits. She had always considered her children and not wanting to see their father in prison. She did not want them to be ashamed of their parents' situation. Angus had grown red in the face, before grabbing the holy man by the very collar and marching him down the corridor to fling him from the front door. The pastor stumbled ungraciously onto the street, but managed not to fall on his arse. He looked back as Angus was moving to slam the door shut, and reminded him that if he did not receive a more positive answer by noon tomorrow, he would be taking everything that he had to the sheriff.

The door was slammed.

"Angus, we must do as he says," Eleanor started as her husband returned to the parlour. "I can't face you going to prison. I can't lose you as well."

"How long has this been going on?"

"I..." she felt embarrassed. Eleanor didn't usually let people get the better of her. "Perhaps a year."

Angus knelt down in front of her. For a minute or so he said nothing, and it was impossible to say if he was angry or heartbroken. "I am touched that you care so much for my well being, but you cannot give in to blackmailers. That man will see you in the poorhouse or debtor's prison, and then he will speak to the sheriff anyway. All I am doing is bringing the end about a little quicker."

"People are not kind. What of the children's reputations? I don't know how it will go with business. I am already struggling with folk wanting to sail in to Hull now. I suppose I should open an office down there, but I just can't be bothered," she sighed. She gazed wistfully into the fire for a moment. Nothing had seemed quite so important with Stewart dead. She knew she had neglected her girls these past months. Elizabeth did not mind for she was happy in Scarborough, although she really needed bringing home for this Percival Farrow was dangerous. And little Muriel, little wall flower Muriel, had been so affected by her brother's death and how it had affected her mother.

"At least this will be out in the open and finished whilst we still have a little money in our pockets."

"You may get taken to prison."

"Aye." Angus got up, feeling his knees crick. "I will not be able to stay here any longer, for the sheriff will be obliged to act."

"You won't be able to return to Falkirk."

"I'll start up somewhere new. Perhaps as someone else. We could go on a drove. You've never seen the country."

"Oh, I have so much to do here. I don't know how it will be after tomorrow of course."

"You've said yourself business is starting to wain. You've been on with this twenty years now. Time to try something new?"

"I don't know what to think."

"Well, think on it. We'll see what happens tomorrow and take it from there. But I need to quit Whitby tonight."

Eleanor wiped at her tearful eyes. "It's all over now, isn't it?"

"Things will change. Let's try to see it as a new start."

"You need to go now, get a good distance between you and Whitby. I couldn't bare it if you were arrested."

"I'll write, tell you where to meet me. We will get through this. And just remember that you never knew. You were the innocent victim in all this."

"Oh, Angus," Eleanor sighed. Once again he was off and she would be alone to deal with the problems and the everyday. This had always been the deal in getting married to a drover but it got harder with the years. The world was changing. She wasn't sure if she would be able to keep up with it all.

When Eleanor's world finally changed, the changes were faster and harder than even she had expected. She cursed Angus's name for slinking off into the night and leaving her to deal with the fall out on her own. He had to leave, for he would have been arrested, but even so she felt very alone, standing before a sea of fury. And for what? They had not stolen nor hurt anyone but themselves. This nonsense about God and moral corruption was irrational, for she had seen many a legal and godly marriage in Whitby that made the couple miserable. There were the beaten, disillusioned wives and drunken husbands, affairs and rapes in alleyways, children that were not truly the offspring of their legal father. Children whose mothers were never certain of the father. Yet those people had the moral high ground.

The pastor had returned the following day in vain hope he could squeeze the money from the family. He had guessed correctly that Angus was long gone from, but was content enough to think that the Scotsman would never be able to show his face in town for risk of arrest. With a final no from Eleanor, he had strutted off to the sheriff, glowing in the knowledge that he was going to make another person's life a misery. And this was the work of God.

At first little happened, for the sheriff was not a gossip, and the news had to be planned and digested. Two days later the sheriff arrived, to advise Eleanor of what he had been told, and what his legal duty was. If Angus was seen in Yorkshire he would be arrested. In Whitby he was known, having lived there part time for a great number of years. Other parts of Yorkshire he may well get away with passing through, what with folk not knowing of his crime nor his face. After a lengthy interview the sheriff decided that Eleanor had been duped by her husband, as was, and had entered into the sham marriage in the belief that she was marrying a single man. She would not be taken to court. But he left with a warning that things like this had a habit of getting out onto the street. He was no gossip, but sooner or later people would know, and she ought to prepare herself.

Whether it was the pastor spreading idle gossip in revenge, or that the news seeped out from other sources, out it came, and the claws of society dug in by the end of the week. Muriel found herself faced with a gang of children screaming bastard and pelting pebbles at her back as she ran away. On her way home she bumped into William Scoresby Junior, her friend of adventuring fame, who was ambling back from school and had his mind on higher plains. He had not heard the news and was a little surprised as Muriel blurted everything out between tearful gulps. Her mother had warned her a few days ago and had explained the situation between her and Pappa, but Muriel just saw the same people and the same happy home and didn't understand why the townsfolk would be so angry.

"But your mother has been living in sin before God for twenty years," William explained to the fourteen year old girl. "That is why they scream bastard at you."

"I've done nothing wrong."

"Your parents' sin is upon you."

"My Mamma and Pappa love me. They're not sinners."

William smiled kindly upon her. Muriel was a sweet girl, and in many ways very intelligent, at least as far as a girl could be, but she was also so naive of the ways of the world. It was a shame for her best prospects had been tied to the family name and money. She did not have Elizabeth's beauty nor figure, in fact if it weren't for the fact she was in a dress, she would have looked quite androgynous. Now that she was tarred with the bastard name, her prospects of marriage were not promising. He was not quite sure how to comfort her, and so petted her hand. "Perhaps some tradesman in another town won't mind, and will still marry you."

Muriel's tears stuttered in pause as she gawped at him. "But what about Edinburgh? We were going to study there."

"I will go on and study, but women don't go to university," William laughed. "It is just the same as when I was planning to go sailing with my father. You took on my stories as if you'd be capable of the same thing. Women are here to marry and keep house and have children. I am sorry for you that your mother and father have spoiled your prospects so. But perhaps with time, and widening the search throughout the county, you'll be able to find a suitable suitor..."

"William Scoresby!" Muriel snapped, shaking off his patronising hand. "I am every bit as clever as you are."

"Muriel..."

"I'm going home."

She came through the front door, rushing like thunder and bumping in to Lucy-Ann Argument who was worrying at Eleanor about the shopping. The butcher had refused to serve her, on account of her wanting to buy food for that depraved lot the MacCaskills. His wife had been muttering over his shoulder. That woman, marching about like a man and showing off her money. And she'd had the nerve to strut about town the other year asking folk how many they had crammed in their houses. And how many marriages there had been. Ha! What a nerve. No marriages in her own property.

Eleanor did not look as though she had slept for days. The morning's post did not help either. The business community at large were turning against her. They had never liked dealing with a woman, and memories were long, harking back to the days when her father, Hobart Hurst, had been at the head of the ship. And what a shrewd and cunning business man he had been. Then he had just vanished. There was something rum about the entire family, and the letters they had received from Whitby only proved what they had suspected all of these years. Her main buyer for timber had written to say he would be severing his contract with her, for he did not think it right to deal with someone of such poor reputation. Eleanor could have cried, for only last week she had bought a load of timber from a Russian vessel. Timber that was now sitting in the yard waiting to be sold on. Her main buyer had added as a postscript that he could buy the last load from her as a personal favour, but at a quarter of the price.

"How does he even know about this?" Lucy-Ann asked. "He lives miles away."

"He received a letter he says. They've all mentioned letters." Her hand tightened around the collection of correspondence. "I am sure this is the pastor's work. He is set to ruin us. I do not know what I will do." She felt tearful. She had been out this morning and complete strangers had spat in the street at her. "I will have to sell the timber at a pittance for I've nothing else to do with it, and this vulture knows it well."

"Mamma, is this the end of us?" Muriel whispered.

Eleanor looked to her daughter and her face grew grey as if she had not realised before that Muriel was in the house. "There will have to be some changes." She peered more closely at her daughter. "What are those bruises on your arm?"

"The children threw stones at me and called me a bastard."

"Oh Lord," Lucy-Ann exclaimed. "She can't say here. What will you do? Send her to Commondale? Your late sister's family is still there, are they not?"

Eleanor's face soured. "I'll not have her staying there. Folk have told me that he was seeing that woman for years before my sister was murdered. And now he's married her and moved her in as mistress of the house. And everyone treats them with respect. It is all right for a man to behave immorally..."

"But what are we to do?"

"I need to think. I need to write some letters." She looked towards her writing desk in distraction. "Muriel, sweet, I think it best if you stay in the house for the next couple of days. Let things calm down. I will make a plan, just give me some time." She hugged her daughter closely. She had no idea how to go forward.

Time and a little help worked things out as best as they could be resolved. Eleanor wrote to her mother, who knew and had always known of Angus' circumstances, but not of the recent exposure in Whitby. Eleanor wrote to her trading partners with the intention of selling off what she could and essentially ceasing her business. Where she was merely a silent partner with shares in shipping or blubberhouses, she retained her stake where the other partners were willing to keep her, or sold out for an insultingly low price where they were not either so open minded or desperate. She wrote to Elizabeth to find out how the land lay in Scarborough. Elizabeth had known the facts for years, but until now it had been a well-kept secret. Eleanor had no doubt that as soon as the Gaskins of Whitby had heard the rumours they would have written directly to the elderly Miss Gaskin. They had held a grudge under the surface of courteous nods ever since Eleanor had pulled herself out of a marriage her father had been arranging. Hobart had planned to hitch her with one of the revolting Gaskin sons in the name of improving his business stakes. She had wriggled out of it, and they had lost access to a fortune. They would have heard with joy of her final downfall. Her letter to Elizabeth was returned to her the day her mother arrived in Whitby, with a brief note from Miss Gaskin explaining that she could not abide scandal, and had asked Elizabeth to quit her service and apartments the same day. She did not care to know where Elizabeth now was.

"Surely she would have come home," Eleanor said as she finished reading the note to Maud. "She is only eighteen. What else could she have done? I must go to Scarborough and find her."

"Find her then come to Haworth," Maud advised. "I'll go back tomorrow and take Muriel with me. My employers are very understanding. She will be able to stay with me, study her books and help out until you know what you will do."

"Thank you."

"You can't be planning on staying in Whitby?"

"I think it is time for a change," Eleanor looked about the parlour. It was her home, but it felt more like a prison. "I am not sure what, but I am winding down my active business interests, then I will meet with Angus..."

"He can't come back here."

She shook her head. "But folk won't recognise him in other parts of Yorkshire. We'll think of something. I'm going to rent out the house. It's an asset and I can't give it up. This could be an inheritance for the girls. Lucy-Ann has said she will stay on as housekeeper and manage it for whoever decides to rent. I know in my mind what I will do about most things. It is just Elizabeth I worry over. She has not written and Miss Gaskin says she has no idea where she is."

"How could she have thrown a young girl out onto the street?"

"No doubt the letter from her relatives has exaggerated all of the charges. You know the hob had plans on marrying me to one of the sons? He was a slobbering pig of a man as well." Eleanor wrinkled her nose. "It is lucky Jayne is already married and away or else they would have been busy to stop that alliance as well. Not that Jayne is one of my children even, but her connection with us would have done her no favours had she still been here."

Although she was practical and tried to be positive – a change after twenty years of business was not necessarily a bad thing – that night when she had retired to bed, Eleanor sat and sobbed until her body was wrenched dry of tears. This was the end of an era in such miserable circumstances. Everything she had built up for her children was falling apart. She did not know what future Muriel would have now, and she was terrified of what she might find in Scarborough when she travelled there tomorrow. She had not been able to get in touch with her daughter. Elizabeth might have quit the town, but it was the starting point for Eleanor's search.

As things worked out, she located Elizabeth on the day of her arrival. Eleanor had first gone to old Miss Gaskin's apartment to ask if Elizabeth had left any details of what she might do next. A maid had answered the door with a pleasant look until Eleanor had told her name. The woman's smile had crumpled to worry and she had informed Eleanor that Miss Gaskin was unavailable to receive guests. Obviously the name was now poison and Miss Gaskin had no intention of trying to help her find her daughter.

"I'm just looking for Elizabeth. I don't know where to start."

The maid's worry deepened. "She did not leave a forwarding address. She did not know when she left..."

"I knew it was a long shot."

The maid glanced back into the corridor then slipped out of the door, almost shutting it but retaining her re-entry with a toe in the way. "Madam, I don't know if this is true, but I've heard talk in town that she moved into a place on Tollergate a couple of days ago."

"Tollergate? I'm not familiar with..."

"Up the hill, towards the castle. If it is true, you'd be best getting her away from here."

"If what's true?" Eleanor was worried.

"I've stayed too long now. Very sorry."

The door was closed in her face. The maid had probably been lectured on Eleanor's sins, and that she was not to speak to anyone from the MacCaskill family. At least she had some compassion to pass on what she knew. Or at least some of her knowledge. Why would she not speak of all the rumours? It could only bode ill, that Elizabeth had gotten herself involved in some other mischief.

After locating the street in question, and several walks up and down in search of her daughter and questioning locals, one old fishwife eventually acknowledged the question and that she knew of the young woman Eleanor was asking after. Number thirty, she had told Eleanor, before heaving up her basket and walking away, keen to avoid any more involvement.

What would she find here, Eleanor wondered as she stood in front of the door to number thirty. It was a narrow terraced town house with black painted front door, neatly washed windows and in general perfectly respectable. Was it purely that everyone had heard about the illegitimacy and were horrified? Or was Eleanor going to walk into a den of ill repute.

She knocked on the door and a rather surprised Elizabeth, in a satin dress of dusky grey rose, answered. "Mamma."

"Elizabeth, I have been trying to find you. Miss Gaskin only wrote and told me that she had severed your services..."

"And thrown me out on the street," Elizabeth almost growled. "I am still the same person and yet she treated me as if I had the plague..."

"Elizabeth," Eleanor interrupted her, aware that people on the street were slowing down in their walking, and lowering conversations so that they might better hear. "Perhaps we could continue inside?"

"Oh yes, of course, do come in."

The interior of the house was a respectable little home, well furnished for comfort and with taste and good quality but not so to be overly lavish. Why would anyone be upset or wary of Elizabeth coming to such a place?

"She's a narrow minded old bag," Elizabeth continued as she followed her mother into the sitting room, now speaking freely. "She looked at me as if I was filth and told me to pack my things and get out. I haven't done anything wrong."

"I'm sorry this has all come about this way."

"Yes, well," Elizabeth shrugged off her mother's advancing embrace and went to sit down. "I am lucky to have more open minded friends who have come to me in my moment of need. I am luckily settled here and have no worries at present."

Eleanor looked around, half expecting the mistress of the property to put in an appearance. "Who is it that lives here?"

"Why, I live here."

"But you are staying with a friend?"

"No, I am living here alone. I am planning on hiring a maid."

She stared at her daughter in consternation and felt as though she was looking at a stranger. It had only been a few days and yet her daughter was so well settled? Miss Gaskin certainly would not have paid enough that Elizabeth could have afforded to buy and furnish a house like this. "I don't understand. You're not telling me that this is your house."

"Well, I don't own it if that is what you mean. But it is my home now. A friend has given it to me for as long as I find I require it."

"But you cannot afford rent. Elizabeth, I must tell you that I can't afford to keep you in this house. We are to rent out the property at Whitby and go to Haworth until I work out what to do next."

"There is no rent. Do not worry for me."

"No rent? You have been given this property for free? Who is the friend who has furnished houses to throw away?"

Elizabeth shuffled awkwardly.

"Elizabeth?"

"If you must know, it is my dear friend Percival Farrow."

Eleanor sat down and closed her eyes. Her daughter could not be this naive, could she? "Daughter, you must politely thank him for his help and quit this property immediately."

Elizabeth laughed. "I will not. I am queen of my castle here. Just because you've gotten yourself into a mess..."

"Elizabeth there is a rent connected to this property, but it is not in coin."

"I will not do anything I do not wish to do," Elizabeth responded stubbornly. "Percival is a dear friend. He has helped me in a moment of need and this arrangement suits us very well. He comes to town for a break from his country estate and is in need of entertaining conversation."

"He should get that from his wife."

"His wife does not understand him."

Eleanor did not know whether to groan or laugh. How many women had tried to convince themselves with such nonsense before? "You must come away before this goes any further. He will expect attentions that only a wife should..."

"We have already worked out the terms and have been very honest with one another."

"You have not already…?" Eleanor felt a sinking horror as she watched her daughter's cheeks heat up in a blush. So convinced of being the sophisticated woman and yet still a girl. But no longer innocent. "Oh Elizabeth, how could you?"

"It is nothing worse than you have done."

"Excuse me? You do not speak to your mother…"

"You knew Pappa was already married and yet you set up house with him, bore his children."

"Including you, I will remind you. And we married in a church."

"Knowing it was illegal."

"We lived as man and wife. It is not the same and you will not talk back to your mother. What you are suggesting is prostitution."

Elizabeth laughed. "I'm not out on the streets offering myself to strangers."

"You are taking a man to your bed in exchange for a house. Coin or accommodation…"

"Isn't that what all wives do? Most women can't earn their livelihood, so they must marry it. And part of that contract is to let the man do what he wishes to them. I have it far better here, for I am queen of this castle and Percival is only a visitor."

"And you a plaything he can cast aside when he is bored."

"He'll never get bored of me."

"A man cannot cast aside his wife so easily. Doing this, you will never be able to get back into respectable society. Women who are kept women… they are despised. And you are youthful and fresh now, but in a few years he will throw you out. How do you think the streetwalkers ended up where they are now?"

"By various means. Such as marrying married men. Having illegitimate children." Elizabeth's eyes narrowed. "I am eighteen and I know my own mind. I will live a better life than you, for there is no hypocrisy."

"You are young and foolish."

"I'm not leaving."

"I will write your father…"

"Tell him what you want," Elizabeth spoke brazenly. "Percival cares deeply for me and I will not abandon him. Now, you have seen that I am well and tragedy has not struck me despite the mischief you and Pappa have conducted. I am very happy here and will not leave."

"Elizabeth, you are coming with me."

Elizabeth stood up haughtily. "Thank you for your visit. I find that I have a slight headache and I need to retire."

How have I failed my children so terribly? Eleanor wanted to tear her hair out. She should never have allowed this work in Scarborough. Even when Elizabeth had come with the first blackmail attempt, she should have held fast and refused. She would have saved everyone a lot of misery.

"Your father will hear of this."

"Good."

Elizabeth stood at the window and watched her mother retreat down the road. When she turned away there were tears streaming down her face. The truth was she was a little frightened at what she was embarking on, but she did not dare tell her mother the full truth. How could she go home now after what she had done? Last night Percival's arguments for their arrangement had all made perfect sense and logic. They were above society's nonsense. Two kindred spirits helping one another in the best way they could. He had plied her with more wine, then reminded her that one good turn deserved another, and ripped her dress from her. Elizabeth had been sobbing, terrified, but he had promised her a new, and finer dress, which she indeed wore now, and then he took her innocence before collapsing into the bed in a fit of snores. The deed was done, Elizabeth had made her choice and would have to live with the consequences. The next time Percival was here she would get him to write down all the reasons why she had made a good choice so that she would not so easily forget.

Emmerline was now twelve. Clara would never acknowledge anyone who suggested such a thing, privately, secretly, she knew that the daughter was starting to oust the mother. Every day she had moments when she felt she hated the girl for it. She had such luscious loose curls, a fine complexion and a happy countenance, and she was beginning to turn from girl to woman as her body began to fill out. Clara was hardly an old hag, only at thirty seven, and the fact that she had not conceived or carried any more children had helped her figure and complexion greatly. She was nearing the time when a woman might not have any children, and given that her only child was twelve, most had assumed there would be no more little parcels of joy in the Mowbray family. Yet her husband persisted with the possibility that one more cure, one more quack idea might just kick start her reproductive system and produce the boy he wanted. This summer he had decided that they would not go to Commondale to stay in the ancestral home – as much as one generation born could create an ancestral home – but that his wife would spend the season at Scarborough to take both the fresh sea air, and the spa waters. The spa, or rather spa house where the wells were enclosed, stood at the sea front near the cliffs. The natural spring was enclosed in a building where one could go and take the waters. It was all stuff and nonsense and the only effect Clara took was a bitter taste in her mouth. If one wanted to become with child, she knew all the remedies and this was not one of them. She had no intention of illuminating her husband on the matter, and went to the spa diligently every day to take a cup of that revolting water.

Having completed her wifely duties for the day she quitted the spa and walked along the beach. They were not having horse racing on the sand this day and people were taking advantage of the peace. Up ahead Emmerline walked with her governess, the two talking and pointing out things at the sea or up at the castle ruins ahead on the promontory rocks. Clara did not much care. The governess was an intelligent and engaging woman and seemed entirely wasted on Emmerline, but no matter. Clara was content to wander quietly and mysteriously, carrying her pretty parasol to keep the sun directly off her face, and watch the other idle rich enjoy the summer.

Ahead a small group were swiftly walking down from the front promenade to the sands, two men and a woman, chattering loudly and gaily. The woman laughed and frolicked like a young child, although her figure of waspish waist constricted by whalebone corsetry, bursting forth top and bottom with her womanly form said otherwise. She was laughing so much Clara was surprised she did not pass out, given how restricted her lungs ought to be in such heavy duty underwear. The grey-blue hues of the satin skirts rustled as she swooped around in the arms of one of the men, shrieking that he was quite the beast. They were not paying attention to their surroundings and almost collided with Clara. As the woman came up to right her stance, her eyes met with Clara's, unknowing and seeing her merely as the scenery, but Clara felt a spark of recognition. There was something of a young Eleanor in the woman's countenance.

The moment was broken as a respectable family man, out with muttering wife and daughters, came to Clara's rescue and hurried the youthful group away.

"I hope they did not alarm you, madam."

"I am quite well, please do not worry."

"My dear husband was concerned you might be knocked over." The wife had scurried up to her husband's side now that the disreputable lot were out of her way. "They clearly have no concern for the other good people on the beach, but if they had any ounce of consideration they wouldn't do what they do. She certainly wouldn't."

Clara regarded the woman's gaze, and wondered if there wasn't a touch of envy hiding under the disapproval. "I am not acquainted with those people, I am afraid."

"And so it should be. Upstanding women such as us can't consort with such types," the wife explained earnestly. "She fancies herself a courtesan of some adventurous spirit, but she is just a kept woman in Scarborough. Living in sin for money."

"Come now, we do not indulge in gossip," the husband lectured his wife, taking her arm. "We are going to take the spa waters."

"Yes, I've just come from there," Clara said distractedly, watching the vivacious young woman cavort with her male companions. Could that be Elizabeth MacCaskill, or whatever she was called, for Clara had heard that it had become public knowledge that Eleanor's husband was a bigamist. Eleanor had the unfortunate timing of being the second wife.

"And how did you find the waters?"

"Quite bitter. Excuse me." Clara started to walk again, ignoring the shocked and scandalous mutterings of unintelligent snobs from one of the local towns. Folk who reassured themselves of their importance whilst pretending to be richer and more sophisticated than they actually were. Clara had grown bored of much of society. It was so bogged down by moral righteousness that it was dull, so unimaginative and tediously competitive over trivial issues. She sometimes wondered how these were considered the social betters of many a person living in this kingdom. Such was her scorn that of late she had taken to writing to Mary Bateman on a regular basis to conduct yet more mischief. Her latest suggestion had been in response to Mary's worry that she was old news and no longer trusted by her target audience. Why not predict some doom? Fear held such a power in getting people to behave and return to the fold. There was nothing like a tale of the end of the world. Mary had liked the idea but hadn't been sure of quite how to go about frightening people. A little drunk on wine, Clara had thought up a ridiculous plot, where Mary ought to get herself a chicken of the apocalypse. A week later she had been hysterically delighted when she read in Mary's letter that Mary had taken her at her word. She was now peddling the prophet hen of Leeds, who apparently laid eggs stating that 'Crist was coming'. It was a shame about the poor spelling, Clara reflected, but one couldn't expect too much from a chicken.

On returning to their apartments, Clara was delighted to find she, or rather Miss Blyth had received more correspondence from her contact in Leeds. There was a parcel containing a petticoat from a Miss Stead, as payment for some talisman or wise woman words from Miss Blyth. Who was Miss Stead, Clara wondered, and placed a finger to her forehead to try and recall. Mary was a busy one for schemes, and tended to send a multitude of letters to Clara, some written as if in genuine belief of Miss Blyth and the fiction they cooked up between them. Others were direct communication between Mary and Clara, although Clara made certain her own name never appeared. On paper she remained Miss Blyth. Today Mary was complaining that Clara's handwriting had been growing worse over the months and she could see what she was doing, mimicking Mary's own hand. Over the months, Clara laughed. She had been forging Mary's very handwriting for the past two years, only that Mary had been too stupid to see it until now. These little tricks amused Clara. They all played their little tricks. She knew when she sent requests for items for Miss Blyth, Mary always increased the demands to the face of the customer, so that she could cream off a little for herself.

Oh yes, the Perigos, Clara snapped her fingers as she remembered who Miss Stead was. A niece who had put a gullible couple into Mary's path. From what Clara surmised, Mary had every intention of draining them dry. That little leech didn't like to leave survivors.

Mary finished on a note that she had picked up a sense of Clara's tiredness in recent letters, and was worried for her friend's well being. A wise woman by the name of Mrs Moore had mixed up a healthy brew of tea which would improve her restitution and invigorate her body. She should find the aforementioned mix in a paper packet in the parcel. Mrs Moore advised strongly against the use of a tea strainer, but to leave the mix in the bottom of the cup. A little sugar might be added as the taste was a little bitter, but Clara was to be assured that every sip would cleanse her soul.

Clara found the packet rolled up in the petticoat and held it up to the light. She sniffed and smiled to herself. Mary was so transparent. There was a heavy dose of arsenic in that tea, sure to kill her if she was stupid enough to drink it. "Oh Mary," she sighed as she stood up, folding the packet into a tight little square. "You never were that subtle." She opened her little tea chest and slipped the packet into the back corner. Cleansing her soul it would not, but one never knew when one might have need of such tea. Besides, it amused her to have Mary's pathetic attempt at assassination in a box where she could look and laugh at it now and then. At some point their partnership was going to become a liability and the connection would have to be severed, but that would be at Clara's choosing, and in the meantime she was having too much fun.

Returning to her writing desk, Clara pulled forth a fresh sheet of paper and began one of her Miss Blyth letters to Mary.

The nonsense continued for many months and into the following year. Clara delighted in providing ever more ridiculous suggestions for Mary to aid the health of this Rebecca Perigo character. From what Mary reported back to shadow sponsor, it seemed that Rebecca and her husband, William, took it all at face value and followed their instructions to the letter. They genuinely believed that Rebecca would succumb to a curse if she didn't do what was asked. Guinea notes were stitched into silk bags, supposedly to be stuffed into the four corners of Rebecca's bed – naturally Mary made sure that by the time the bags were in place the money was long gone, along with the compensatory guinea notes William had given her for the expenditure. Money was of little use to Clara, so she started to ask for objects; pincers, tea caddies and camp beds, hundreds of eggs, shirts, stockings, linen from Knaresborough and all kinds of ridiculous items that would no more save a woman from her illness than all the silk bags stitched hither and thither would keep their money safe. Some of the items eventually made their way to Clara in Leeds, who kept everything in a wardrobe and out of sight from her own husband. Many of the requested trinkets remained with Mary as additional items added to the original letters sent from Clara. Mary was never shy about adding her own commission. Whatever nonsense Clara contrived, the goods continued to arrive. Neither she nor Mary could quite believe how gullible these people were. Surely one day the Perigos would run out of money or idiocy, but as 1806 rolled into 1807 and then crept towards 1808, the scam was still working well.

Not all of Mary's scams were sucessful. Her prophet hen of the apocalypse had been quickly revealed as a charlatan when a local doctor, convinced of the lies, snuck in to the hen house and saw Mary forcing the etched egg back up the hen's arse. Clara had heard of this discovery through her acquaintances Patricia Varsey and Margaret Lawson who were idle wives with little to do but delight in gossip. They had been to Mary years ago for little charms, and had kept up with the news as Mary's name grew well known. Mary had connected herself to the followers of Joanna Southcott, which had for a time worked, until the lies surrounding that chicken had proved her to be a fake and she had been forced to move again. And yet the Perigos continued to lap up her lies and give all that she asked for.

"Do you still go to Mary Bateman for little charms?" Clara watched her breath twist up from her mouth in the January chill as she turned to Patricia Varsey, the thought suddenly occurring to her. She had just been thinking of that evening when they had ventured to one of Mary's old abodes.

Patricia, sat on a little canvas stool whilst she sketched, looked up at Clara and blushed. "Oh, don't speak of such things, especially in the hearing of my husband or anyone important. That was so many years ago, and just a silly passing notion."

"So that's a no?"

"She was proved to be a fake. There was such talk her predicting the future through her chickens. They laid eggs that foretold things." Patricia stared up at Clara, wide-eyed and earnest. "Of course I didn't fall for such rubbish, but there were many who were taken in."

"Of course not." Clara did not believe her for a moment. "I do not know how you can sit and sketch in these temperatures. There is still ice on the grass in the shadows. I must take a turn around the ruins."

They were at Kirkstall Abbey, a ruined monastery north of Leeds and on the banks of the river Aire. Battered and roofless, stone stolen after the reformation for local farm buildings, it was now a point of amusement for passing gentry who had read too many gothic novels and wanted to sketch the crumbling walls and grey stone columns. Even in January when people of sense ought to be inside. Clara shivered and stuffed her hands deeper into her little lambskin muff as she walked through the crisp crunching grass. The ground underfoot was frozen solid. She was not quite sure why she had allowed Patricia to persuade her to come out on such a cold day. She had left her daughter Emmerline at the fireside playing with a little puppy her father had seen fit to give her for Christmas. Clara had been on the settee close by, peering into her tea cup with a touch of distress. It wasn't often she bothered looking at the leaves, and it was nothing she had ever admitted being able to do. It didn't happen often but every now and then she would glance into the dregs of the cup and get an inkling of things to come. She had been pondering on her next Miss Blyth letter and idly glanced into the teacup. Nothing more than a glance, but she found herself illuminated on some facts on the future. Mary Bateman's time was drawing to an end and her tricks would catch up with her once and for all. Their tricks had been fun, but Clara would find some new entertainment. She harboured no distress that she would not associate with Mary for much longer. What troubled her was her own connection to the law catching up with Mary. Clara might be brought down with her. She must make her contingency plans now. She had a number of items Mary had coerced from the Perigos in her wardrobe, and some letters from Mary. Every time Mary made the silly request that the letters were burnt once read. Clara did as she pleased. Not that she needed to hoard Mary's correspondence, for Clara could easily forge her hand and style. Clara was prepared to defend her position and had plenty of ammunition. She was just not certain yet how she would arrange to severe all connections.

Whilst she had been worrying over these factors, Patricia had called and asked if she might accompany her in a carriage ride to Kirkstall Abbey. Distracted, Clara had agreed, and soon regretted it whilst she listened to Patricia's babble about some silly novel she had recently read and how it had inspired her to take up sketching again. She wished to produce a winter scene of ruins for would it not just been the most romantically desolate scene Clara could imagine? This was declared as they stepped down from the carriage and Clara had caught sight of the coachman's expression, which eloquently communicated what she felt in her own heart. Her face remained blank as she had taken his hand to step down from the carriage. It did not do to let the staff think they had a point of common opinion with their social betters.

Leaving Patricia to her numb-fingered amateur sketches, Clara wandered through the hallowed ruins of Kirkstall. Stepping through a tumbled down wall that now served as an exit, she gazed up at the surrounding trees. Leafless, and like a collection of dried witches' brooms reaching up to the unfeeling grey sky. It was just right for one of Patricia's mournful literary ghosts to come strolling by. But this was reality, and the only figures were real. Clara stopped and watched a middle aged couple walk up from the tree-lined river, arm in arm and deep in conversation. She had never seen them before and yet they were familiar. As they grew closer she could hear something of their conversation.

"As I said before, I am much better. I wonder if we should continue with it all. We can scare afford it."

The man petted the woman's arm. "It is not for you to worry of the money."

"Oh, but I do."

"I do not wish to severe the connection, for what if all our good work is thwarted should we neglect to complete the tasks."

The woman looked grave. "I just sometimes think of how much we have done for Miss Blyth already..."

Clara's ears pricked at the mention of her pseudonym. As the couple passed her, she casually started to walk, following at a safe distance with a gaze to the crumbled medieval architecture but an ear firmly to their words.

"Oh William," the woman sighed. "We have spent all our money."

William? Could this be William Perigo, Clara wondered. Mary had told her that the couple lived in Bramley, and that was just across the river from Kirkstall.

"A compromise then, my dear," William spoke. "We have had the letter thanks to Mrs Bateman, but perhaps we delay some weeks. See what happens. That way we have not closed the door on their help, but we can be settled in our minds that we do not always jump when told do."

"You do not think we are being taken for fools?" The wife, Rebecca, asked uncertainly.

"I cannot believe it. There is always such a good natured sense in Miss Blyth's letters. She genuinely wants to help us with our problems."

You liar, Clara thought as she stared at William's back. You doubt it all but you speak out of shame. You think over all that you have given to Mary Bateman and are too embarrassed to say now that you think it may be a fraud. You will continue to follow her orders if only to avoid admitting to yourself that you might have been duped. Clara pursed her lips. It would end badly for the Perigos and Mary, but she felt she could navigate her way neatly out of this coming tragedy.

It was the end of May that same year when Clara next heard of Mary. She had received no correspondence from Mary for many weeks, if not months, and her mind had been more focused on dealing with her husband who was putting all in for a final push on the second child front. Clara would be thirty eight this year, but he would not give up, and had it on good authority that the waters of Buxton worked wonders. He had arranged that Clara would spend her summer there with Emmerline. Clearly this spa water had something that the waters of Scarborough and Harrogate could not compete with.

That particular evening they had been to dine at one of Andrew Mowbray's colleague's properties in Leeds, and the line up had been a fine selection of the best professionals Leeds had to offer. A variety of intelligent and officious men with leading city roles, accompanied by wives decked out in the latest fabrics and fashions. Margaret Lawson had gotten hold of a very clever little French dressmaker who had fled the country due to the ongoing wars. England was perhaps not the best choice for a French refugee, what with the war with Napoleon, France was certainly not the most popular of countries, but the woman had personality and flair. Besides which, she could turn even the dumpiest of women into something resembling form with the cunning angle of her seams.

Now that the dining was complete and the sexes had retired to their separate rooms to discuss, this was the subject Margaret was prattling on about. The other women were the usual unexciting crowd, bar a new face, and a recent bride, Emma, now Mrs Clark, the second wife of George Clark. His first wife had died some years back in childbirth. George was now in his forties, but Emma was a mere nineteen. The age difference in itself was not shocking, for many women were married at that age, and to men older, but her age was very apparent in a room of wives and mothers of some years. She was unformed, gullible and empty headed, and sat beside Margaret, soaking up every word that tumbled from the woman's mouth without remembering a thing. Clara, stood by the windows gazing out onto the garden, would occasionally glance back in to the room and could not help being drawn to Emma, both for her empty headed nature and her youth which irritated her immensely. George would certainly not be at his wife all the time reminding her of how old she was getting, almost far too old to be worthy of creating life. If there was one thing Clara knew, it was that if she hadn't wanted children in her twenties, she certainly did not want the fuss and burden now that she was heading towards forty. She diligently took her potion to repress her fertility.

Bored by the level of conversation, she draped her shawl over the back of a vacant chair and wandered out into the corridor unnoticed. The door to the study, where the gentlemen had gathered to smoke and talk, was partially open. Did they prattle of French fashions as well? Slipping off her shoes, she crept across the corridor and placed herself by the side of the door.

"I believe you promised us an account of a curious case at dinner," Varsey, such a distinguishable voice, guffawed at an unseen party. Clara recalled overhearing a man start to tell of an odd case that had come to his work room, before he had faltered and declared it would not be a suitable subject in front of ladies. She had been irritated at the time, for the man was a surgeon and all kinds of odd things must pass his office. Some of the ladies had tittered and declared they would feint if they had to hear of such things. Clara thought it nonsense, for in her experience it was generally the women who could cope with the gore and the bloody reality of life. They didn't really have any choice, between Eve's bloody curse and children, it was a brutal life their bodies forced them to endure.

"Yes, Chorley," this was her husband's voice. "Do not renege on a vow."

"It began when a sick man came to my premises. He told me of headaches and vomiting, and that at one point his lips had even turned black. He was very distraught for his wife had suffered the same but to a far greater violence, and had died the day before."

"How dreadful."

"Come, come, Mr Chorley is a surgeon. He is more than used to patients dying on him."

"Tell us, have you discovered a new disease about to destroy Leeds?" one of the men laughed.

"Hardly. For I believe it was poison that sickened Mr Perigo and killed his wife."

Clara's eyes widened slightly and she pressed her back to the wall at the name. Mr and Mrs Perigo were a couple Mary had been fleecing for months. The very same Clara had seen at the ruins of

Kirkstall Abbey. What was this mischief then, the wife was dead and the surgeon suspected poison? It wasn't the first time. When people either ran out of money or credulity, Mary tended to sweep away the problem with a little poison. It didn't always work of course; Clara was living proof of that. But she was wise to Mary's tricks.

"Do you think the husband did away with the wife? Took a little poison by accident himself?"

"Perhaps not an accident. It would be a cunning alibi."

"Gentlemen, I am not a professional of the law. Science and human anatomy is my field. Mr Perigo told me a strange tale of his wife having been under threat of a curse for a good many months. They have been purchasing the services of a wise woman who has had them perform all kinds of services and tricks for her..."

"A fraud and a con artist in other words."

"And perhaps a poisoner. I am not sure. The couple had been sent powder and flour and told to make puddings that they would eat for six days. They also were given honey that they should take if they were to feel sick. Mr Perigo reported that his wife consumed a great amount of honey. I took some of this flour that had not been used and mixed up a paste which I fed to a chicken to see if there was anything in it."

"And the chicken died a terrible death?"

"I sincerely hope it wasn't served up to us this evening."

This brought forth a round of chortles.

"No." The surgeon, Mr Chorley, sounded a little disgruntled at this. "To date the chicken thrives."

"So they were not poisoned?"

"Just a malady of the house perhaps?"

"Inconclusive," the surgeon stubbornly responded. "I have taken the honey with the aim of making some pills from it. I will purchase a hound or some such animal to feed the pills to and then observe closely."

"You may be watching for something that is not there."

"I have seen poisoning before. I am sure of what happened to the Perigos. But one cannot accuse without evidence."

This was interesting, Clara thought to herself as she stared into the semi darkness of the corridor. Mary had poisoned people she had no more use for before now. She had driven others to suicide. But this was the first time an outsider to the case had suspected poison, and talk of evidence and accusation had come up. Perhaps the Perigos had been a step too far and Mary would shortly be apprehended. It would make life a little dull not to have the entertainment of Mary Bateman's cons and nonsense, but supposedly wise women and witches were two a penny and becoming all the more popular. She'd find someone else. So long Mary, she thought with a smile, and headed back for the ladies' room.

If Clara had expected Mary's arrest in the coming weeks, she had been extremely wrong. Much later she learned that the surgeon's experiments with the dog had been successful in that the beast had died, and the autopsy had shown poison in the stomach. Damning evidence perhaps, but nothing was done with it. No word on Mary's arrest was heard, in fact the woman continued to go free. When Clara was in Buxton trying another one of her husband's ideas of a 'cure', she was surprised to find a note from Mary in her forwarded correspondence from Leeds. Mary was oblivious and quite happy in her enterprises. What was particularly shocking was that she continued to fleece Mr Perigo. Despite the death of his wife, the suspicions of his surgeon and everything that he had suffered, he still danced to the woman's whim. Clara had to begrudgingly admit finally that Mary did have some talent.

Of further coincidence, Clara saw Mr Perigo from a distance, himself at Buxton to take the waters to improve his health after the poisoning. Was the man an utter fool, she wondered? Many fell into the web, utterly gullible, but there was usually a point at which the rational self woke up and called a halt. If the death of a wife would not do this, there was no hope for Mr Perigo. Clara wrote to Mary to let her know she had seen him in Buxton. When he was returned to Leeds she should go and see him and scold him for not letting her know where he was going. Didn't he know Miss Blyth was going to Buxton? He ought to send her the family bible so that she might sit on it in her carriage travelling back home from Buxton. Clara laughed at this last request. If he was stupid enough to comply, he deserved no compassion.

The bible never made its way to Clara, so whether he had complied but Mary had kept the winnings, she did not know, but over the next months, through to the following year, in fact through to the autumn, Mr Perigo continued to comply with all of the ridiculous requests of Mary Bateman and her Miss Blyth letters. It was in the year 1808 that it all started to fall apart, but before Mr Perigo finally called time on Mary Bateman's great con, some very odd things did happen.

Andrew Mowbray finally admitted defeat when his last ditch hopes on the spa waters of the north of England failed to bring about a second child. He had his Emmerline, now a beautiful young woman fourteen years of age and outshining her mother in youth, beauty and good temperament. With acceptance came freedom over travel plans for Clara; no longer badgered to holiday at spa towns and take odd treatments. That summer she, Emmerline, the maid and governess went to Commondale to spend several weeks at Pines Lodge. Clara commandeered the governess to adhere to her whims and vanity and Emmerline found herself alone and unnoticed for much of the daytime. Not that she minded, for there was the moorland to tramp across, and a little pony her father had bought that had been brought over for the summer to be kept on the farm for her entertainment.

She would go out on the pony across the moorland, letting her hair fly loose on the breeze, savouring the feel of the sun on her skin. Really she ought not to do it, without a hat at least, for all the young ladies were terrified of blemishing their fine pale features. But she wasn't with society here, and the country folk she occasionally came across, trekking over the moorland paths to get from village to village, were only mildly amused. Just a young girl, let her be before marriage sets down its strict rules. Most were on foot, but there was a man on horseback she passed one day at noon. He doffed his hat at her, and being the young inexperienced girl she was, Emmerline found herself blushing the moment he caught her eye. He noticed, his grin widening, and she had to look away as she smiled in greeting. He was a very handsome young man. She did not know who he was, for he did not look like any of the locals she remembered from the village. The following day she quizzed one of the village girls who had come up to the house to help with chores. The lass did not know who he might be. The horse, a brown creature with a streak of white across the forehead like a scar did not sound like any horse known to the village. Perhaps he was a passing merchant, or a traveller away to Whitby. Just passing through the once.

Emmerline never heard word of the stranger from others, but she found herself falling into a routine of going out for a ride so that she would be on the moors at noon. And more often than not, she was passing the same young man on the same horse. Sometimes she noticed a silver haired woman in the distance, untied hair blowing in the breeze, watching and never moving, but mostly Emmerline's attention was consumed by the young man. For young girls of fourteen are very silly and do not question what is in front of them.

At first only a few words were exchanged: a good afternoon, a smile to acknowledge that they had seen one another again. Words came to sentences, then the horses were brought to a halt so that they might speak a few minutes before riding on. He had a curious accent, bounding up and down, fast flowing and keen of chatter. He did not tell her much of himself, but he did tell her that he came from a place close to Newcastle, further north in the country to Commondale. That was all she learned, for information was not something he gave easily. He was keen with questions and flattery. Eventually he told her of his dreams of sailing across to the continent to seek his fortune and adventure. Two things held him back: a lack of riches and the absence of a pretty young wife. For he would not wish to leave his homeland shores without his soul mate. Emmerline felt the blush reach for her toes and her heart rate flutter.

The following few days she did not see him. She stayed out on the moors longer and longer, riding the pony hard in hopes of catching sight of him. There was nothing. It was true what they said, that absence made the heart grow fonder, for her whole body ached for sight of this young man. Then the rains came for two days and she was housebound and miserable. On the third she rode out despondently. What euphoria she felt when she saw her young man again. He told her he had been away putting his plans in place as he intended to set out soon and follow his dreams. He just needed to wed his bride and then the happy couple could set sail.

Her heart broke at this news. Emmerline wished she had worn a hat or a veil or something that might have shaded the disappointment in her face. "And your sweet bride," she said. "Does she also come from Newcastle like yourself?"

The young man laughed. "My sweet treasure. She comes from here, from a place I believe they call Pines Lodge. You'll run away and be my little wife?"

She felt breathless and ecstatic. But surely she was too young and ought he not to ask her Pappa first? Her mother barely noticed her and rarely took an interest in her daughter. Emmerline frequently felt as though her mother looked at her with an appraising and cold look, as if she were competition although she knew not what for. Her Pappa doted on her when he was not working, but rather in the way one spoils a little dog. Emmerline was a young woman, and this young man was the first that had noticed.

He would come for her before dawn the next day. She was to put all the money and jewellery she could find into a little bag to bring with her, so that they could sell it, for they would need money for the journey. Get her little pony saddled, and he would meet her just outside the farm yard. Then they would ride together across the moors, be wed in a little village and then take a ship across to Holland. Their lives would begin and she would no longer be a little doll for her parents to dress so finely. She would be a real woman.

She did as asked, and could not sleep that night at all. In her finest dress, as requested for one ought to look stunning at the wedding, and a purse full of all the jewels she could find, Emmerline crept out of the house whilst still dark, saddled her pony, who was such a good natured creature that she took no distress in being woken in the night, and led the beast out of the farmyard. As promised, her young man was waiting for her, and as dawn rose upon the moorlands the two rode out up onto the open ground and away to their destiny.

Had Emmerline studied her geography or generally been more familiar with the land of her mother's childhood, she would have known that they were not heading in the direction of Whitby, from whence she had assumed they would sail out to the rest of their lives. Instead they took a more north-easterly direction up over the high moors and met the sea at the rocky, cliff-looming coastline just north of Runswick Bay. They had ridden past moorland, farmland and copses of trees, to come down towards grasslands and scrub before the ground petered out to a sudden drop to the briny sea below. The tide was high and the waves smashed at the rocks below.

The young man brought his horse to a halt and nimbly hopped down from the saddle before helping Emmerline down from her pony.

"I thought we were going to be married somewhere?"

"I wanted to show you something," he said, taking her hand. "This is a special place to me. Come and look."

They walked up to the edge of the cliffs and peered over the edge. Some gorse bushes clung to nooks of earth and outcrops but beyond that the drop was sheer. Just in front of them was some low lying gorse, the flowers long since past their bloom, the bushes keeping low to the wind and out of the way. Emmerline felt the sea breeze whip up and rustle through her heavy skirts, tousling through her hair. She stared down at the broiling water but could not see anything in particular.

The young man let out a sigh. "It is high tide. I did not think. You won't be able to see them right now."

She looked across at him. "Them?"

He pointed down at the sea far below them. "Six girls have I brought to this place, and they have flown down there to be crushed upon the rocks once I have given them a good ride. You will be the seventh."

Emmerline went to flee, but he grabbed at her arm whilst simultaneously swinging around with his right fist to punch her squarely in the face. Emmerline gasped and felt a hot burst rush over her mouth. She staggered backwards and landed in the grass on her rump. Flopping onto her side, she moved onto her hands and knees and saw the blood come splattering into the grass from her face.

"Now throw that little purse of treasures my way, girl."

She shifted to look up at him.

"Now."

Emmerline felt all her fourteen years of inexperience fill up in her eyes as the salty tears began to flow. She had never faced aggression or hostility of this sort before, and she was all alone. No one knew where she was. He towered above her in authority. What else was she to do? She found the purse in her pocket and threw it to him.

He left it in the grass, noting where it had landed. It would be to pick up once his work was done. He smiled watching the horror form on her face as he started to unbuckle his trousers. These rich young girls often had no idea of a man's anatomy or what he might do with it. That had been the way with the second girl, and lord how she had screamed through the entire event. At least the poor country lasses understood the facts of life, and when resigned to their fate, had at least gotten themselves into a suitable position.

"Up on your feet," he said. "And get that dress off you, lass. Let's not get any more blood stains on it. Besides, it would be a shame to throw such finery to the sea, especially when I can get a bob or two for it."

A stronger person would have fought, or at least had the notion to refuse. With shaking fingers Emmerline started to unbutton her dress, pushing down skirts around her ankles, removing the blouse, until she was left in her shift and stays.

He eyed her whilst he warmed himself. "I bet that's fine whalebone you have there. And that long smock'll have a value too, I bet. Only the finest for Pappa's little angle, what?"

Emmerline shivered and hugged her arms around herself.

"Take them off."

She started to wail. "I cannot. I cannot shame myself. I would be naked if I..."

"That's the idea." He grabbed a fistful of her hair and shook her head violently, not minding the blood and snot that came from her face onto his shirt. Rutching up the skirt of her shift, he roughly forced his fingers up between her legs, eliciting a sharp scream from her. He took his hand away, covered in blood, and glared at her before slapping her about the face. "You'll start that right now, will you, you little witch? Think you'll pour your poison blood onto me?"

"Please just let me go," Emmerline sobbed. "My Pappa is very rich. He'll pay you anything..."

"I know who your Pappa is, you silly slut. Your jewels and dress is payment enough for me." He struggled across to the cliff edge with her and pointed down at the sea. "You'll be down there with the other six girls with your broken face and smashed bones. A deep briny sleep you'll have. And no one but I will know that's where your bones tumble in the swell of the sea."

"You can't thrown me down there."

"Why ever not?"

"The gorse will tear at my skin as I go over."

He laughed loudly. "The vanity of foolish women."

"Let me keep my shift on."

"That has value to me." He flicked back the side of his overcoat and pulled forth a large knife. Pushing Emmerline away so that she tumbled back into the grass, he leaned forward to hack at the gorse. "That a suitable passage for her ladyship to fly through?" The words were barely out of his mouth before he huffed up a breath of shock as something furious and heavy pushed into his side. He lost hold of the knife and felt himself going headfirst over the edge. His arms thrashed out wildly, blindly grasping for anything. He screamed in pain and fury as his fingers wrapped around branches of lower lying gorse bushes. They were hardy, thick shrubs with vicious thorns that ripped directly through skin and flesh, hooking into bone. But it was the only thing stopping his fall and he clung on. His booted feet scrabbled at the cliff edge trying to find a hold. He would not die today. Looking up to the cliff top, he saw his attacker watching him coldly, her bloodied nose beginning to clot. There was menstrual blood smeared across her cheek. Hair torn from its brushed and curled stylings. He ceased in his screams and the two regarded each other in silence for a moment.

"You're a clever lass, I'll grant you that," he started. His mind was racing. "Indeed, I believe you've passed the test. Cleverer than those other girls. You are more than worthy to be my sweet bride. Now, you reach down and pull me back up, then we'll see about getting to a church..." Panic rose in his throat as Emmerline stepped away from the edge of the cliff and out of his line of sight. "Wouldn't you be proud of a fine looking husband like me? You'll be the envy of all the finest ladies."

Emmerline reappeared, his lost knife in her hand.

"You don't want to do anything stupid now..."

"Oh do be quiet!" she interrupted. "You may well have had your way with six girls here, but the seventh girl will have her way with you."

She lunged to the edge of the cliff, brandishing the knife as if to lash out and hack off his hand. Logic dictated that she would not be able to reach without falling over the edge herself, and indeed Emmerline had no intention other than making a pretence of attack. It was enough, and instinct had him shifting his hands to protect his face. He screamed, bloodied torn hands reaching for the air and the image of his brutalised seventh girl. He fell down and with a splash was swallowed up by the sea.

Emmerline went to throw the knife in after him, then thought better of it. She carefully put her dress back on, then found a cloth in the young man's saddle that she used to wipe her face before wrapping up the knife. Clearly one never knew when one might need a knife. Taking the young man's reigns, she hopped back up onto her faithful pony, and began the ride back to Commondale with her prizes. The silver haired woman watched her come back with a smile on her lips. Emmerline ignored the queried looks of passers by as she rode. She did not answer the occasional questions as to her health. She did not stop until she reached the door of Pine's Lodge. The maid complained of the state of her clothes and how would they ever get the blood out of such fine fabrics. Her mother took one look at her and made a comment about her having finally fallen off her horse. Yet for the next couple of weeks, whilst Emmerline's face swelled and bloomed up in bruises and healing, Clara was quite happy to spend many hours in her young daughter's company. No one asked about the strange horse that was now in the stables until the farm manager returned and then Emmerline merely said she had decided to purchase another horse for her father's estate. The knife had since been removed from the saddle, and such a fine horse as it was, the estate manager was more than happy to take it on as his new stead to ride about the property as if he were lord of the manner. As if things were on the way up and the might of the Mowbray family would know no bounds.

When the summer was waning the Mowbrays reunited in the main family home in Leeds. They enjoyed a short and uneventful period before things started to unravel. An outsider's downfall triggered a chain of events. The precipitation end was not quite as predicted by Clara although she saw something coming in her tea leaves that morning.

It was mid October and Andrew had been absent from dinner without word regarding his delay. Clara was irritated. Andrew knew the mind of his demanding wife and was by now well trained to send word if he would not keep to what had been agreed that morning. It was not until almost ten o'clock that night when he returned home in a fluster of excitement.

"My dear sweet woman, I have been engaged with Mr Duffield, speaking of how to proceed tomorrow in a very terrible case. They are expecting evidence, attempted murder and an arrest..."

"I thought you already had enough work on," Clara interrupted with a bored expression. "Clearly you don't have any more time for new work if you are to return this late."

"This will not be a prosecution case for me. I was merely fortunate enough to find myself in the offices when Duffield arrived asking for advice."

"Duffield. The name is vaguely familiar."

"He is the Chief Constable of Leeds. William Duffield. You have met him at several dinners." Andrew Mowbray sat down at the opposite side of the fireplace to his wife, his eyes sparkling with the boyhood excitement of scandal and adventure. Clara's reception of his news did not meet expectation. "I completely lost track of time, otherwise I would have sent word..."

"No doubt it is a very interesting case to legal minds, but I think I shall retire..."

"You do not want to hear it?"

"No."

"It will bring down a woman of many years conning and murdering. Only today a Mr Perigo came to Mr Duffield in need of advice."

Clara stopped at the doorway.

"He has been asked to meet with the woman at the canal tomorrow morning, alone, but he does not trust her. He believes she has poisoned his wife."

The Perigos. The couple that Mary had been scamming for years. The wife, Rebecca had perished over a year ago and yet still the husband gullibly followed the game. Had even his slow wit finally touched upon the fool he was being made? Clara turned and looked back at her husband. "A recent poisoning?"

"No. It's been a year since the good lady died. I remember Chorley telling us about it at the time, as Perigo had called upon his services. He'd conducted some experiments on some animals, but it would seem it came to naught, for the woman, Bateman, she's called by the way, Mary Bateman, had never been brought to account. I don't know if you've heard of her from some of your friends. I'm told she used to sell lucky trinkets and such rubbish. A witch they call her. A fraudulent harlot says I."

"But if this has been going on for so long, why has the man only thought to question her motives now?"

"He'd checked these silken purses she'd had them stitch in the corners of the bed. Apparently with money in, but of course when he checked, the money had disappeared. Duffield tells me the fellow has been running all kinds of errands, purchasing a veritable shopping list over the past couple of years for this Bateman. Quite frankly, if a man is that gullible for that long, it begs whether he deserves his worldly goods back. But a murderess can not be allowed to walk unpunished. Duffield will go with Perigo tomorrow, when he is to meet with Mary Bateman."

"When is this?"

"Early tomorrow morning, at the canal."

Clara's brain was working through the scenario. She knew where Mary was living at the moment, and she knew how long it would take her to walk to the canal. Of course, the children might still be at the house, or the husband, but they could be easily distracted. If this was to be the end of Mary Bateman, then Clara needed to be sure there would be no doubt left hanging over the woman's head. It had been fun, but all things grew tiresome eventually. "I need to leave some instructions with the staff," she told her husband as she turned back to the door. "And then I am tired and must retire. Do not over excite yourself with all of this. You know how it puts a strain on your heart."

She almost bumped into the maid as she moved through the doorway. Listening at keyholes? Clara's eyes narrowed. "Go fetch me our carriage man. I need a word with him now."

Instructions were duly despatched. Clara took the carriage man to her stores, where she had kept the items Mary had sent onwards in regards to the Miss Blythe letters. Petticoats and tea urns, a camp bed and a bag of flour were collected, along with other small articles. He was instructed to pack it all into the carriage and that she would be leaving early the next morning. The remaining letters that Clara had kept, she held fast herself, trusting them to no other.

The next morning, very early, before her husband had risen, she was out and in the carriage. She had not disclosed the address to the driver in advance, and paid him extra on the understanding that he would speak to no one about what they were about to do. A good deed, she told him, delivering goods to needy folk.

Mary had already left for her rendez vous when they arrived, and the husband was off to his work. Clara paid some local urchins to get the children out to play, then she and the coachman carried the items into the house. She had him wait outside with the carriage whilst she arranged the property appropriately, and secreted the letters in various places, where they might look long forgotten and part of Mary's own secrets. She paused for a moment to survey her handiwork, satisfied with the matter. She thought back to the time when Mary had come to work for her briefly, when she had just inherited the property in Commondale. Even then Mary had the audacity to steal from Clara. Such actions would always come up and catch her eventually. Only yesterday morning Clara had seen the hangman's noose in her tea leaves. That was for Mary. It was coming to an end.

Clara learned the facts through Andrew over the next few weeks. He had too much work on already, and was growing more tired and weary each day yet he couldn't keep away from his colleague's offices to catch up with the drama. At the canal-side meeting Mary had turned up with a little bottle that was later proven to contain poison. When she realised the game was up she had claimed William Perigo had been planning to do away with her. A desperate claim that no one, probably not even Mary believed. Mary, William Perigo, Mr William Duffield and sergeants then went to Mary's lodgings to find all the items William had been purchasing for a woman called Miss Blyth. Everything was clearly for Mary's personal benefit, and even letters of blackmail, nonsense supposedly written by a "Miss Blyth" but which Mary's husband's employer would later confirm in court as Mary's own hand, were found in the property. According to the eye witnesses, Mary had seemed a little stunned to see so many things there, but had made no attempt to explain it all away. Perhaps she was resigned to her lot.

In fact, the next day when she was taken in front of the Leeds magistrate and charged with fraud, Mary even admitted that Miss Blyth did not exist. Clara was happy with that; Mary knew when she was beat. Searches at Scarborough brought up no evidence of such a character and it was accepted that Miss Blyth was of Mary's imagination. A fantasy that continued as Mary then blamed a Hannah Potts for the letters. Hannah Potts, Clara laughed to herself. What was this, a pathetic plea for Clara to come forward and speak on Mary's behalf? It would never happen.

Mary was transferred to York's women's gaol to await trial at the lent assizes in March the following year and Clara relaxed. Her fun with Mary was at an end, but there would be new tricks in the future, and quite frankly she was well shot of Mary. The woman had been getting sloppy in her work and was a liability.

Andrew was working later, and to keep his wife happy that he was not up to mischief, he undertook a greater amount of his paperwork at home. To keep his mind awake and revitalise himself, he took to drinking a great amount of tea. He kept a ready pot of hot water on his desk, and a strainer and tea urn to the side. One evening when he had run out of tea, he went in search of some more. He did not wish to wake up the servants at such a late hour. In his searches he came across his wife's tea box. In the corner, wrapped up in paper was some loose tea. There was a handwritten note about reliving stress, and so he took the little package and made a drink. The hour was late, and his headache grew bad, so after the tea he decided to retire. On his way up to his chamber, a spasm of the stomach hit and he did not make it to his room to the basin, instead throwing up a green and noxious stuff upon the stair. A maid was called for to clean it up.

He woke late the following morning and felt dreadful. His tongue felt thick and heavy. He looked ashen in the mirror. Yet there was so much work to be done. He returned to the study, and brewed up a strong mix of tea from the package he had taken. His condition worsened. The housemaid came in at lunch and was horrified by his appearance, especially the blackened lips, and ran for the housekeeper. Clara was informed, but waved it aside without going to her husband, saying he was just overworked and needed to rest. Andrew finished his tea, then collapsed to the floor in convulsions. He was taken to bed and in the drama the mess in the study was ignored. The doctor was sent for, but by the time he arrived Andrew was taking his last breaths. Emmerline had been terrified, and sobbing in the hallway until Clara had angrily sent her to her room. She herself remained in the doorway, watching Andrew. Poison. She knew it as if she could smell it on the air, but who would wish to attack her husband?

The doctor knew it as well, and was most concerned as to where the contagion had come from and whether the rest of the family were in danger. Andrew had been working in the study a lot recently, so the doctor was escorted there by Clara, the housekeeper, footman and little maid. The chaos left by Andrew's struggling hand was still spread across the room. The dregs of the tea in the cup. Vomit across the desk. The doctor poured the remains of the tea into an empty bottle, then noted the package with a little of the tea unused remaining.

"Has anyone else been in here drinking this?"

"No sir."

"And where did this come from?"

The little maid, who had been with them for some years, stepped up to regard the packet then looked back through the door to Clara's opened little tea chest. "Why, that is madam's tea. She's had it there but never drank it."

Clara stared dumbly at the packet. Mary had sent it years ago in a pathetic attempt to take her life. Why had she not thrown it away at the time? Damn you, Mary Bateman, have you killed my husband as well? She stepped out from her thoughts to find the other people in the room staring strangely at her. Almost leaning away from her.

"Can you account for this, madam?"

She looked from the doctor to the hallway. Emmerline was on the staircase, her face tear stained. "Pappa is dead," she wailed. "How has this happened?"

"I shall investigate this and I will have to return," the doctor said.

Clara felt a numbness sink upon her. I am done for, she thought. Mary Bateman will have her way, even if she does not realise what she has done.

It was soon proved to be poison, arsenic to be exact, and the Chief Constable, that very William Duffield, appeared at the Mowbray residence to arrest Clara Mowbray for the murder of her husband. Clara did not deign to speak to him or respond to his accusations, and was led away in dignified silence. She was not yet worried. She knew Mary would hang, for the woman could not afford legal counsel, and the trial would see that there would be no doubt to her guilt. Clara had money. She would hire lawyers. They would wipe this problem away.

There were certainly many loopholes and so many assumptions that it could have been done, especially with such a sweet looking woman. But Clara's husband had been well respected in legal circles, and it seemed no one was prepared to take on her case. Before Clara knew what was happening, she had been charged with murder and was being transported to York in readiness for trial in March. There was no regular court, as judges travelled about handing out justice as they went. York took two annual visits, and the accused simply had to sit and wait until the judge was next in town. Indeed Clara had the money to make sure she had every comfort possible whilst she was in York gaol, but in gaol she was, the door locked and the miserable sound of other beings waiting for the end surrounded her. After all she had done throughout her life, that she had ended up here. Day after day she sat dumbly in her cell and stared at the wall in horrified consternation. How could she have ever let this happen?

Four and a half years had passed since Angus MacCaskill's bigamy had been made public, and his second and therefore illegitimate family shunned from Whitby. The family town house in Whitby remained as one of their assets, although rented out to provide an income. Eleanor's business interests had been reduced to sleeping partners, and she was never seen in the coastal port again. Likewise she would not to set foot in Commondale, for the memory of her estranged sister, Gillian, now deceased, bit at her even to be close to the site of her suspect death. Her family, or what remained of it, had spread across Yorkshire. Elizabeth, her eldest daughter, essentially shunned her family as though she somehow had the moral high ground. At twenty three she was young and beautiful. Rich men sought out her vivacious personality. She had enough talent and cunning not to need to take to the streets with strangers, but dress it up as you will, the girl was a prostitute, albeit a very well heeled one. Her parties were talked of for months, if not years afterwards, and many gentrified and nouveu riche men sought invitations. It was just about acceptable for respectable men to attend, but that a decent woman could even meet Elizabeth's eye on the street was unthinkable. For now she was having too much fun to consider the long term repercussions. The only thought she would give to the future was when she considered her sponsor, Percival Farrow's, face and the hatching of wrinkles and lines. Scarborough was getting a little provincial, and she was sure in the next few years she would be spreading her wings to something far grander.

Eleanor's income and funds had allowed her to purchase and pay the upkeep of a small property on the hills just outside of Haworth. Without the notoriety that her name carried in Whitby, what with the gleeful avarice of seeing a successful person knocked down, it had been possible to set up a quiet life in Haworth. Maud had handed in her notice on her current position and moved into the house, which Eleanor hoped would be some comfort for her now that she was in her sixties. She was in a much better position than many women at that age, what with still being alive and not taken by birthing. She had worked hard domestically through many periods of her life, and at other points been able to take it a little easier. Good eating and fresh air and an inherited healthy constitution meant that she was still able in body and mind to walk and work at what she wished. Muriel, now nineteen and to turn twenty that summer, lived at the house and spent most of her time in her books. Study study study. She was fluent in French and German, as well as her old Estonian learned in the old offices at Whitby, and read much science and anatomy. She dreamed of going to a great place of study, to be with other such inclined minds to learn and to discover, but it seemed that the notion of women studying to such a degree was not entertained. She might purchase the same books and inside know she matched their intellect, but university admissions were nothing but a little amused by her letters.

As for Eleanor, she was only at home in phases, and had easily taken to a drover's time keeping if not the profession. She and Angus had set their feet to the road and travelled the length and breadth of the country, not out of any need to herd animals from pasture to slaughterhouse or take letters to the intended, but for the simple pleasure of discovering the world around them. She picked up the travel bug from Angus, and for those four years they did not worry about Whitby, about the first wife at Falkirk, or responsibility and duty, and instead merely lived for the day. Eleanor's mental atlas of the United Kingdom mushroomed, not only of roads and rivers, cities and villages, but of the landscapes, the people and habits. She became a compendium of local stories and folk beliefs.

In the Peak District she overheard an odd tale about a shoemaker hobgoblin, long since disappeared from the parts, who was said to have kept his house up on the moors about Chatsworth. Angus admitted to her later that many years ago he had heard folk joking about the place, referred to as Hob Hurst's House, as the place of her father. Having met him briefly the once, he could understand where the goblin rumours would have come from, but surely it was a coincidence of name, and had her father even come from that part of the country? The Hob had never been her biological father, but in truth Eleanor knew next to nothing of the man's past prior to his marriage with her mother. She had no love for his memory, and yet time had dulled some of the pain and she found herself a little morbidly curious. Paying a local lad as a guide, they trekked out onto the moors above Chatsworth, the lad nervously keeping a distance from a heather hillock and pointing to declare that was where folk said the hob lived. It was drizzling and chill when they were there. Whatever had been or happened there in the past, it was now an empty and lifeless place void of magic. They travelled on to the market town of Bakewell as the wind picked up and the rain increased. Angus coughed his way down the hills from a chill he had picked up some weeks back that had never gone away. When they were settled by a fire in an inn in Bakewell, Eleanor found him feverish and glowing, with a high temperature yet complaining of a chill in his bones. He took to his bed and weakened from there on and a week later he had passed on.

Eleanor remained in Bakewell for a month, numb and lost, simply unable to think what to do. Her mental map of the country provided many routes back to Haworth, but without Angus she was no longer sure what she was supposed to do. Her mind shut down and she spent the festive period at the inn as a paying ghost. Her maternal instinct told her that she needed to get back to Yorkshire for Muriel's sake, but the girl was used to her mother's travels and absences. The most she could manage was to pen two letters, one to Haworth and one to Scarborough to inform her two surviving daughters of their father's passing.

It was eventually travellers' gossip that woke her out of her mournful state. Eleanor was in a shadowy corner of the inn, picking over her pie and peas. Two tall men in long overcoats strode into the inn, ordering ale and mutton, before sitting down to loudly continue their gossip. They were from Yorkshire, heading south on business, but were keen to get back to their native county in time for lent. They wanted to attend the trials and executions at York at the Lent Assizes when the judges arrived to set up court. There was a notorious local witch up on murder charges and rumour had it that she may well fly away on a broomstick or other such trickery if she were indeed found guilty. One of the men laughed loudly, and shook the paper at his compatriot. As if. There was no doubt that the old witch would hang.

When they had quitted the inn, Eleanor was careful to fetch the discarded paper, and by candle light in her room, she took her fill of news. It was a first awakening, and it may have simply been a link to home but nothing to tempt her forth had she not seen a name she knew. Beyond the stories of some Mary Bateman who had been arrested for fraud and murder – a well known witch and con artist of Leeds - a lesser murder charge was also noted. A Mrs Andrew Mowbray had been arrested for poisoning her husband with arsenic. The family was rich, and normally one would have expected a troop of well crafted lawyers to deal with the defence, yet as Andrew Mowbray himself had been a man of the law and his death a tragedy, leaving a single daughter, Emmerline, behind, it seemed that no self respecting man of the law was prepared to defend the widow. What an oxymoron: self respecting man of the law, Eleanor thought wryly. There was a nag in her mind that Andrew and Emmerline were familiar to her but it was not until she saw the brief history of the murderess, a certain Clara Mowbray, nee Hurst, that she realised the article was about her own younger sister.

Eleanor lowered the paper, unable to quite believe what she had read. In many ways she was not surprised. Clara had always been up to mischief, even as a child, and she had wondered if she had not seen Clara's hand waving in the background of many a sad event at Commondale over the years. The only real thing that surprised her was that Clara had been caught. Surely age and experience would have honed her talent, not weakened it. Either that or she had simply become lazy. Eleanor paused in consideration. She'd had no doubt that Clara was guilty of the charge, and that in itself was interesting.

It was time to leave Bakewell, but before she went back to Haworth, she needed to go to York.

The medieval city of York, jewel in the crown of Yorkshire, was a compact and buzzing place in the farming lowlands at the feet of the Vale of Mowbray. There had been a settlement of some description on that site on the banks of the River Ouse for as long as humans had settled in the area. The narrow twisting snickelways and alleys that wound their secret paths between buildings and under first floors were watched over by the imposing construction of York Minster. The busy city was surrounded by heavy stone city walls, and the remains of the old castle, now a tower on a mound. It was at this side of town that the city prisons, along with the courthouse stood, almost cowering before the castle remains. The executions had been performed out on the Knavesmire, beyond the city walls, but the number of people and carriages stopping to watch the hangings had caused blockages, and so the site for eternal justice had been brought closer to the prison. Now people were to be executed around the back of the castle, at the Castle Mills Bridge area. Not that it was a foregone conclusion, for when Eleanor arrived, the court was only being established and no one had yet been convicted, but the city was excited with the show trials to come and there was an atmosphere about town that it would be an event to be seen. Further afield many who would not come to the trials were keeping their eyes and ears to the news. If certain people were found guilty, a trip would be made to York to watch them dance the jig of death; or as some hoped, watch the witch fly away or disappear in a puff of smoke.

All the talk was of Mary Bateman, the Yorkshire Witch. Clara Mowbray, the elite husband poisoner was almost ignored due to lack of drama. If it weren't for the staff of the prison, the court officials and constables and all those in charge of managing the law, Clara might have slunk out of York on foot, such was the disinterest in her case. It was the first to be tried in court that week by Mr Justice Simon Le Blanc, who sat at the head of the court in his fine scarlet robes in a calm and wise state. Occasionally he would glance at the public gallery when a particular sigh or rough comment came from someone who did not respect his court as they ought. Eleanor sat towards the back and wondered how it would be when the main feature was brought to court at the end of the week.

She was a little surprised to hear that Clara did not have legal representation, not due to lack of funds but rather that no one wished to serve as the defence against the death of such a respected member of the legal community. She had not thought lawyers to be such an emotional bunch, and regardless, surely someone would have wanted the post, even if to give it the barest of attention but to be able to say that justice was fairly done and the wife had recieved legal counsel. Or perhaps a man newly admitted to the bar would wish to make his mark. Yet no, and even on the day, when the judge raised his eyebrows to hear there was no defence, did any of the legal personalities watching in the public gallery, step forward to help the woman. Eleanor could only see her sister's back. She seemed passive, tall and unapologetic, and yet somehow resigned.

What Clara would not admit to was the fact that she was innocent, for in explaining the origin of the tea, she would have been forced to bring up Mary Bateman's name. She did not want to connect herself in any way to that woman, or the sensationalist trial that would be starting soon. Similarly, it would eventually lead to necessitating an explanation of Miss Blythe, and Clara would not wish to facilitate any kind of leniency for Mary Bateman. If the tea had been taken from her tea chest, so what? Surely the judge and jury would only need to take one look at her to understand that such a sweet looking woman was not capable of murder. And the evidence to be offered was circumstantial at best.

The trial was short and bored her. The law stated that the accused could not speak in their own defence, and therefore without any kind of a legal counsel, a very short selection of evidence and the particulars of her husband's death, there was not all that much to be said. The jury were sent away to consider their verdict, and were back within the hour. Clara watched the jurymen file in to their pews and wondered for the first time if she would have been better in a black dress and unbrushed hair, to show the picture of a grieving widow, rather than an angelic young girl. It would be her fortieth birthday later this year and whilst she did not like to think of herself as ageing, perhaps there were times when she ought to play more to what society thought she was. It was too late now to consider tactics.

Too late, but she would have an entire week to regret her apathy to proceedings up until now when the jury came back with a unanimous verdict of guilty. It was ridiculous and gormless, but Clara felt her mouth drop open at the horror. Not only was she innocent of this particular charge, but she was out of control of the situation. These men who knew nothing about her or what she had really done, were passing judgement upon her. Men who were mere worms in comparison.

The judge set the black cap upon his head before proceeding to sentence her to death. It was the only option available in regards to capital offences. He began by explaining that the law stated women found guilty of murdering their husbands ought to be burned alive.

Clara's eyelids fluttered at this news. The stereotypical death of a witch. Another woman on the bonfire.

"However," the judge coughed, caught for a moment by Clara's face. "In consideration of taking a more humanitarian stance on the matter..."

Would she not be executed?

"You shall be taken to a place of execution and hung by the neck until you are dead."

Her hope of life, her vibrancy, which had been tuned out since the shock of her husband's death, only to reignite this week, stumbled and fell into hopelessness at this final statement. The Clerk of the Arraigns asked Clara what she had to say in response, and if there was any reason immediate execution should not be awarded. The only reason women could postpone and hope for a pardon was the age old excuse of a pregnancy. Clara, whose husband had pushed her down all kinds of paths for an infertility remedy for years. If only she had had the foresight to let it work last summer. She would be safe now. But a woman not serving her purpose was just as well dangling on the three legged mare. Clara felt a terrible rage well up. She had suppressed her emotions all this time, numbed by a strange shock that her husband was dead. No one had allowed her to speak in her own defence, and only now, that they had decided the 'truth', would they ask her what she had to say. It was the same all through her life. A woman could not speak for herself. A woman could not even own her own inheritance. A woman only had the life and the independence the man decided she could have. "You are wrong," she began. "I am innocent. You can not kill me."

The judge regarded her coolly. He'd had his share of hysterical women in the dock taking on board the guilty verdict. "You have been found guilty by a jury of your peers..."

"Those men are not my peers. They are ignorant worms. I will not have my life decided by men anymore."

There was uproar in the public gallery as Clara began to shout and protest. Eleanor had to stand up to try and see, but could only catch sight of her sister's glowing blonde hair. Angelic but hiding a demon. The judge was red faced, demanding that Clara be taken away. Clara lost her cool demeanour and screeched, pulling against the jailors who caught hold of her arms to drag her back to her cell. They would all rot in hell, Clara shrieked. She had sent others to hell, and a few more worms were no challenge to her. The men in the public gallery rushed to the front, shaking their fists and shaking their jowls. The few women laughed at the display. Eleanor closed her eyes and sank back down to her seat. She did not know what to think.

Because she was in town and did not know what to do with her time, unable to leave until Clara had taken her final walk, Eleanor found herself drawn to the other trials that were conducted during the week. The highlight and the pinnacle of the Lent Assizes was the Mary Bateman trial, which people were fighting to get in to, hoping to hear of scandal or witness magic performed in the courtroom. Eleanor had been early, not sleeping or settling in York, and had managed to get a place in the gallery. It was a long day's work, the trial stretching out to eleven hours, whilst witness after witness came to talk of the work and trickery of Mary Bateman. There were stories of imaginary wise women who had written instructions to gullible patrons. The entire story of the Perigos was recounted. Eleanor could not quite believe that someone could be so gullible for so long. It was the kind of manipulative con she could imagine her younger sister plotting. A niece of the Perigos accounted for how she had unwittingly first put them in contact with Mary Bateman. A certain Winifred Bond, once employed by Mary, told of how she used to take letters to Bramley for the Perigos. Letters she could not read, on account of being illiterate. Most had been burned, but some were available as evidence at the trial, including some having been penned by an imaginary character called Miss Blythe. Eleanor sat in a sea of whispered comments, gasps, and excited faces, all enjoying a good day's entertainment.

The jury were not gone long, and returned with the guilty verdict. The judge, Mr Justice Simon Le Blanc, who had also presided over Clara's trial, gave a long speech on the wicked nature of Mary Bateman, and advised that she was to be hanged until dead, then her body would be handed over to the surgeons to be dissected and anatomised, as was the fate with all murderers. As with Clara, Mary was asked if she had anything to say, or any reason why she could not be executed immediately. Clara had met the court with rage but Mary broke down in tears and declared she was with child. Eleanor considered the way the woman hunched forward, hands to her face, but out of a chink of fingers, watching. She was lying, Eleanor thought, then felt disgusted with herself that she had sat through a week of these miserable stories, as if they were just tales from novels and not the ruined lives they actually were.

She stood up just as the judge announced Mary would have to be examined and asked for the courthouse doors to be locked. There was panic amongst the public, but he decreed that twelve married women from the public audience would have to come forward to examine Mary Bateman in a room to decide if she was telling the truth. I don't want to be here, Eleanor thought, wondering if she could shrink back into her seat unnoticed. She looked around. Some other women were on their feet, having looked to flee the building before the requirement of examiner could be forced upon them. And it was the women on their feet who drew the attention of the court officials. Eleanor felt a hand at her elbow, and a grey whiskered man, a court official, asked if she was prepared to do her duty and see if there was any truth to these claims. I have brought this upon myself she thought, to watch other people's miseries, I must now bring a woman even closer to her death. She was a murderess, but Eleanor did not feel qualified to pass any judgement over her. As she was brought forward into the courtroom with eleven other women, she wondered how it would have been had Angus been arrested for bigamy. It did not carry the death sentence, but he would have been locked away for seven years, and who knew if he would have survived the prison. For a man so used to wandering the country, being restricted to one building would have been hell.

She felt her eyes water up as she thought of her deceased husband. She and the other women were sworn in, before being led to a room where Mary Bateman had already been taken. Here they were supposed to find out if she was telling the truth. Mary Bateman looked frightened, as did some of the women. It was hard to know quite what they ought to do or how to start. One of the woman asked Mary if she already had any children. She did, she confirmed, her youngest was even now waiting for her back in her cell. The women muttered amongst themselves. She knew what it was to be pregnant, they could not ask questions for she would know the answers.

A woman next to Eleanor, who looked like a nervous rabbit, whispered to Eleanor that they were not surgeons. If Mary said she was only half way through her pregnancy, they could not expect a large belly, and how were they to know?

"I heard if you put a needle in her piss and it turns black, it's a sure sign she's with child," someone else said.

"Get her clothes off," another woman demanded. "I've had twelve babies. I know what I'm looking for."

A couple of woman went towards Mary to start undressing her. Mary shrieked and tried to back away, lashing out at the women. Four of their impromptu jury went towards the accused to bodily check her. Someone in the room told Mary to calm down. She didn't want to hurt the baby, and she wanted these good women to confirm her pregnancy, didn't she? Where is the dignity, Eleanor wondered as she watched the women scrabble and tear at cloth. Although where was the dignity for Mary's victims? And what was life really? All just flesh and bone, gently rotting towards the end goal. Was it sensible to be so precious over a body that would sooner or later rot in the ground?

Mary cried and spat as the woman felt at her breasts and belly, shoving their hands between her legs and pulling at her skin, more often out of morbid curiosity and a joy at such sudden power than at any knowledge or intention of discovering a pregnancy. The menstrual blood, unfortunate in its timing, soon finished the question, and Mary was discarded to a laughing crowd. A desperate attempt at the very end, but one proved false.

The woman who had claimed twelve babies and had particularly vigorous hands in the examination, shook her head at Mary before spitting in her general direction. "Murdering, lying bitch," she muttered. "Didn't you manage to get the jailors to knock you up in time, then? Looks like you'll be swinging next week."

Mary merely glared at the woman, pulling her clothes about herself. Had she known this is what happened to a claimant of pregnancy, she would not have even attempted this last final fraud.

The jury of matrons and the defendant were returned to the courtroom, and Mary Bateman's lack of pregnancy was confirmed. Mary, along with her fellow convicted criminals, would be hung that coming Monday until dead. Their bodies would be shipped off for dissection so that they might serve some final purpose to society in extra punishment for their crimes. And so the wait for the gallows began.

What was one supposed to feel on facing the last few minutes of life? Terror of pain? Perhaps one ought to snivel and plead to be allowed a longer life? Or perhaps a furious rage would be more fitting. Screaming and cursing, attacking the fools that might try to end one's life. It all seemed rather futile. In fact the entire affair had been rather underwhelming, and now that she stood on the platform before the gallows, Clara mostly felt irritation. There were three people to hang this Monday morning, and out of the three two claimed mystical powers and only one, the one who did not brag about her abilities, had really achieved anything in that realm. Yet she was an unknown on the day of her death. The crowds, and there were a lot of people, were here for that pathetic fraud, Mary Bateman who stood at the head of the line. Between the two women was a man, Joseph Brown who was here to hang for the murder of his landlady. Those two were guilty, whereas Clara was innocent of her husband's death. There was something rather insulting about the entire proceeding.

It was possibly the drama that was getting the women through the horrible experience. Mary had been extremely amused when she had heard that Clara was also locked up in York Gaol, accused of her husband's murder. That she and the fine lady, Clara Mowbray, were to be hanged together as equals had brought some joy into her otherwise miserable last days. She had been woken early that morning, taken away from her sleeping little boy, who had been in prison with her, and taken to the chapel for her last communion. Clara was also there, scorning the priest, and sizzling with a despising energy. It had relaxed Mary's nerves to see her, and taken her mind off what was to come. She gave a cackling laugh, and Clara had looked around and caught sight of her with disgust.

"Not so high and mighty now, Miss Blythe, eh?"

If Clara could have ripped her tongue from her mouth, she would have done so there at the feet of God. "You can go to the devil, Mary Bateman."

"Time enough for that."

"Ladies!" The priest had looked horrified.

Clara didn't know how this Joseph Brown had managed through his last communion and confession, what with him being the only man to hang, he had been separate in the men's gaol. Now, at their final moments, men and women were finally treated as equal.

She gazed out at the crowds. Hundreds, nay thousands of people, and she doubted that any of them knew who she was. Everyone was here to see Mary Bateman turn into a bat and fly away, or perhaps hover in the air when everyone else took the drop and final dance at the gallows. The air was electric, eyes feverish, people gossiping and whispering, trying to guess what they might see. Hawkers were selling their papers on the histories of the murderers, a little souvenir from a fine day out. Families held their children's hands and pointed at the no-good murderers. Mind that for a lesson of what happens to the wicked. I have not seen my daughter in weeks, Clara thought. And now I never will.

The hangman stumbled on the platform in front of the condemned, tripping over his own feet, and eliciting a mixture of cheering and boos from the audience. William Mutton Curry, Clara wrinkled her nose. She had heard her husband mention him in the past. He'd been at the job for six or seven years, accepting the vile post to avoid deportation. Nothing but a greasy little sheep rustler, and a drunken ignoramus at that. He was often drunk at executions, on one occasion even falling through the trapdoor. This was not the grand exit Clara had imagined to complete her life story.

Behind the condemned loitered the sheriff and his attendants, who had led the prisoners out on their final walk. Clara glanced off to the side, where the surgeons waited beside the cart, ready for the spoils of brutality. As a final insult, all three of them would be carted back off to Leeds for dissection. Mary would be the star attraction even in death, and Clara was sure they'd be charging money to see her corpse before it was finally sliced up. Vultures, she thought. These people are all vultures and beneath my contempt.

Her eyes scanned back across the crowds, searching for who knew what, before looking up to the sky. She felt tears prick her eyes. She was not ready to die, but what could she do now? It was too late.

Mary gave a muffled curse as the hangman pushed her forward. He drew a sack hood over her head before wrenching the noose around her neck. All three would be lined up and ready before the trapdoor was opened up beneath them. Someone somewhere on the platform was reading the Lord's Prayer. That wouldn't help anyone. The executioner took the man, Joseph Brown forward. Clara started to feel sick. She wanted to cry. I don't want to die. The blood started to rush through her fingers. Think of some clever trick to get yourself out of this. Her mind was blank.

A sweaty meaty hand pushed between her shoulder blades, urging her forward to position. Clara stared desperately out to the crowds. Someone save me. No friendly faces. Just as the sack cloth came down to obscure her vision, she was sure she caught sight of her father's face amongst the throngs of people. Pappa! Her ears filled up with the scratching sound of rope against sacking as the noose was fastened around her neck. The executioner, his breath hot with a tinge of gin, roughly tugged the noose around her neck, pulling awkwardly at it to make it a close fit around her slender neck. The knot pushed up from under her jaw, forcing her head up at an arrogant angle.

People were jeering at the condemned, like wild frenzied animals as the prisoners had sacking pulled over their faces. They had taken innocent lives, they were wicked and were about to receive what they deserved. This was a spectacle, Eleanor observed as she looked about her. Families were here. People clutched souvenir papers, describing in sensationalist terms the wicked lives and deeds of those to be hung today. She was not sure what she felt, but this did not seem right, and she felt quite sick. She was not sure why she had come, as much as she hated her little sister for all the misery she had caused, she had no desire to dance upon her grave.

"Eleanor?"

She looked about the throngs of strange faces, then suddenly her mother was upon her, clutching her forearm.

"Mamma, what are you doing here?" Eleanor looked aghast at her mother.

"I travelled down with Winifred, she lives in the village. She knew all about the trial. Well, she was called as a witness. Not for my Clara, of course, but that witch Mary Bateman. She used to run errands for the woman back when she lived in Leeds."

"You came to York last week?"

"Yes."

"Muriel, she's not..."

Maud shook her head. "Back at the inn, she's here in York but I did not want her to see this. She's with her cousin, Emmerline."

"Emmerline?" Eleanor had never met the little girl. The next generation of Clara, she shuddered. Although she ought not to be so uncharitable. The girl had lost both her parents, and how old would she be now, fourteen or fifteen?

"She's such a sweet girl, but a shadow at the moment. I had never met her until after Clara was arrested." Maud shook her head, tears in her eyes. "Her aunt's husband is fighting for control of her wealth, what with her not being of age. She's a wealthy girl, certainly will be after... but the child needs comfort, and her Mowbray kin are only interested in the money. I've taken her in at Haworth for now." She paused, still holding on to Eleanor's arm. "Muriel needs you. She's frightened she's lost you as well as her father."

"I am coming back. I just needed to..."

The crowd and Eleanor's thoughts were interrupted by a drum roll, by a burp erupting from the hangman's throat as he shuffled in to position. An unnerving silence filtered across the air. The moment was nigh. The trapdoor was wrenched back and Clara

242

felt a sharp, iron-heavy jolt wrench up from her neck and up to the back of her head. There was a clear, definite snap. The bodies bounced on rebound against the ropes. Joseph Brown thrashed against the rope, suffocating to death as he danced the dance of the doomed, his own neck holding up against the trauma for two long minutes. Clara's legs did not move, her body swinging in reaction to the drop, but already an inanimate object. Mary writhed for some moments before her body grew still. An almighty roar of triumph went up from the crowds. The men at the side shuffled and shared glances. Everyone wanted a look at Mary Bateman. The sooner they could get those bodies down and on the road to Leeds, the better.

Maud gasped and turned away from the scene. Eleanor put an arm around her mother's shoulders. "I think we should go now."

"I did not think I would outlive three of my four children," Maud said, her voice weakened. "I never would have imagined it would have worked out like this. I remember when I first moved to Commondale, when my family was only just starting with you and Gillian. Then Clara was born. I remember that little angel."

"Mamma, don't upset yourself." Eleanor clutched on to Maud's coat, feeling a surge of bodies around them. People wanted to get up close to see the corpse of Mary Bateman. Mother and daughter pushed back against the movement of bodies, aiming to get away from the sorry scene.

"Three children and two husbands," Maud said, wiping her eyes with her sleeve as she let Eleanor pull her through the crowds. "I did not think I would outlive so many. You know some of this pain. Your son, your husband..."

Eleanor pursed her lips together and tried not to think of her little boy, stolen and eaten up by the navy, or her husband, burned up in the end by a fever. "Clara was a murderess. I know you think she was an angel, but she manipulated her way through life. Destroyed people. Look how she behaved over Pine's Lodge."

"I never understood that girl."

The two women stumbled out of the back of the crowds, through a narrow alley between two buildings, and out onto a somewhat calmer lane. Eleanor straightened her overcoat, then turned to her mother. "Well, she is gone now."

Maud nodded sadly. "She is gone to God."

"I don't know about that," Eleanor murmured. "She's gone to the Hob at least. Wherever he did finish up." It would soon be thirty years since the Hob had died, she reflected. So much had happened since. So much he would never have believed had he still been alive. Imagine if the Hob was still alive, she mused; he would be nearing ninety now.

"He was good to me once,"

"Sorry?" Eleanor looked at her mother in confusion.

"You call him the Hob, but he was good to me once. He got me out of a very bad situation."

"That doesn't excuse subsequent behaviour. None of it does. Come now," she linked arms with her mother. "Take me to this inn. I wish to see my daughter."

Hob Hurst's Daughter is a fictional history of Yorkshire. The Hurst family and all their offspring are entirely fictitious. It therefore goes that everything they do, and every interaction they have with other people never actually happened. Having said this, there are some highly fictionalised versions of real figures who were alive at the time portrayed in the story, Mary Bateman and William Scoresby Junior being the principal two. The prophet hen of Leeds being a minor personality (I can't take the credit for making up that story). The Miss Blyth letters and the murder/attempted murder of the Perigos is also a matter of record.

Some of the small subplots within this book are inspired by/adapted of actual local stories, local folklore, local legends and folksongs of elsewhere. They have provided inspiration for this work, and any further coincidences are nothing more than that. All inaccuracies are purely the error of the author. The details of folk stories have been adapted for my purpose, be it principal characters, location, circumstance or even geography. It is not my intention to detail every reference here.

The drummer boy legend of Richmond is well known in the area. Reputedly there is a tunnel going from the castle to Easby Abbey, and a drummer boy was lost in the tunnel, so the story goes. Egton Bridge has been enjoying an annual gooseberry competition for over a hundred years and even has a Gooseberry Society. The rock in Farndale where Mr Hodgkins meets his end is called Hangman Stone, and has a similar tale attached to it. Elizabeth's friend who pushed her sister off a cliff was in part inspired by a real life incident in Whitby in 1810 when 9 year old PS Hubbersty was killed falling from the cliffs at St Marys. It wasn't until the surviving sister was dying of old age that she confessed she had pushed her sister off the cliff in a tantrum. And Clara and Emmerline's defensive murderous adventures have their inspiration in other folktales and songs.

Curious?

Go back to the year Maud Hurst first came to Commondale in *Hob Hurst's House*.